A MOUTHFUL OF MURDER

ANDREA CARTER

Published by Konstellation Press, San Diego

ISBN: 978-0-9991989-5-7

Copyeditor: Lisa Wolff

Cover design: Kim Keeline

For my Mom

CONTENTS

CHAPTER 1

We leaned against the back of a black-and-yellow plaid living-room love seat, not too sure of our next move. My best friend, Rachel, and I had landed inside a major vortex of high school coolness, a Friday night party at Joey Ballard's house with Led Zeppelin amped up close to deafness. The potted plants in the macramé hangers looked like they were vibrating. We needed to make our move or we'd disappear into the wood paneling. We'd wind up like the two sad clown paintings above the beige brick fireplace. Should we head outside the sliding glass door behind us to the back patio, where people sat on lawn furniture around a fire pit that snapped with flames? As sophomore guppies in the exotic fish tank of popular seniors, our mission was to swim up to status. At least that's what I'd promised Rachel. We had to mingle again.

"I don't know if this is going to work, Addie!" Rachel yelled out to me. She kept looking around to see if her on-again-off-again senior boyfriend, Perry, showed up.

I'd promised her Perry would realize how much he loved her when he saw her here tonight. Of course, I promised her because, well, I didn't want to deal with her and her broken heart. A girl and her broken heart are bad news. Plus, deep down, I thought maybe being popular would be fun. Even deeper down, I thought maybe not.

"Hey, we invaded cool central—we can do anything!" I yelled back.

I met Rachel in second grade. We played pretend-spy, endured sponge curler headaches, and tried to stop waiting for knights in shining armor. Rachel's dark hair, olive skin, and chocolate confetti freckles on her nose and cheeks were a contrast to my pale skin and hair the color of beach sand on an overcast day. Plus, I'd practically plucked my eyebrows into nonexistence.

Even though we were pretty much dweeb central, we were at party number four. We tried to share a shot of vodka, smoked two puffs each of a joint that someone accidentally shared with us, petted the Ballards' labrador, and then noticed that the four ex-cheers were here: Jaycee, Lisa, Myla, and Lorelei. We didn't see Merry Jacobs, who wasn't a cheerleader but was the most popular girl at Santa Raymunda High, and she was the ex-cheers' ringleader. Rachel and I weren't close to the major coolness, but we were orbiting.

Someone had come in from the back patio and left the screen door open, and I went to go shut it after a moth winged my ear. That's when a senior linebacker the size of a walk-in freezer batted at the screen door, staggered toward us, and barfed away.

"Blaacchhggg."

"Hey—" I started to say something to him, and then I looked down. Yep, splatter on my no-fail summer sundress, right at waist level. Granted it was still spring, but it was hot for May. Gross me out.

"*Move*, blockhead." Rachel pushed him into the living room. We ducked into the kitchen.

"Grody city," said a girl getting a glass of water at the sink. She was the only one in here. Her black afro was held down on both sides by sparkly blue hair combs.

"Hey, it's not *mine*," I said.

"That is *so* disgusting." She ran the tap and wetted a dish towel before handing it to me. Rachel grabbed a vegetable brush and dribbled liquid soap on it.

"Didn't you just move here?" I asked the girl. I recognized her from English class. She was a new transplant from somewhere.

"Yeah, but I am so moving back home. This town, man, I can't deal." She put her hands on her hips. I noticed her platform rainbow sandals.

"Thanks," I said, taking the damp towel. Her eyebrows were perfect commas. "I'm Addie, by the way."

"I know," she said. "I'm Gina."

"I'm Rachel." Rachel stopped scrubbing with the soapy brush.

I started to wipe with the towel. "But you haven't been here that long."

"Since December, man. My mom, my sister. From Chicago. My mom's the editor of *The Santa Raymunda Gazette*."

"Wow," I said.

Rachel nodded.

"No, *how*," Gina asked us, "could my mom do this? Take us to this, this deadbeat town full of prejudiced comatose idiots? Oh, right, my mom talks about women's lib and all, but women's lib doesn't tell people to up and leave their husbands for brain-dead Southern California surferville, no way."

Technically, the beach was another three miles west, so we weren't exactly surferville, and Santa Raymunda was a mission town—you know, adobes, enslaved Indians, tourism. Okay, bo-ring.

"I mean," said Gina, "I'm like a bug in a package of Wonder Bread!"

Rachel and I stared at each other. I mean, what to say? I kept trying to think of another kid who was black at our school, but there wasn't one. Then we tried to relate to Gina's situation. See, my mom divorced my dad when I was little because she found out my dad had a girlfriend, and they had three children together. Rachel's mother was widowed when Rachel's father died in Vietnam piloting a helicopter. Gina threw her shoulders back. Not relating at all. *Oh, smooth move, Ex-Lax.* Rae and I were just as boring as Santa Raymunda.

"My mom is so for women's lib, the ERA—she even excused me from saying the Pledge of Allegiance in seventh grade," I said.

"Yeah," said Rachel, leaning way into Gina's personal space probably due to the vodka-and-joint combination. "I mean, Addie here, *she* is a radical! A force to be reckoned with. I mean, she almost burned her bra last year."

Gina burst into laughter.

"Thanks." I felt my face get red. I mean, please, I wasn't microscopic.

"Way, man," we heard a boy's voice booming. It was Nick Stanley, all-time-all-time fantasy, surfer and senior star running back in football. He was so beautiful I couldn't swallow. I grabbed Gina's arm, so I could disappear behind her and Rachel.

"He can't see me like this," I whispered.

"You've got it for that guy?" asked Gina. "Oh, no," she sighed.

"I know, I know. But he's not with Merry Jacobs—they broke up again," I said.

"Yeah, weird. Merry's not here tonight," said Rachel. "But the ex-cheerleaders are."

"But if the ex-cheers *are* here, where is *she*?"

Merry Jacobs was the senior vice president of the student body. She was best friends with Lorelei Miller, who was a senior and on the cheerleading squad until Lorelei and the other senior cheerleaders got kicked off even though it was so close to graduation. I mean, I have no idea how people get to be as popular as Merry. Sure, she was beautiful, with long, glossy auburn hair, was a volleyball slammer and track team record-breaker, had a sexy voice, and was smart. I mean, I'd be lying if I said I didn't want to be like her. I hated her because of that. She even tried out for the football team when she was a freshman, but the coach said people wouldn't come to the games if a girl was playing, so she forfeited. She just did these *things*—ran for VP and got it, was valedictorian and loud about it, became prom queen and then didn't even want it—but I loved hating her because I was jealous of her being Nick's regular girlfriend. And that I was not going to ever tell anybody.

"Why are they *ex*-cheers?" Gina asked.

"Someone narced on them for drinking and smoking pot," I said as Rachel dragged me into the thumping noise, low lights, and wall-to-wall bodies in the living room.

"Why do we have to get in the middle of the crowd?" I yelled to

Rachel. We clapped, raised our hands in the air, turned around and around. Marvin Gaye sang, "You got to get it / Got to give it up."

"This place is way too lame!" Gina yelled to me. "Who kicks their cheerleaders off the cheerleading squad?"

I shrugged. "Well, not the entire squad. There's still Valerie. She's the sole survivor." She was the lone junior who didn't get kicked off.

"C'mon." Rachel spun around me. "It's 1977, you don't need a guy to dance."

When I clapped and turned around again, I saw Nick Stanley on the plaid love seat talking to Lorelei Miller. I had to look away or my heart would definitely explode through my eyeballs. That would be after I tied Lorelei's long, wavy blond hair around her graceful little neck. Puke city. Where was Merry Jacobs?

Monday morning, I drove Rachel and Gina to school in my fixer-upper powder-blue Pinto. Yes, I had the license and the wheels. Santa Raymunda High, built in 1925, pale pink and art deco style, was at the south end of town. Students walked or biked or rode the school bus, but you were way cooler driving. If you could get there early you parked in the lot behind the school by the soccer field, but if you were late like we were today, you parked up the hill on Calle Antonio, the street behind the school, and then walked down the long, steep set of concrete stairs, around the football stadium, and across the grass, which was a drag.

"If you hadn't taken forever," I said to Rachel. I slowed to see where we could park. We were doomed to the long walk.

"You could at least try the lot. You're so negative," said Rae.

"Hey, I just got done yelling my lungs out with my mom. Just park the car," said Gina. "Man, I should have taken the bus."

"Well, I resent that you think I am the cause of this problem." Rae crunched on her cinnamon toast, which did smell good.

"Oh, right, because the bus picks you up in front of your house," I said.

"Just drop me off—forget it," said Gina.

"We'll take the shortcut," I offered.

"The shortcut?" Rachel coughed on the last bite of her toast. "That's where all the stoners go, and it's so dirty."

I parked, and we hustled across the street.

"Look, we go down that way." I pointed past the sloping chained-off driveway that led to three maintenance buildings with faded pink paint and dusty windows. The warehouse still looked like an army barracks and the other two outbuildings like bomb shelters. Of course, we weren't supposed to go down there because all the sage, long grasses, weeds, and sycamore tree branches hid the prickly pear cactus, and the slope was steep.

"You want us to walk through *that*?" asked Gina.

"Two minutes tops." I galloped up to her.

"I swear." Rachel swished through the grass behind me.

"This," Gina made progress past me but still delicately pushed aside a mass of spider webs clinging to a dead yucca stalk, "is completely unauthorized."

"See?" I said once we hit the flat space between the warehouse and the two smaller buildings that were peeling like they had sunburn. "Right there's the girls' locker room." True, but there were more weeds to wade through. "Come on," I said. We heard someone with a bandsaw or something. We could go behind the second building and at a fast run, around the corner of the girls' locker room, and head down the slope. We were good on time. Not yet eight by my watch.

"Aahhhh!" Rachel yelled.

I looked back to watch her right before she face-planted into a pile of leaves and flailed her arms. Dark brittle shapes floated in a cloud.

"What's with all the leaves?" said Gina.

"There's spiders in here, man!" Rachel tried to pull herself up but slipped again. "Ugh, something's really gross in here." She shook her head. I could see she was trying not to breathe. The pile was really big.

"It's mulch, Rae." I reached over the island of leaves to help her take a gigantic step over it.

"Addie." Rachel looked at me. "There's something there. It's on my foot." Her whole face squeezed up like a juiced orange half.

I bent down to sweep at her foot.

"Oh, man," said Rachel, "what if it's a rat!"

"It's okay, it's not a rat. You know—"

I grabbed up a hunk of leaves and saw a weird non-leaf color where the leaves had been. *Gross me out to the max.* It wasn't a rat. It was worse. I pushed away another clump of wet leaves that clung together. I could see what it was now. It was someone's face. I could make out a profile because I had stripped off some of the leaf skin that had been sticking to the face. It was a girl's face. A girl's face I knew. I couldn't close my mouth. I could feel my whole stomach bubble up to the back of my throat.

"Well, tell me what it is!" said Gina. "I can't see anything with your fat head in the way."

I looked up at Rachel. There were tears in her eyes. "It's a body," she said, her voice shaking and hoarse like she had laryngitis.

"No way," I heard Gina say.

Everything was swimming up into my eyeballs. It was so hard to focus. I looked down at the face in the leaves. There were two slimy purple bougainvillea petals stuck to her cheekbone. The muscles in my face and arms and legs started twitching. I squeezed my lips together to keep my mouth closed. I thought I was going to puke and cry at the same time. If I opened my mouth, an endless stream of blind black eels would come out of me. I shook my head and swallowed. I looked up at the sky. At least this way whatever came out might not go everywhere.

"It's her," I said. "Merry." I sounded like some other person. Maybe I was dreaming. A nightmare.

"It's *her*?" said Rachel. "Merry Jacobs?"

"We need an ambulance." I kept looking at the sky.

"Okay." Gina's voice sounded far away.

"I don't think she's alive," said Rachel.

I let my head drop. I saw Rachel's face; a tear full of mascara raced down to the corner of her mouth.

I bent my head down. "Merry?" I pulled a lock of her hair—red, gold, and brown—I could see the strands in the light. I brushed more leaves away. She was lying on her side. I saw where her tan ended at her hairline and the freckles on her forehead, but the skin wasn't her normal color, more like gray or blue, and there was her—this open eye.

Rachel tried to lift Merry's bent arm, but it was molded into place. The leaves crunched under her like dry cereal flakes.

"Hey, what's this?" I saw something like cloth, but, like, part of it bunched up, coming out of Merry's mouth, soiled, yellow and black with white edging. "Can you see this?"

"It's—that's a skirt, that's a cheerleader skirt," said Rachel. "Oh, man. Oh, man."

And then I thought I was going to hurl, and weep, and black out. I hated myself for hating Merry Jacobs because, because now I was hating a dead girl, and that is really bad.

CHAPTER 2

Maybe I got this head-rush-city phenomenon because I was kneeling. Like Niagara Falls, but it wasn't like the water was falling inside my brain, more like water was coming in fire-hose bursts, flooding down under my skin. Then the dizziness. I couldn't tell where my body was. The "me" part of myself was out near, like, Jupiter, and I didn't know how to get it back into my body. I saw a guy race out of the building with Gina chasing him, and he was talking too fast. He came up to me and put his hand up, waving it in front of my face and telling Rachel and me to step back.

"Don't touch, don't touch." He was breathless. His blue shirt had his name sewn on the label—oh, right, Carlos. He was in charge of all the building stuff and the grounds, facilities, all that. His dark blue work pants had sawdust up and down, a big ring of keys on the belt loop at his side.

"But I touched her hair." I tried to pronounce the words.

"Wait." He took a breath. "I called the front office. The police will be here."

Rachel and I, still on our knees, leaned back on our heels. Gina stood behind Carlos. He raised Merry's stiff arm just a half inch and held the wrist with his thumb at the pulse point.

"No pulse. This isn't good." He was taking big breaths and pushing the leaves back up as if Merry needed to stay warm or something.

"No, please," I could hear Rachel say. It was so strange, like we were looking at everything from about ten feet in the air.

"This is insane, man." Gina shook her head from side to side, her hands on her hips.

We heard the sirens.

"Police," said Carlos.

The police cars' doors slammed and the sheriff was the first one out of his car, walking over. A red paramedic truck pulled up behind the sheriff's car.

"What the hell is going on here?" He wore mirrored sunglasses and his body looked like a walking slab of cement, square and straight and cold.

"They just found her, these girls—they had no idea the body was here," said Carlos.

"Well, now." The sheriff stood above the body.

A shorter bald man wearing glasses and carrying a small medical case knelt down beside the body and started examining it.

"Let's leave the man to do his job," said the sheriff, and we all moved back toward the warehouse building.

"They were just trying to shortcut it to get to school on time, weren't you?" Carlos looked at us. His skin was the color of milk chocolate, and he was thin and wiry in blue work pants and his blue maintenance shirt. "Right?"

We nodded.

"Uribe," said the sheriff. "You let *us* figure out what their story is. *Comprende?*"

"I was just trying to see if she was still alive, and I speak English," said Carlos.

"Well, excuse me." The sheriff didn't take off his glasses, but it seemed like he was trying to stare the other man down.

"They need to go home—they're in shock," said Carlos. He straightened his back.

"Okay, I see how we play this." The sheriff stood between Carlos and us. "You and your crew come down to the station, and you talk to my officers, who will be only too happy to hear every single thing you have to say. Ladies, I'm walking you down to someplace where we can talk."

I wondered why the sheriff called Carlos by his last name and why they had to question him at the police station. I wanted to ask Rachel, but it all hit me at once. I started to feel light-headed. Merry Jacobs was dead. Then we were all walking, the sheriff escorting Rae and me and Gina across the grass, along the walk that led from the girls' locker room to the back of the school.

At first, I just saw the badge, the olive-colored uniform, the mirrored sunglasses, the thick dark brown mustache combed above his upper lip, the slicked-back hair from the 1950s. The sun shimmered around his face the opposite of Merry Jacobs's face, which I was trying to remember and trying not to remember. I didn't really hear Sheriff Griffin. I just stared at how his mouth moved. I thought about how I once saw him save a little boy from drowning in Santa Raymunda Creek. But that was a long time ago.

I didn't really start thinking clearly until we sat across from the sheriff, trying to answer his questions.

"So, you know this girl, this young woman?" He breathed heavily through his nose like the breath had been stored up for a really long time.

"Yes," I heard myself say.

"She was right out in plain sight?"

"No."

"No? Where was she?"

"There, but under the leaves. That's why we didn't see her." I put my hands over my eyes to try to make myself see it better, because maybe there was a better way to answer.

"Did you touch her?" he asked. He held a pencil in his right hand and wrote in a little flip book. He sat opposite the three of us at one of the round orange lunch tables in the outdoor eating area that backed up to the parking lot and basketball courts. The thin morning fog was lifting. Behind him, I could see the two concession windows where you lined up to buy snacks and lunches.

"I tried to," said Rachel in between tearing off hunks of fingernail, and then sucking the finger after biting off too much.

"I did." I felt sick to my stomach again and really cold. I gripped the edge of the table.

"And?"

"I saw her face," I said.

"What about you?" Griffin asked Gina.

"I only saw part of her face." Gina cupped her hands over her nose and mouth.

"Did you touch her face?" he asked.

"I touched her hair," I said. "I had to see her face."

"See, the thing is, you guys went out of your way to come through that area." Griffin nodded his head back to indicate where; farther up behind the girls' locker room to the maintenance buildings.

"Because we were late." Gina started rummaging in her purse and took out a clear bottle of lip gloss. She couldn't get it open and then just held onto it.

"And no one else was there." I could feel the sun, but it wasn't making me warm. I crossed my arms tight around me.

"Except Carlos," said Rachel. "He took her pulse." She gnawed again at her right index finger.

"Yes, we're talking to him," said Griffin; his wide nostrils flared. He flipped the pencil back and forth between his index and middle fingers.

"Where is he?" asked Gina. She dropped her fist that still held the lip gloss on the table, and it made the plastic reverberate.

"Never mind. You just pay attention to the questions I'm asking, all right? I have to ask if you had any sort of," he paused, "problems with the victim."

I looked at Rachel, Rachel looked at Gina, and Gina looked at me.

"You saw the skirt?" asked Rachel.

"What?"

"The skirt," I said.

"She was wearing pants." He flicked the pencil, and the eraser head thumped his flipbook.

"No," I said. "Like, in her mouth."

"We saw a cheerleader's skirt," said Rachel.

A pigeon flew down near the table and pecked at some old piece of a sugar cookie wedged in a crack in the gray concrete.

"So, you guys, you're in shock. It's okay."

"No," said Rachel. "Tell us you saw it."

"Sure, we collect all the evidence," he sighed. "That's our job."

"But I can show you." I started to get up.

"Whoa, whoa, whoa." He shook his head at me.

"Look, there was a cheerleader's skirt that somebody, the killer probably, like, gagged her with maybe," said Rachel.

"I know what I saw," I said.

"Whatever is at the scene will be in our possession. Okay?" The sunglasses masked his eyes. He paused. "So, did you have any sort of problems with the victim?"

"No," I said. "And even if we did, we wouldn't kill her."

Rachel and Gina shook their heads no.

"Right." Griffin wrote something quickly and clapped the little book closed.

They had brought us apple juice and Fritos corn chips, which sat unopened on the table in front of us.

"She—it was there," said Rachel, staring at Griffin.

"You ladies just need to go home, lie down, and quit thinking. You're—you're emotional."

"Well, if you won't write that down about the skirt then we should tell my mom. She's the editor of the *Gazette*." Gina stood up.

Griffin rose to his feet, and his billy club hit the edge of the table. "You are not talking to anyone but me right now." He leaned toward her. "The reporters will come to us for the facts of the case. Do I make myself clear?"

I tugged at Gina's skirt, and she sat down slowly, and stared at me like I was the stupidest person in the world, and then she just looked away.

"Sheriff?" Phyllis, our school secretary, walked toward us. She was my mom's age, but she always looked like she didn't understand you, even if you didn't say anything. She wore a yellow-and-white checkered shirtdress and platform sandals and glasses that hung from her neck.

"They're free to go," he said.

"Good. I've called your moms, so you can get picked up." I could see the tendrils of her brown hair falling out of the big barrette she used to keep her hair in a ponytail.

"My car's up there," I said, "on Antonio. There's no other way to get it back, and my mom's at work." I jangled my keys, fingering the leather key chain with a butterfly on it.

"You will do no such thing. We're escorting students in groups, so come with me, ladies." She nodded to Griffin and clicked her sandals behind us.

We stood in front of the round deco admin building with its beveled glass and watched for our moms. There were about twenty other students doing the same. No student was leaving the classrooms or the grounds without supervision. The vice principal and three teachers walked students down the wide concrete steps with thick stone borders that led to the long driveway where normally buses picked up and dropped off students. A line of old date palms had left stains from the dropping fruit.

"This is insane," said Gina. "Man, this place is seriously over, as in over and out. I am out. Get me out of here."

"Wait, you can't leave now," I said. "We have to do something."

"You are insane, too," said Gina. She grabbed my hand and Rachel's, and we stood there for a second. Then we watched Gina hustle down the steps to where her mom hugged her. It looked like maybe her mom was crying. I started to tear up and looked at Rachel. We held hands. I couldn't wait for my mom to get here. Or Rachel's mom. I promised I wouldn't leave until we could both go at the same time.

"Thanks, Addie," she said and tried not to cry.

"I can't get her out of my mind," I said.

"I know. I just don't understand why Carlos and the maintenance guys had to go to the police station."

"Yeah," I said. "Weird. Like everything else."

Carlos Uribe had been the one person who helped me jump-start my car the first day I drove it to school. In addition to that, he didn't give me that look that says, *how could you be so stupid to leave the lights on and drain your battery the first day you drive to school?* I got a little emotional when I realized what I'd done, especially because I only had my learner's permit. My mom had already gone to work, so I'd figured I could drive Rachel and me to school, drive back, and my mom would not know a thing. It was the perfect plan. Except when I tried to leave and the car wouldn't start, and Rachel started to complain. Thank God for Carlos, or I would never have been able to keep the car—well, I wouldn't even have lived through the humiliation of seeing that look I knew my mom would give me after she found out I'd driven illegally and left the lights on. That guy had no idea how much he'd saved my bacon.

Everyone got two days off school. Rachel's mom didn't want her going anywhere, and she called me about being scared. I couldn't get Merry's dead face out of my mind, so I called Gina, and she invited us to go swimming and help babysit her little six-year-old sister, Triana, at the pool at their complex.

"Wicked city, you guys," I said. "What do you think?"

I mean, we were supposed to be on, like, high alert. There was a murderer, who had murdered Merry Jacobs, her royal pain of a highness, senior prom queen of Santa Raymunda High School, first female vice president of the student body association, captain of volleyball and track, and now, of course, not keeping me from fantasizing about Nick Stanley, but that was really grossing me out.

Lots of kids from Gina's neighborhood were hitting the pool today. Right behind us, my sixth-grade math teacher and his wife, inveterate tanners and dachshund owners, read the newspaper, which so far didn't tell us a whole lot. We sat with our feet dangling in the shallow end and watched Triana paddle and splash with the other little kids.

"Doesn't your mom want to interview us?" I asked. "I mean, we were on the scene."

"The sheriff told her not to," said Gina. "Like, it'll compromise the investigation right now."

"Please! And he said we were too emotional! Come on," I said.

"Hey, I know," said Gina. "Look, it's not easy for my mom."

"I think it's a cheerleader," said Rachel, keeping her voice low. "The murderer."

Gina got in the pool and steadied Triana in her lime-green-and-orange-red inflatable ring. "It's possible." Two long braids with tons of butterfly barrettes flowed down Triana's back.

"Way too obvious," I said.

"You really saw it, saw this cheerleader's skirt?" asked Gina.

"Yes," I said. "I'm not making it up."

"Me either," said Rachel. "I found the body. It's a cheerleader, I swear."

"It's definitely creepy," said Gina.

"I'm talking about the *ex*-cheerleaders," said Rachel.

Yes, our cheerleading squad had been cut down to one because the cheerleader coach, Stevens, had lopped them off, all four seniors. Only Valerie, or Val as she was known to her friends, who was a junior, maintained her cheer-status. Normally, I could care less about those bouncing, joyful, type-A personalities, but it was completely staggering to be at a high school where almost all of the cheerleaders got fired.

"The police did talk to them," said Gina.

"But they didn't arrest them," I said. "I get it. Merry Jacobs might bad-mouth one of the cheerleaders, but even then, I don't buy that she had a hand in getting them kicked off."

"No? They were caught at Steve Ryan's party drinking and smoking pot," said Rachel. "Except Val."

"Yeah?" said Gina. "So, who doesn't drink and smoke pot at Steve's?"

"Exactly," I said. "They must have made Coach Stevens mad to fire them like that," I said. Stevens was in charge of the cheerleaders.

"Merry was so bossy," said Rachel. "This one time she came to talk to Coach Zamora, and, I mean, I have a hard enough time getting picked to be on someone's team. Merry stops what she's doing, walks over, and serves the volleyball *for* me."

"That hurts," said Gina.

"Oh, and then get this: she says, 'If you were wondering how to serve, that's how you do it.'" Rachel pulled her feet out of the water and hugged her knees. "Man."

"I didn't really *hate* her." I cleared my throat. "But she wasn't . . . I don't know. Like, I want to give her credit for being the first female VP, you know, but then, she was kind of mean. It made it hard to like her."

"Okay, so," said Gina. "Possibly cheerleader."

"No, it's got to be someone else, but who?" I asked. I was getting burned.

"We've got the cheerleader skirt. I mean, that's a clue," said Rachel.

"There's Nick," said Gina.

"The police talked to him too," I said. Yes, he was a total squeeze-your-knees-together hunk. Yes, I was totally in love with him. "Can't be him."

"Yeah, but Merry dumped him before the squad's big amputation," said Rachel.

"So, she booted the perfect boyfriend?" Gina looked at me. "He could be a suspect."

Nick sat behind me in Calculus and wanted me to share my answers to the tests, so he would blow softly on my neck, even though I was just a sophomore, oh, my God, while other students watched and giggled because it made me blush like candy Red Hots. Nick did this to a lot of girls he sat behind in his classes. When Rachel went to the winter prom with Perry, her sometimes boyfriend who was bright and wrote poetry but also had an overbite that gave him the nickname Bugs, she told me how bad she felt that I didn't have a date. But she said I should forget about Nick, that conceited dick.

"I do think it's a guy," I said. "Just not Nick."

"Why a guy?" asked Rachel.

"Merry Jacobs?" I said. "Later days, man. She could totally beat up a cheerleader." I tried not to think of Nick Stanley's incredible biceps. Man, I had to get my head on straight about Nick Stanley as much as I did about calculus, physics, women's rights, and playing the cello. I mean, get real.

Talk about majorly awful! I mean, okay, so I didn't like her. But, now, Merry wouldn't be bossing people around during volleyball anymore or talking down to us at student assemblies about sagging school spirit, as in everyone needed to be more proud, "You're Santa Raymunda Jaguars, let me heeeeaaaar you!" I kept seeing Merry lying on a dissecting tray like the frogs we cut open in Mr. Boatman's biology class, her clammy skin pulled open and pinned to the tar backing.

Poor Merry Jacobs. I mean, she couldn't even be poor because she was dead. Life definitely wasn't happening for Merry anymore. For no reason whatsoever she ended up dead on a Monday morning. Murdered. It said it in the paper. And who was next? I mean, we'd seen that cheerleader skirt. We'd totally seen it. Totally creepy. I had to know that it really wasn't Nick.

Triana swam out from under her inflatable ring and popped up with a splash in front of Gina. "I am a shark, and I will have to eat you!"

"We have to find him, you guys," I said. "We have to find the killer."

CHAPTER 3

We did not have to worry about the whole "found-a-dead-girl-at-school-curiosity" thing. If I thought I couldn't be any more unpopular, well, I was. I mean, I'd actually touched the dead girl's hair. Bummer. I cut a swathe like Charlton Heston as Moses in *The Ten Commandments* parting the sea.

At the special assembly we listened to Principal Ennis, a large, barrel-chested man with standard block-head hair, thank the police for coming and state that no students were allowed to be alone on school property. Sheriff Griffin with his Teddy Roosevelt mustache and mirrored aviator sunglasses, two other officers also in shades standing beside him, said he was on to a suspect but gave no details. Before Ennis dismissed us, he told us, "Now, of course, you must all be on guard, but remember, you have a higher chance of becoming the victim of instantaneous human combustion than murder." In the super-silent auditorium, students mostly swallowed hard and looked at the ground.

Afterward we sat at the plastic lunch table at the far edge of the cement courtyard away from the cafeteria service windows. Another twenty feet behind us, two metal gates opened to basketball courts, then baseball and soccer fields, and finally up to the football stadium.

"Okay, finally, I got something out of my mom." Gina wore a striped T-shirt with a scoop neckline that would probably get a comment from Mr. Angel, our English teacher. Girls could get sent home if they wore a "distracting" outfit.

"Okay, so?" Rachel hugged herself in her vanilla-colored sweater. Even though the overcast of this morning had lifted, she had the blood temperature of a lizard. But this morning even I was chilled. My butterfly top had little cap sleeves, and I could feel my goose bumps.

We sort of had this plan to find the killer. The first part involved Gina getting all she could from her mom. Before the murder, Gina and her mother, Peggy, had had a big blow-out over whether Gina was going to go back to her dad's in Chicago over the summer; so, like, complete nuclear winter between Gina and her mom. But then came Monday with Merry's murder, and some swift emergency diplomacy on Gina's part. So, would Peggy pour forth details from the investigation to Gina like an endless M&M's supply? I mean, of course, totally confidential.

Most of Gina's dark berry-colored lip gloss had faded even though she applied it at least six times an hour. "She said Merry was killed sometime between Friday afternoon and Saturday morning. So that's the good part. Then there's something that's not so good."

"What do you mean, not so good?" I asked.

"They think it's a cheerleader," said Rachel. "I bet you anything the police think it's a cheerleader. Some girls, seriously nasty."

"No, it's a guy," I said.

"Don't have a cow, okay? So, cause of death," Gina lowered her voice, "asphyxiation."

"Oh, my God," said Rachel. "What did I tell you? Those cheerleaders choked her to death with that skirt. Proof positive. It is. It's a cheerleader!"

"Wait, that's not what it looked like." I glanced around at the other tables. It seemed like everything was so quiet after Monday. Locker doors shutting not as loud. People talking at simmer instead of boil or burning engine level.

"So, whose is it?" Rachel pulled at her sweater cuffs to reach over her thumbs.

"They must know who the skirt belonged to, right?" I asked.

"*That's* the not-so-good part," said Gina. "My mom said there's no skirt." She looked over her shoulder to make sure no one around us heard anything.

"What do you mean?" I put my hands on my head to keep my anger from exploding out of my brain.

"That's impossible. We saw it. We told the sheriff." Rachel spoke really fast.

"It didn't come up in the police report. It wasn't in the evidence from the scene," said Gina. "There, that's from my mom's lips. Took me forever to get it out of her."

I tried to remember when the sheriff was there, when we got told to walk with him down to the lunch area. I should have grabbed the thing.

"But where does that leave us? I mean, we saw it," I said.

"I know," said Gina applying her lip gloss.

"What does your mom think?" I asked.

"She thinks anything's possible; they could have lost it or—" Gina looked up. "She's under a lot of pressure to cooperate with the police."

"We did see it, Addie," said Rachel. "That's why we are going to find this killer. Because it is a cheerleader, with that skirt. How could the police not have found it?"

"I don't know. It's just got crime of passion written all over it," said Gina with lips so shiny you could almost see your reflection. "There's the boyfriend."

Yes, deep in my dark recesses, I fed this fantasy of being Nick's girlfriend in a future No Place and No Time. But it kept getting interrupted by the whole criminal element thing, like, this image of Nick rising out of the foam at the beach, his surfboard snug under one arm and dragging Merry's dead body across the sand by her hair with the other. It kind of bothered me.

Still. All those breakups and make-ups between Nick and Merry. How many times had he given me the lowdown that Merry had dumped him? Couldn't I do, I mean, help him with his homework? Then, after he'd passed an exam thanks to some of my work I let him copy to be cool, he would lean back in his chair and tell me how he and Merry were back on. Back on? After their most recent back-on, I ate a whole box of Fudgsicles, and I'd only recently been able to get that box in the trash without my mom seeing it.

"I can't believe there's no skirt," I said. "Hey, Carlos saw it, right?"

"I don't know," said Gina. "He was making you guys get away from the body, and the cops were swarming around."

"It's a cheerleader. Girls can be that mean," said Rachel. "Who was that girl they sprayed with that sugar-water lemon-balm stuff? And then she got stung by all those bees?"

"That was Melanie Hollis. That was extreme," I said.

Melanie Hollis had made the mistake of sleeping with an upper-esher girl's boyfriend.

"See?" said Rachel. "How awful was that?"

"But they didn't kill her," I said.

The thing was, Merry Jacobs didn't even have to physically kick your butt into yesterday. She could just shame you with her artillery of facial expressions. Once, a couple of freshmen got "the look" because they blocked the breezeway to the Biology classroom with the aquarium that Mr. Boatman swam in on Fridays. Yes, it was that big, and he swam in it in a wet-suit. Those hopeless freshman girls, completely hypnotized by Merry's gaze, fell forward, got trampled on by the students coming out of class, and survived with four skinned knees, a broken wrist, and a concussion.

"Oh, my God, what about Alex?" I asked. Alex Stapleton was the smarmy ASB president. All teeth, all the time.

"You just don't want it to be Nick," said Gina.

"No. I'm being serious—look at him," I said. "Merry practically did all the work on those student activities. He just took credit for it. Maybe she refused to do his bidding. He gets mad at her. You know, guys-in-high-places type of deal?"

Gina's eyebrows, like two dark paramecia, slowly moved closer toward the bridge of her nose. "Come on, Alex isn't going to kill his meal ticket. He relied on her to take credit for all the rallies, the fund-raisers, all that high-quality school spirit. *Now* he's going screw that up? His scholarships? His reputation? Nuh-uh. Get this: I saw Nick after third period today. He's Mr. Cool Dude, talking with his friends," said Gina.

"So, he's here? He's not missing school?" Rachel squeezed the plastic wrapper of her cheese snack.

"He doesn't look like he's lost a lot of sleep," said Gina.

I pulled out the rubber band holding my ponytail, shook my straight hair loose, and inspected my split ends. Yeah, they'd hit a nerve. "Just so you guys know. I am not in love with Nick Stanley. We're just friends, okay? He teases me in Calculus. I help him with his homework. But guess what? He does, in fact, thank me for it. Genuinely thanks me." I felt a spray of something. I turned around to look at a group of guys stomping milk cartons and screaming as spurts and gushers of milk splattered everywhere.

"Either way," Rachel asked, "why was Merry's body out by the maintenance building in the first place?"

"Right, didn't her parents wonder where she was?" I asked.

"You know," said Rachel, "with Nick. Guys don't show emotion. He probably is sad."

"I say it's someone who had some big problem with Merry. Someone she, like, screwed over or something. Okay, after she and Nick broke up, who was she seeing? The cheerleaders would know that, right? Nick always went back to her, not the other way around. You guys, he sits behind me in Calculus. I've heard the saga for almost a year, please. He told Martin Hellman that he promised Merry he was going to stop flirting with sophomore girls." I winced when I thought about how Nick tapped me on the neck, and I turned around breathless. He and Martin busted out laughing, and Mr. Vargas asked me to turn around and face the board. I was the lone sophomore girl in a sea of mostly senior students in that class. "We should look at the rest of the football lineup. And he's friends with Martin. Maybe Martin knows something. Maybe Merry met her secret love out there and, you know?"

"That's lame. Forget it. Think about the skirt. The cheerleader skirt? Like, where is this mystery guy going to get that? The thing is," Gina's hands made fists on the table, "what about the police? They eat their donuts and lose the evidence? Like, I want *those* guys finding a murderer?"

"But that's not right. Merry Jacobs was a superstar. Track, volleyball, softball, vice president, valedictorian. Okay, not anymore. But the police are going to want to find out who did this," said Rachel.

"Or they'll find who they want to find," said Gina.

"We have got to get up close and personal with those ex-cheerleaders," I said. "But how?"

CHAPTER 4

Friday morning, we floored the Pinto into the student lot and parked in the spot with the diagonal lines that read NO PARKING. Plenty of time. A good, solid ten minutes before classes started. We were going to get noticed.

"I feel kind of naked," said Rachel.

"You are not naked," said Gina. "But. Tube top? Very risky. Didn't know you had it in you."

"Me neither," said Rachel.

Gina wore a crocheted top from The Bikini Stop in San Felipe. It barely had a front and the back was just a couple of crisscrossed strings. My choice was a bandana-print halter and cutoffs.

"We're all going to get sent to Ennis," said Gina.

"Hey, trust me," I said. "This is totally going to work."

We marched through the outdoor eating area. A group of sullen boys stared at us and dropped their books with uneven smacks on the concrete. *Yes!*

"Where's that boyfriend of yours?" Gina asked Rachel. "Don't you think you ought to give him a thrill?"

I waved to the boys.

"Addie," said Rachel.

"This is part of the plan, Rae." I stumbled in the high-rise wedge sandals I'd borrowed from my mom's closet.

Rachel stopped at her locker. A loud whistle echoed. "What was that?" gasped Rachel. It was like when you're walking back from the beach and the girls in their cat's-cradle bikinis ahead of you get whistled at, and cars slow down, so the guys can tell the girls they are "gnarly babes." We waited for Rachel to regroup. She pulled her tube top up.

"We are on a mission." I stared ahead as Gina and Rachel fell in step with me to enter the quad. People looked up from behind their open locker doors.

"The ex-cheers got kicked off the squad. We get kicked out of school. We are instant friends with the ex-cheers." Gina winked at me. "Genius to the max."

"Ditto," said Rachel.

"De nada," I said, as I felt the blisters erupting on the tops of my little toes.

A stunned girl dropped her breakfast sandwich in front of us before she got to take a bite. A boy throwing his boomerang fixated on us, and the boomerang socked his forehead while he remained frozen in place. Once we got to the quad, a row of people had stopped in their tracks under the eaves with their arms out like a human picket fence. I swear, I was not thinking we would get this reaction. But it was totally boss.

Then we took a short right and continued to walk, passing the outdoor stage where the most popular of the most popular, the upper eshers, reigned, and among them the ex-cheers. I paused, thinking we should try to slow down.

Rachel turned to me. "Are they looking?"

"I don't know." I searched for Jaycee or Myla. They were the loudest of the ex-cheers. Myla had long dark brown hair with one section in the front that fell across half of her face and a crazy-thin nose. Jaycee was the captain. She had curly brown hair, thick dark eyebrows, and blue eyes the color of dark metal. She always got one foot out in front of the ex-cheers traveling as a pack of four with Lisa, the quiet blonde, and Lorelei, too beautiful for words.

Talk about awkward. We were taking smaller and smaller steps and still no sign of the ex- cheers. Oh, man, had I totally miscalculated? We might have to wait until the ultimate, the suspension, but if the ex-cheers didn't see us first, they might not understand that we were trying to be like them, that we wanted to be liked by them. Getting a suspension would prove it.

"Addie." Gina leaned into me and looked up.

At the edge of the concrete outdoor stage platform, I saw the four ex-cheers standing in front of the upper-esher crowd. I stopped walking, and so did Gina and Rachel.

"Wave," I said.

The three of us raised our left hands to the ex-cheers. They waved back.

"Radical," Rachel whispered.

"Far out," Gina whispered back.

"Hey!" Jaycee yelled to us. Her voice had a sharp, cutting quality. "You are so busted."

I smiled. I hiked my shorts up.

Jaycee gave us a thumbs-up.

"Psych," I said under my breath.

"Busted!" someone yelled out from the upper-esher group on stage.

"Busted, busted, busted!" people on stage repeated and then people in the quad and in the breezeways next to their lockers started chanting.

"Over and out," said Gina.

"Now do you want to go back to Chicago?" I said.

"Stellar to the max!" Rachel waved to Perry.

The bell for first period blared.

We all landed in Ennis's office by break time. Outside his open bay windows, you could see the date palms outside. He looked weary. Block-head hair you could serve a pizza on. Bags under the eyes and a nose you couldn't help staring at because there was a dark curlicue of hair growing out of it. I wondered if he had thought of using Nair, because that would loosen the hair at the root. But shaving it, it would just grow back.

He made no effort at direct eye contact. He looked above our heads, into the jars of his leafy creeping Charlie plants on his desk, and at the folded newspaper in front of him. Décor category: boring. American flag, the state flag, don't forget the George Washington portrait, plus, a framed photo of the Apollo-number-something-or-other during liftoff. And dead air.

"Why would three intelligent young women come to school in rags barely covering their bodies?" Ennis sighed.

"It's a protest, sir," I said. "It's a free country; what's wrong with what we wear?" I sat up straighter.

Gina nodded; Rachel was in a bit of a shock. Would he just suspend us for the day? Or more?

"Okay. I see where this is going." He took a deep breath and contemplated the ceiling. "We have suffered a great loss with Merry Jacobs's death—"

"Murder, sir," said Gina. "Merry was murdered."

Ennis closed his eyes as if to make that fact go away. "Yes, right." He leaned back in his chair, his hand on his forehead. "Do you have any idea how awful this is? Do you know how many parents are calling me? Not just during the day but at night? When are they going to be able to stop worrying? When are the police going to make an arrest? I read about it every morning." He slapped the newspaper in front of him.

"Sir," I said.

"Tell you what I'm going to do." He reached into a drawer and pulled out three yellow slips with carbon backing. "These are suspension notices. Phyllis," he called out, "these young women are not allowed on school property until Monday. Please show them out." Just as we got to the doorway, he called after us. "Wait." I thought he might be able to say something profound. "You go home, you put some decent clothes on, and you come back here alive, you hear me?"

"Wicked," said Gina.

"Psych," I squealed as we pushed open the admin door to the outside.

"Yeah, I guess so," said Rachel. "But what about these?"

"He doesn't have time for stupid paperwork," I said.

"I'm saving mine," said Rachel. "Just in case."

I shook my head. "No one is getting in trouble."

"Rae, don't you get it?" Gina looked at Rachel. "We are just getting our plan into action."

"Right." I scanned the break crowd as we pushed through. People stopped and pointed at us. Yes, now we were the students who found the dead body and just got suspended. I wanted the ex-cheers to know we were ex-communicated for the day.

"Okay," said Rachel.

The bell for third period went off. People started evaporating.

"Hey, you!" The Swiss Army knife voice of Jaycee made me turn my head like an owl. The four ex-cheers were still on the stage, but the steps that led down to the concession lines coated them in shadow.

"You guys," Rachel whispered.

"Hey, you, too!" I yelled back to her.

"We like your style." Jaycee waved.

"Like yours too." I tried to move toward her, but students in twos and threes were running past. "Had to get suspended for it." I waved my yellow slip.

"We can dig you," said Myla.

"You're cool," said Jaycee.

The divide was still between us.

Then the four ex-cheers turned around and walked back into sunshine across the stage and down the stairs.

"Check it out," said Rachel.

"Victory." I rubbed my hands together. "They know who we are."

"Right on," said Gina. "They think we're cool."

We walked fast past the lockers under the eaves near the deserted lunch area.

"Whoa, foxy, huh?" It was Nick Stanley.

Oh, my God. Oh. My. God. Gina and Rachel were afraid I was going to faint.

"Um . . ." I went all warm inside. I looked around. *Oh, don't blow it. Act natural.*

"Looking good. I like those legs. Guess I'll have to check them out in Calculus. Mmm-mmm." He smiled, then trooped off toward the boys' bathroom across the walkway, a stained two-by-four hall pass in his back pocket.

"Major." I braced myself against the lockers so my knees didn't buckle.

"Mellow out," said Gina.

"Addie, let's go," Rachel commanded.

"Now," Gina barked.

"But he, but we—" I stared at the wake he left in the air.

"We are jamming," said Rachel.

"You guys . . ." I wanted to wait. He'd definitely be coming back.

"Yeah, he's a guy, he got an eyeful, you'll live. We are wasting time," said Gina.

"Maybe I should stay for Calculus," I said.

"Hand me the keys," Gina demanded.

"The keys?" I asked.

"Your car, ding-dong," said Rachel.

"What? Hey, no way. I'm driving."

We went to my house. My mom would be proud. I was taking a stand against authority, and, well, we needed to figure out how to get close to the ex-cheerleaders. But my mom never got home before five p.m., so I'd have to tell her later. Since protesting makes you hungry, we ate baloney sandwiches outside on the little porch with geraniums and marigolds in little pots. My room would have been way too stuffy. I still had that white French colonial girly furniture and that trippy pink wallpaper. Plus, I piled. Papers, music scores, books, on the bed, the floor, the desk, the bureau. I was lucky there was room for me.

"So," said Gina, "I gave it one more try last night. I asked my mom about this thing with the police saying they have a suspect. They have this big lead, and they're going to make this big arrest." She stopped speaking when a dark orange butterfly flew past. "But they won't give her a name."

"Does she have the police report? Can we get a copy?" I asked.

"No," sighed Gina.

"So, I know we asked this, but all the cheerleaders were questioned, right?" asked Rachel.

"Yeah. They got asked about Merry, what they did Friday, stuff like that," said Gina.

"Well, the skirt was from an outfit of one of the cheerleaders, so wouldn't they have asked about the skirt?" Rachel asked.

"*That* I don't know," said Gina.

"Okay. How about this? Maybe they turned all their stuff in when they were cut from the squad," said Rachel.

"It's possible," said Gina. "I mean, I looked through my mom's desk. She must sleep with those files or something."

"You guys, we got the attention of the ex-cheers," I said. "Now we need an excuse to pick their brains without them realizing what we're doing."

"But why would *we* be interested in Merry unless it's about her murder?" asked Gina.

"Yeah, I mean, people are now weird about me in art class because I found her body," said Rachel.

I watched the butterfly dart to a pot of marigolds and fold its wings while it worked to get the sticky pollen onto its legs. It was hard not to think about Merry, dead and over with, and these butterflies, random nobodies, kind of like Rachel and Gina and me, working for pollen.

"I think people are dying to say stuff," said Gina, "and, I mean, dying."

"It's the police who are so clueless." I couldn't get the image of Merry's body lying there in the leaves out of my mind. "She deserves justice."

"That's what people are talking about," said Rachel. "We need to know who did it and resolve this thing. It's like she just keeps getting more murdered every day."

"We need a major lightning bolt." I took a bite of sandwich and the white bread melted onto the roof of my mouth, rendering me speechless.

"Maybe we could get someone to spy on the police for us," said Rachel.

"Oh, right. Why didn't I think of that," said Gina.

"Hey, you don't have to get petty," said Rachel.

"Hey, you don't have to get so sensitive," said Gina.

"You guys." I was finally able to un-adhere the gluey bread. "I've got it. Check it out—it's totally perfect. Perfection city. So, here's what we do." I swallowed several times. "There's a memorial for her tomorrow, for Merry. We go."

"Wait, it's been almost a full week since she died and no funeral?" asked Rachel.

"Did you not read the paper this morning?" asked Gina. "Rae, that's the story Ennis was looking at when we were there. 'Family finally gets memorial for murdered daughter.'"

"So why did it take so long?" asked Rachel.

"Well, they can't technically bury the body until they have the suspect or something. Man, I don't know," Gina said.

"But I thought you said they have a suspect?" I said.

"Not behind bars, they don't," said Gina.

"Okay, so we go to her memorial; I'm with you," said Rachel.

"Yeah, but there's more," I said. "The yearbook's already gone to the printer's, right?"

"Yeah." Rachel did artwork on the yearbook.

Gina rolled her eyes. "The yearbook? Which means?"

"Listen. It's so brilliant. We put together a commemorative book, a special publication, just on Merry, right? Okay, limited edition for seniors? And we've got to interview the people who knew her. That means family, friends, *cheerleaders,* I mean the ex-cheers, who we are already cool with, the whole nine yards. It's totally airtight. We put it together. Give it out at graduation. Genius." I could barely contain myself.

CHAPTER 5

Let's just say Gloria Dei Lutheran Church was a bit of a killjoy, especially if you were used to the chapel of Mission Santa Raymunda like my friend Rachel. A thick blanket of golden poppies covered the slope up to Gloria Dei, perched a few blocks west of the high school. But no earthy smells, no incense mixed with warm candle wax, no stained glass, no distraction from the business at hand: just cold, hard sin-sifting.

The modern rectangular structure of wood and glass was all 90-degree angles. When you first entered, you thought, okay, with that wall of windows at the front there'll be light in there, but that only permeated a few rows into the church like a stagnant tide. The contrast between the bright outside and the darkness within caused people momentary blindness, which led to this weird un-churchly groping you'd be subjected to if you weren't careful on your way to your pew.

We arrived, noted the vision problem, and waited until one of us could see. This was definitely not an occasion for overthinking your fashion getup; Gina had said to wear something tasteful. Besides, we were all sitting in the dark anyway; everything and everyone was swallowed in shadow. Gina and I wore identical navy wraparound skirts with some silver disco shimmer. Rachel was in a Qiana polyester dress—yikes—for special occasions, and her new Dr. Scholl's sandals made a distinct snick-snick sound with every step.

We signed the guest book and slipped as solemnly as possible into some seating near the back. Of course, no interviewing anyone just yet. We were only going to observe. We sat getting used to the stern dry air inside and taking the pulse of the people already in the rows half-whispering, adjusting suit jackets, and offering little sticks of mint gum. We saw the minister's pulpit raised at a diagonal to the left. A simple wood cross hung above the altar and, in front of this, an easel with Merry's portrait surrounded by bouquets of white flowers.

"Look." My heart jumped. "Nick's here." I stuck up my hand and waved wildly to him. What can I say?

"Control yourself," said Gina.

"Thank God he didn't see you, Addie. This is for a dead person," Rachel scolded.

"But see?" I mean, I was sincere. "He's not a total dick like you guys think."

"Right, okay. So, like, coming to the funeral of your dead girlfriend? That is a supreme humanitarian gesture? I can definitely see that," said Gina.

"Okay, message received," I said, but I was not embarrassed. His coming was supreme to me.

We watched the arrival of the Jacobs family greeting people on the way to their seats at the front. I could feel a lump in my throat. These poor people lost more than a loud, aggressive pillar of high school popularity. Rachel kept nudging me. I knew she was thinking about her dad. She told me that even a year after his death she kept thinking she saw him, driving down the street, in a supermarket aisle, or at the beach with a different family. It seemed like a long time before she realized that it was just her mind playing tricks. I wondered if something similar might affect Merry's mother, a tall, thin woman in a gray pantsuit and pixie-cut blond hair. She walked arm in arm with Merry's dad, a beefy man with a freckled face and a few strands of reddish-brown hair combed across his balding forehead.

Merry's six brothers followed their parents in dark striped ties and dress shirts tucked into trousers. Each brother had the same hair, with long bangs that swept across their foreheads in different shades of reddish brown. The family picked their way to the front of the church, putting out their hands now and then to touch those thrust at them in signs of comfort. Merry's mother stopped occasionally and touched a handkerchief to her eyes, looking majorly bummed.

"You know, we'll have to interview the family," I said. "What they say about her friends and stuff."

"You really think they'll tell us about Merry's enemies, Addie? They just lost the light of their life. They're going to be way too worked up over the murder," said Rachel.

"I wonder," said Gina, "about Merry's dad."

"You can't be serious." Rachel's whisper was a gasp. "You think her dad? No way!"

"Come on, Rae. The guy pushes his kids to be straight-A, star-athlete superhuman. Merry didn't totally measure up to the ideal." Gina watched Glenn Jacobs taking a long time to lower himself to his seat.

"Just because she didn't set every school track record, her dad murders her? You are so sick," said Rachel.

"Hey, I thought we were here to consider possible suspects," said Gina.

"Her dad really pushed her for the football tryout when she was a freshman four years ago, and then he went ballistic when she didn't make it on the team," I said.

"Her dad murders her for something that happened four years ago?" Rachel demanded. "Besides, everyone knows Ennis didn't want a girl on the team."

"Chauvinist pig, man," I said. "But, yeah, not murder material."

"Look," said Gina. "I'm not saying he did, I'm just saying it happens."

"It's got to be some guy. Like, Merry led them down a path of romance and then she let Nick get back with her, and he, this other guy, couldn't take it," I said.

"You guys, you are forgetting the cheerleader skirt," said Rachel.

"Right," I said.

"I do not see any of those ex-cheerleaders," said Gina.

"There's Stevens." Rachel pointed. The women's volleyball coach was also the cheer coach, a tanned woman who looked like Tammy Wynette and favored wide headbands to hold back her thick coils of blond hair. Why had she kicked all the senior girls off the cheerleading squad?

"You don't think she would kill Merry?" asked Gina.

"About as much as her own dad," said Rachel.

"You guys." I pointed to Hugh Donnelly, the girls' track coach, a Slim Jim jerky stick of a man. A couple of people behind him stood Alex Stapleton, the ASB president.

"Piece of work, Alex," said Gina. "That guy can even smile at a funeral."

"He is so two-faced, you just have to consider him way up on the list of suspects," I said. "She could have had some dirt on him, something. Or maybe he was in love with Merry—think about it."

"You guys," said Rachel, so excited she pushed herself back against the pew, which creaked and set a flank of faces turning with a domino effect to see who was responsible for the eerie noise. "Sorry," she murmured.

"Stellar, you guys. She's here." I'd spotted her.

Lorelei Miller. Merry's best friend. She floated in a river of people jamming the aisle. She could have been a model out of *Seventeen* magazine. I mean, you know how some girls are just, wow, just appear out of thin air like Botticelli's Venus? Okay, Lorelei was Santa Raymunda's version of that. Venus with a serious tan. Even her thighs were perfect. It made you want to slice off every imperfection from yourself, but you'd just end up as one big pile of bleeding human chunks: too chubby here, too skinny there, that bumpy acne on one cheek that your mother told you would clear up if you just got outside more. Oh, Lorelei. Could you consider Lorelei real, much less a real friend? And now *she* was my mortal enemy because she was talking to Nick on Friday night. All we could do was watch the head of Lorelei and her hair in the one concentrated beam of light down the center of the church.

"She is so pretty," Rachel sighed.

"I know," I said.

Lorelei's hair wasn't even blond; her hair was, like, that burnished gold in those illuminated manuscripts where the Christ looks pregnant and the Virgin Mary's eyes are closed. We watched her move over to the right-hand side and then fill in a space in the sea of other heads. All of the other ex-cheerleaders materialized one by one, but none of them sat together.

"What's up with that?" said Gina.

"I don't know," said Rachel. "But they're on the program."

"What?" I looked at Rachel.

"Here." She showed me the listing of a routine from the Jaguar cheerleading squad.

"A routine?" I could feel my eyebrows lifting up into my hairline.

"Don't ask me," said Rachel.

"This is just too bizarre," said Gina.

The organ music started, and there was a hush as the church filled with quiet. The only sound was from the back-and-forth movement of memorial programs being used as fans. The temperature rose with so many bodies accordioned together. People cleared their throats or coughed between that weird silence you hear when you are waiting.

Reverend Perrault made his entrance. He was a tall man whose clerical garb flagged behind him as he approached the pulpit from the vestry and stepped up past the altar's flower arrangements. The organ music continued for a few more seconds while he shuffled his notes and adjusted his glasses.

Okay, so if solving Merry Jacobs's murder means we've got to start at the Lutheran church, Jesus Christ, so be it.

The minister spoke for a good thirty minutes before he finally introduced Mr. Jacobs.

"I'm just saying," Gina whispered.

"Really?" Rachel whispered back.

Glenn Jacobs dwarfed the pulpit, sort of like King Kong on a lecture series. He had sweat marks under his arms that you could see when he reached out to his sides and took hold of the podium like it was something he was going to drive. His face was bright pink and his eyebrows made two straight dashes; his eyeglasses were propped on his forehead. He made a slight bow to the microphone and then pulled his glasses down and took out a piece of paper, which he unfolded seven times.

"My daughter," he said, "was a shining star. She was generous; she wanted everyone she knew to be her friend. Her family, me, her mom, her brothers, all here today, we're still in shock. We can't believe that someone would take the life of our dear girl." He stopped to sniff back some tears. "As you may know, I love sports, and up until Merry, it was me and the boys and a ball and a playing area. But then we had our little girl." He sniffed again. "Her mother was so excited. She had all these little dresses for Merry. But my girl refused every bow, every bonnet, every dress. No, sir. She grabbed her brother's old mitt and followed us to the baseball field almost before she could walk." He sniffed again. "She said, 'Dad, I want to be on your team.' And that was my Merry. You know, she was always on your team." He paused. "I just miss her so much." He paused again and looked out at the dimness in the ark of the church filled with tiny dust motes like plankton in the deep sea. "Thank you all. God bless." He sat down in silence.

"Still think he murdered his daughter?" Rachel whispered to Gina.

"He does sound pretty torn up, but it could be all that guilt, too, you know," Gina answered.

Next came Merry's eldest brother, who gave a short speech about his sister's need to help others and how much he missed her. Then the second eldest took the podium and started speaking.

"Dang, didn't the brother before say the exact same thing?" asked Gina.

"It is a memorial," said Rachel.

The rest of the brothers repeated the same lines when they got up too, while Merry's mom cried the whole time.

Finally, the organist started. At first it sounded like church music, but no one reached for the thick hymnals to start singing. Gradually, we heard what sounded like a medley of pop tunes. "Your Song" by Elton John, "Rhiannon" by Fleetwood Mac, and "Turn to Stone" by ELO.

"Trippy," said Gina.

That's when Coach Stevens stepped up to the podium, and just as the organist finished her last flourish, the cheerleaders filed one by one up to the stage. You had to be there.

"Ladies and gentlemen, the cheerleading squad of Santa Raymunda High would now like to pay tribute to Merry, who not only supported the team in all of its competitions but also helped choreograph many of our routines." She stopped and blotted her eyes with a Kleenex.

The cheerleaders, all five of them, wore dark skirts and pastel blouses. They started a slow wave with their left arms, then began a cheer clapping in rhythm, though much slower than any school or game chant. There were the ex-cheers: Myla's dark flowing hair always covered one eye; Jaycee, the captain, who could smile while doing five handsprings in a row; Lisa, the shy blonde with ballerina posture; Lorelei, the Venus; and then Val, the only cheerleader on the team, with her long straight black hair, bangs, and intense dark brown eyes. Jaycee stepped out in front. "We're here," *clap-cla*p. And the rest echoed, "We're here, we're here, for a very important cheer." *Clap-clap, clap-clap*. The cheerleaders rose up on their toes, waiting for a response. A tentative single clap started in the middle row. A long fifteen seconds followed before a *clap-clap* came up from the front somewhere, then two more *clap-claps* to the left of us, and finally you could hear people across the pews clapping back in unison, or trying to.

"Too weird," said Rachel.

Gina and I nodded while we joined in the clapping too.

"We miss our friend, yes we do. We miss our friend, how about you?"

Now the audience responded. "We miss our friend, yes we do. We miss our friend, how about you?"

"She was the greatest, oh, yes, yes, the greatest." *Clap-clap*. "She was the one, who got the job done. How will we live? Out, out, without her. I don't know, I don't know, but heaven's got a winner." *Clap-clap-clap*. The audience and the cheerleaders finished together. Then silence, as if everyone expected something more but there wasn't, so everyone quickly sat back down.

"Well, they got it together to do a cheer for her." Gina leaned into Rachel.

"Purely for show," said Rachel. "What would be more suspicious than them not coming or making a memorable appearance? Well, here it is."

"Remember, Rae, we can't just jump to conclusions. We have to check stuff out," I said.

Finally, Coach Donnelly got up to speak. He described how great a runner Merry was, that he knew he had something special on his hands way back when she ran the 400-meter for him: "Imagine watching this freshman winning by 3.35 seconds, a new record." Merry had come in first ahead of two other Jaguars, followed by the rest of the pack. "She brought all that was good about her into her performance, and she wanted the same for her teammates. Sometimes she yelled at folks on the track more than me." He looked even thinner without his track suit and sweatband.

"Maybe they did the nasty?" said Gina.

"I swear," said Rachel. "Freak me out. That's just too gross to imagine."

"Well, what about Tara Heaney and Mr. Anderson?" I asked.

"Yuck-o-rama," said Rachel. "That was out a of a science-fiction novel. He's, like, an intergalactic alien or something." He was the biology teacher who didn't have an aquarium to swim in, but Tara Heaney had fallen in love, somehow, with Mr. Anderson during a field trip to Joshua Tree in her senior year and got pregnant. There was a shotgun wedding the day after she graduated.

"Defies modern and future science," I said. "But it happened."

"So disgusting," said Rachel. The image of Mr. Anderson wasn't something you could easily get rid of. He sported a toupee that made him look as if he wore half a coconut shell on his head. At least Donnelly was real about being bald. But attractive? To a seventeen-year old girl? To Merry? Later days.

Reverend Perrault cleared his throat and said the Lord's Prayer while the organist began the final dirge.

The whole thing was over, and I still couldn't get who the murderer was, or get Merry's dead face out of my mind. I mean, who was it? Could you discount Coach Donnelly? Her own dad? No way. But Merry Jacobs had been murdered here. Holy Christ! And those cheerleaders with their cheer of—what was that? Too weird. Plus, we wanted to be the ex-cheers' next best friends? It was better than nothing, which was all Merry Jacobs had now.

Merry Jacobs could never bask in her athletic glory again. Merry Jacobs was not even going to graduate. She would never see all these people here paying homage to her. She was gone because someone had cut off her air supply, stopped her breathing, stopped her brain, stopped her heart, and now it was time for action because that someone was probably sitting right here in this church.

CHAPTER 6

The Jacobs family stood to the left of the podium and shook hands with people in the receiving line that ran all the way along the side of the church, as more and more people joined it.

"Okay, we've got to find those ex-cheers." I bolted out of my seat and tried to squeeze through, but I felt someone pulling me back.

"Addie." Rachel kept her voice low. "You can't just cut ahead."

"This is going to take forever." I looked down at the altar with the bouquets and portraits of Merry.

"We've got to do this thing right." Gina applied two layers of lip gloss as we took tiny steps on the worn dark blue carpeting. "If we act too weird in here, we won't get to talk to anyone."

"It's just—they're right there," I sighed. The pastel brigade of ex-cheers stood next in line to give the Jacobses sympathy handshakes. Plus, I didn't really want to meet the grieving parents. Sadness is not my thing. The wood-stained pews looked almost black. The skinny stained-glass windows projected small squares of red, gold, and green light on people's backs. Voices churned in a low rotating hum like an old washing machine.

"We'll get to them." Rachel looked at her watch. "We'll need to talk to the parents anyway, so let's not totally blow it by being crazy when we don't have to be."

"Excellent point," said Gina. "So, I still don't get how we 'get' a commemorative book approved and printed."

"That's Rachel's job," I said. Rachel excelled at art, like a junior Picasso. She was in Ms. Deerfield's art and yearbook classes this year. Drawings. Paintings. Cartoons. Deerfield had marked Rachel for success, contests and scholarships. I knew Rachel could get her to okay our idea. "She talks to Deerfield with the idea. Possibly some tears, too."

"Yeah, yeah." Rachel nodded.

"Just get her to okay it," said Gina.

When we finally shook hands with the Jacobses, I could tell Mrs. Jacobs really wasn't up for it. Shell-shocked but smiling, she looked nervous and weak, and her eyes had a weird clouded stare, painfully distant, totally majorly distant, like the-next-galaxy distant.

Once we were outside, we walked past a grassy area with tiny pink geraniums between the path to the church entrance and the parking lot. A slight breeze relieved the afternoon heat.

"I bet you anything Mrs. Jacobs is on tranquilizers," said Gina.

"Poor thing," said Rachel. "Bummer to the max."

"I thought maybe the ex-cheers would talk to us after we got the thumbs-up from them for getting kicked out yesterday," I said.

"Later days, Addie. They're with their parents. This is not the time or place," said Rachel.

"I mean, we have got to play it cool all the way through with them," said Gina. "You don't think up a genius idea and then set it on fire so you can get a third-degree burn."

"I noticed Nick Stanley got out of there super fast," said Rachel.

"We should too." I felt weird watching people still exiting the church not talking, not smiling, not touching. Death really does a number.

"Please, you guys," said Gina as we hiked through the parked cars in the lot. "What *was* that? Have you ever had a cheerleading squad pump a funeral crowd before? Like, hello?"

"Too trippy," said Rachel.

"I thought I was hallucinating," said Gina.

Then someone bumped into her and she lost her balance, her feet shifting off her platform rainbow sandals. It was Alex Stapleton.

"Sorry for that." The ASB president always wore a navy-blue blazer, and his super-straight black hair had one crazy cowlick at the back of his head that could not sit down. His lips peeled back to show off all those teeth, pretending to know Gina. Several people threaded past us between the metal bumpers of the cars. "I forgot your name."

"That's okay, Alex." Gina's voice dripped with honey. "You know, I have so been meaning to talk to you."

"Really?"

"I'm Gina, you know, from Joey Ballard's party?"

"Gina!" said Alex. "Look, I know this isn't the best place—"

"Would you excuse us?" said Gina. She and Alex wandered in a sea of station wagons and VW Beetles, and disappeared behind a shiny purple van.

"I think she's shaking him down," I said.

Rachel and I made our way to the edge of the parking lot where I'd parked the Pinto. We looked down the cliff of poppies, ice plant, sour grass, and prickly pear cactus to Calle Antonio below. A couple of cars zoomed out toward the Coast Highway.

"Rachel?" a voice spoke behind us.

Dream on. Was it? It was Valerie Muñoz. The one remaining cheerleader coming toward us.

Val and Rachel had been pals in first grade and through the summer before I moved to Santa Raymunda and started second grade. Val lived with her mother, Rosa, two blocks down from Rachel's house. Rosa would come over and have coffee with Adela, Rachel's mother. Val and Rachel spent their summer at the San Felipe public pool and told each other horror stories. That summer you couldn't turn around without hearing about some slasher driving up and down Pacific Coast Highway leaving a trail of chopped hitchhiker heads in his wake. My mom went on and on about it too.

Valerie Muñoz was a basketball forward and the only girl in the chess club. She was as close as we could get to the ex-cheers, and she was standing right in front of us. Stellar! She was the perfect candidate for us to start asking questions about how Merry Jacobs had wound up murdered.

"It's so sad, isn't it?" said Val.

"It's tragic," I said.

"That's the truth." She wrinkled her forehead. Normally, Val gave the impression that her electrons moved at a higher-than-human speed. You almost needed a nap or a cool-down after some time in her presence. Her long black ponytail swished behind her, and her normal facial expression was set at smile on high dazzle. How could a human being be so positive? Was it her eternally clear skin or the ability to move from cheerleading one minute to doing combustion reactions in Chemistry class the next? I'd heard she was the best lab partner, bar none.

"That was nice," said Rachel, "you know, the cheerleaders doing something for Merry's memorial."

"Thanks, but, got to say, that was all Lorelei's idea." Val bounced, but her feet stayed on the ground. "You guys found her, huh?"

Rachel nodded.

"What was that like?"

"The worst," I said. I had told my mom after that morning that I was okay. That was after I spent most of the day and night crying. I would dream the whole thing over and over, but having the job of finding Merry's murderer helped me feel like I wouldn't get trapped in that mire of fear, panic, and visions of what Merry looked like dead. "No one should have to see something like that."

"But at least you found her. I mean, who knows how long she could have been left there. Right? So, thank goodness you did."

"Thanks," I said. It was the nicest thing anyone had said.

"Addie's being modest," said Rachel. "She thought up this idea to make a commemorative book in Merry's memory. We interview her friends and family, you know. So, it's like she's still part of the class. I think it's totally boss." Rachel nodded at me.

"That is rad." Val pressed her hands down her black skirt. She looked back up at us and shaded her eyes from the sun. "You know, no one really liked Merry—I mean, besides Lorelei. But what can you do?"

"About what?" Rachel balanced on one foot, then the other.

"The ex-cheers weren't going to do the cheer thing. But Lorelei begged and begged, so eventually they came. It took a lot. Right before yesterday, I thought it was going to be just me and Lorelei." She sighed. "Let's face it, Merry was not the most mellow person on the planet."

"But you don't think any of them wanted her dead, do you?" Rachel tried not to look like she wanted to hear a "yes."

"No way, not like that. Their vibe was freeze her out."

"Except for Lorelei," I said.

"So that must have been awkward," said Rachel. "With the cheerleaders not liking Merry, and Merry helping with the routines, helping Coach Stevens and everything."

"Well, that was Merry's day job, keeping Stevens from getting in trouble," said Val. "If you know what I mean."

It was fairly common knowledge that the coach hit the bar pretty regularly. Sometimes she hit the bar before she hit the bar.

"Stevens's drinking, you mean?" I asked.

"Merry kept her in line, covered up for her, that kind of thing. I had to respect Merry for that. She ran interference. I mean, the coach could get into a temper, and it would not be G-rated."

"Like violent?" I asked.

"A lot of potential. I didn't see her hit anyone, but she threw things," said Val. "Hey, did you tell the police Merry was wearing a cheerleader outfit?" Val asked.

"We never said that! We said—" Rachel almost said something I thought she'd better not.

"We said she was friends with the cheerleaders." I looked down at the street again and started to feel vertigo. Coach Stevens had a violent streak?

"The whole thing is so totally weird. I just hope they find the guy," said Val.

"You think it's a guy?" I asked.

"I don't know, I just said that." Val looked behind her and waved. "My mom's over there waiting. Later days, you guys."

"Addie, we saw that skirt. What if the cheerleaders think we're pinning the murder on them?"

"Well, we kinda are. Where's Gina?" I wondered.

"I know, but that was after, after we talked to the cops," said Rachel.

"It would be bummer to the max if the police mentioned this to the ex-cheers." I felt like we were too close to the edge of the property. I walked to the back of the Pinto. "We have all this potential to get into their inner circle and the police could come back to them, and then—"

"Guess we just hope they still like us for getting suspended. Gina's mom, that's who we need to talk to," said Rachel.

We heard Gina's rainbow sandals thumping the gravel area along the edge of the parking lot.

"So," said Gina, "I saw you guys talking to Val. That's major."

"So major," said Rachel. "Got anything out of Alex?"

Gina shrugged, "Maybe. Let's go." She looked behind her. "I got rid of him for now."

We jumped into the Pinto and sped out of the lot. When the latch holding down the hatchback had broken, pretty much right after my mom bought it, Rachel helped me tie it down with a piece of rope around the bumper, and then—what ingenuity!—with the leftover length we pulled up the loose tailpipe. It was a thing of beauty. Except that it clunked over bumps if I didn't quite avoid the curb.

"I truly do not understand why funerals make me hungry, but I am starving," Gina sighed.

"Me too," said Rachel.

"Ugh, my feet!" I tore off my wraparound sandals. "What I do for beauty."

"You're not supposed to drive barefoot," said Gina. "You give women on the road a bad name."

"Roll down the window, please! Man, between the exhaust and your stinky feet I'm going to choke to death," Rachel complained.

"My feet need their freedom!" I yelled.

We headed down to Pacific Coast Highway and turned into our

favorite hangout, a burger joint called Doheny Joe's. It was on the side of the road just before the entrance to the State Beach. We ordered burgers, shakes, and French fries and began the ritual of tearing up and squirting little packets of ketchup and mayo into pools on napkins before our meals were ready.

"Tell all." Rachel looked at Gina.

CHAPTER 7

"Alex Stapleton, man. What is my reward here?" Gina demanded.

"What?" I bit into my burger and sucked up a stray onion strand.

"Yeah, come on," said Rachel.

"What did he say? All that smiling, that's got to be covering up something," I said.

Gina savored her bite of burger and washed it down with chocolate shake. "Well, he's an egomaniac, yes. And he did see Merry on Friday, but in the morning. Then," she picked up a fry to point at an invisible Alex, "he went on and on about how much he'd done for ASB, how little Merry actually did."

"When everyone knows *she* did everything," said Rachel.

"That's it. He couldn't stand a girl doing better than him, so he got rid of her," I said.

"I wouldn't say that," said Gina. "But Merry was VP, so normally, he said, they have the ASB meeting in the afternoons on Friday, but they cancelled it that Friday."

"Hey, Lorelei's the treasurer of ASB. Oh, my God, we have to talk to her, too," said Rachel.

"I know, I know, Lorelei," I said. "But why didn't they have a meeting? Did they get in a fight?"

"Who cancelled it?" Rachel dipped three French fries into her chocolate shake and munched.

"How can you do that?" I watched her.

"Look, I'm *not* saying Alex is not a suspect, but he didn't sound like he was that interested in Merry, dead or alive," said Gina. "I asked him why they cancelled the meeting. But it was just something to do with somebody's schedule. It wasn't an out-of-the-ordinary thing."

I dug into my book bag, took out my folder, and started to write on the notebook paper in it.

"Oh, no, I'm doing it. You can't even read your own writing." Rachel grabbed my stuff and started jotting things down. "Okay, so ASB meeting cancelled on Friday. Not uncommon but not usual."

"If someone had to go to a doctor's appointment or something," said Gina.

"Ah-ha," said Rachel. "Or a track meet?"

"No, I asked. Track is over, but anyway, we can find out. I can talk to him again," said Gina.

"Well, okay, she was healthy before lunch," I said. "So where did he see her?"

"She was going to the gym to talk to Stevens at third-period break. He just happened to see her. He wanted to know what her plan was for the last couple of days of school. They were planning some senior prank stuff, and she said she was too busy." Gina stared at her burger.

"See, she did all the work," I said. "No surprise."

"And, of course, I asked what he knew about her, and he gave me the list. Merry was a good planner, had good ideas, creative. Of course, he didn't say she was 'smart.' Also, Lorelei is her best friend. Was, I mean. Anyway, he's trying to get on Ron Miller's state senate campaign." Gina daintily peeled her pickle off her burger and buried it in the napkin pile.

"So?" I asked.

"Hey, that's Lorelei's dad, Ron Miller, right? The signs?" said Rachel.

"He wants to work for *him*? Okay. Hmm." Ron Miller's heads were planted around town on large red, white, and blue signs to remind voters to vote for the rest of him.

"Did Alex talk to the police?" I asked.

"No. But you guys better help me."

"Why?"

"Why? Because I told him I'd go out with him." She sucked noisily on her shake until the liquid stopped sputtering and she got fish lips.

"Gross me out. Are you kidding me? Alex?" I asked.

"No, I'm not." Gina shook her head. "What about Valerie?"

"You can't date him," said Rachel.

"Right now, my strategy is avoidance, but let's just not talk about it."

Rachel and I told Gina what Val had said about Coach Stevens.

"The cheerleading coach has a drinking problem?" said Gina.

"And the violence thing," I said.

"We just have to do everything we can to let the ex-cheers know we're real cool, totally with them," said Gina.

"I didn't try to explain anything to Val. She said nothing about a cheerleader skirt. I mean, it's obvious, isn't it? That skirt wasn't there when the police got there. Or?" I said.

"Or, the police took it for some reason, so nobody would know about it but them," said Gina.

"Man." Rachel finished writing for a minute and looked up. "The police aren't supposed to do that. Isn't that tampering with evidence?"

"I don't think we can trust the police. My mom says they pretty much have a stone wall around the case." Gina sighed. "I mean, I've tried to look at her stuff when I could, like, for the police report or anything else useful."

The shake and burger grease congealed in my stomach.

"Look, if they don't have evidence, if they don't do their job right, whoever they do find may not be the murderer," said Gina.

"That would be worse—I mean, what's worse? Merry being killed or the police getting the wrong person? You guys, we have to talk to more people," I said.

"Yeah, hey," said Rachel, sitting up and taking her straw out of her mouth. "What about Val?"

"What are you talking about?" said Gina.

"You know." Rachel looked at Gina. "Val's mother, Rosa, and Griffin."

"What did you say?" asked Gina.

"Rosa and Griffin." Rachel fiddled with the chain around her neck that had a little gold cross.

"The sheriff?" said Gina.

"She doesn't know, Rae." I looked at Gina.

I knew about Rosa's broken-heart thing, unlucky in love.

Rachel took a long slurp of shake. "Val is actually Griffin's daughter."

"The sheriff? He's her *dad*?" Gina's voice got higher, and she tossed the last of her burger at the pile of used napkins.

"This totally makes your case for Santa Raymunda's lameness," I said.

"He gets around, what can I say?" Rachel explained.

"The sheriff?" Gina insisted.

"He's got at least another four kids that way," I said. "Everyone knows. Of course, no one says anything."

"Great, and so do these babies grow up to be police officers?" Gina bowed her head.

"Do you think that could happen?" I felt somewhat defeated and then mad. My dad left my mom for another woman. Actually, he didn't officially leave until he'd had two kids with this other woman, his girlfriend. Then he left my mom and me. My mom stayed in her bed for a while, with the curtains closed, and I kept trying to feed her: Frosted Flakes, peanut butter cookies, canned ravioli. I slept in her bed with her sometimes to keep her company, but really, I was afraid she might take off too. She told me I didn't make Dad leave. She told him she didn't want me to see him. That made me cry. Later, she went out with several guys who had motorcycles. One of the guys even moved in, but I would have to go find him at Los Buitres, the vultures, the bar in town, to get him. I told my mom he was bad. Luckily, soon after that, he was gone, and my mom burned all the sheets that night. Mine, too.

"Rosa and Val get money from Griffin. I mean, he does that for the other kids in town, too," said Rachel.

"When did you hear that?" I said. "I knew that he was Val's dad, her real dad, but he gives them money?"

"Someone told my mom. It just shows the police, the sheriff, they may be doing their best, but right now, it sure doesn't look like it." Rachel licked shake from her straw. "It looks really lame, actually."

Good old law-and-order man Sheriff Lloyd Griffin. Not the portrait of police purity? I thought about that drowning boy he'd saved. We watched from the bridge at the edge of town. The boy's mother cried and agonized watching her boy floating in Santa Raymunda Creek when it rose after a big rain. Griffin dove in, fished the boy out, and carried him to shore. Straight into his mother's arms. Now, Griffin was all starched uniform, the fit so tight it squeaked, one ironed fresh every night by his washed-out wife. He wore these mirrored sunglasses, so you couldn't really tell what he was looking at. Don't you want to trust the police? But it didn't seem like he was doing the right thing. Gagging the town newspaper? Not reporting evidence? What else had he done?

"Now we know he's totally not trustworthy," said Gina. "Gross me out to the max."

"Dang. That makes me wonder if Merry wasn't Griffin's offspring," I said.

"No," said Rachel.

"This is nuts," said Gina. "So, Val is a cheerleader, and her real dad *is* the sheriff, and you're not going to consider that at all?"

"You're right," I said.

"No, you guys, I know what it seems like," said Rachel. "But Val isn't like him, and she's no murderer."

"She is excellent when it comes to chemical reactions," I sighed.

Gina unscrewed the top of her lip gloss. "Hmmm. You've been saying it's a cheerleader from the get-go, but now that that's possible, you're saying 'no.'"

Rachel checked her watch. "Not her. I said *ex*-cheerleaders. Hey, you guys. It's four thirty; my shift starts at five. I need a ride."

"You know what?" said Gina. "I totally forgot. I saw Merry and Lorelei talking on Friday, at lunch."

"Now you remember?" I asked.

Rachel wrote and tried to shove the folder in her bag at the same time. "You guys, I've got to be there."

We hurried to the Pinto.

"We've got to talk to Lorelei." Gina slammed the passenger-side door. "I'm pretty sure I saw them."

I gunned the Pinto down the little south street back into town, instead of Calle Antonio from the beach, to drop Rachel off. The road went past the high school to the north, along Santa Raymunda Creek, around the Yamashito farm, rows and rows of square plots of strawberries, and past the trailer park between the road and the creek bed. I liked this way better, less traffic. For the first time since discovering it, I forgot about Merry's dead body. The Bee Gees sang "Nights on Broadway," my friends pretended they knew the words, and we were full of shake and lukewarm fry grease. Nice. Small wonder no one got whiplash when the police sirens blared and two cop cars looked like they were going to drive up over the hood of my car and my windshield.

"Hey!" Gina grabbed the dash.

"Wicked," I said.

"Dang, Addie. You don't have your shoes on," said Rachel.

"That's it. They can smell your feet from town." Gina straightened in her seat. "Get ready to be arrested."

I punched the brakes, jolting the Pinto. I was able to steer to the side of the road to give the cops a wide berth, but they slowed down and turned left in front of us onto a road that led to two older clapboard houses sitting on smooth lawns with wood rail fences. We watched the patrol cars stop in the gravel driveway of the first house.

"That's where Carlos lives, you guys," said Rachel.

"Who?" asked Gina.

"Carlos, the guy that checked Merry's pulse—the janitor, you know, person," I said.

"He lives right there, in the yellow house," said Rachel.

"Dang." I couldn't believe they'd arrest him. I stopped the car to watch the cops re-tuck their shirts into their pants, straighten their holsters, and walk up the short set of stairs to the porch. They looked like dark caterpillars on a pale rose petal. The house was an old-fashioned two-story with dormer windows like eyes, and the porch wrapped all the way around it. A white trellis enclosed the south side of the porch, and purple bougainvillea bushes climbed toward the second story. A lawn sprinkler in the middle of the front yard attached to a hose made a small fountain.

"Time. I'm gonna be late," said Rachel.

"I told you," said Gina.

"Total burn! Are they really going to arrest him?" said Rachel.

"I just don't think it's him," said Gina.

"It's so—convenient," I said.

"If he's innocent, what's going to happen?" said Rachel.

"We'll follow them," I said.

"And then?" asked Gina. "We sit in the car and drive and become outraged in the car?"

"Okay, then what? We can't just let this happen," I said.

"I'm sorry, you guys. I already got two lates this month," said Rachel. "We can't stop them."

I put the Pinto in drive, and we didn't say anything. We dropped Rachel off in front of the grocery store for her shift in her funeral dress.

CHAPTER 8

"Murder Suspect Arrested!" the *Santa Raymunda Gazette* headline assaulted in three-foot type, the letter edges serrated. Totally ominous. Accompanied by a grainy black-and-white photo of Carlos Uribe, a jacket pulled over his head, flanked by four police officers. In the caption he was identified as the Head Supervisor of Maintenance at Santa Raymunda High School. Also, in the shot, the sheriff at the far left just happened to face the camera. Sheriff Griffin's Teddy Roosevelt mustache could practically sweep a street, and he wore those mirrored aviator sunglasses, so maybe he wasn't looking directly into the camera, but he was definitely the centerpiece of the photograph. What a scene! What do you do when the absolute worst happens?

"How could it be Carlos?" asked Rachel.

We sat near the back wall in English class. Our teacher was giving us free time to work on our term papers.

"Then they bring up this arrest for stolen property that's totally bogus," I said. In the news story the police were quoted as saying Uribe had been charged in the past for stealing stereo equipment, but the reporter countered that Uribe had driven the van without any knowledge that the vehicle had been used to stash the theft and was exonerated of any wrongdoing. "Carlos Uribe was innocent then, and now this?"

"Hey, they reported that the police got it wrong about him. Totally bogus," said Gina. "But my mom has to keep her job. She got called last night by the sheriff's office."

"You said a guy was the killer," said Rachel.

"Val said it was a guy too," I said. "But it's not Carlos Uribe. I mean, it makes no sense."

"But they have arrested him," said Gina. "It's like he almost got framed before, and now it looks like he might get framed again."

The bell for lunch sounded.

"We start interviewing now," I said.

Rachel fished into her book bag and took out a clipboard with paper.

"Hope they still like our style." Gina applied a fresh coat of lip gloss.

The sunlight blasted us when we stepped outside. We scanned the quad and the stage, the natural cheerleader habitat. We stashed our books and bags in our lockers. I took off my sweater from around my waist. Rachel pulled her hair up in a leather tie and pin, stuck a pencil behind her ear, and carried her clipboard.

"Wait." Gina wiped her lips, applied dark berry lipstick and lip gloss, and then touched up my and Rachel's lips. The rest of us might blend into the background, but not our lips.

By now the whole school was at lunch and there were three groups on the steps of the outdoor stage. We dove in: parts of people's faces, pants pockets, lockets, ankles, Oreos, carrot sticks, arms, hands—total teen motion. As usual, the upper eshers staked out a place at the very top of the stage.

We spotted our first ex-cheer, Myla. Her hair perfectly cascaded across one eye like she was some super-sexy French film star. She stood in a circle of other senior girls talking. We tried to close in.

"I still don't see why she got a nose job," said Rachel.

"Who knows," I said. "It was a perfectly nice nose."

We angled through a bunch of people to position ourselves behind Myla, although there were still a few bodies between us and her.

"What about her nose?" asked Gina.

"Plastic surgery," said Rachel.

"Even her parents must not have liked her nose," I said.

"Wicked. My mom would never say I needed a new nose," said Rachel.

"To me it looks too thin, like she's had a clothespin on it and it just stays that way. Her nostrils are just slits. You wonder if she can get enough air to breathe," I said.

"What's weird," whispered Rachel while we were still slowly pushing toward Myla's crowd, "is after the surgery her butt just grew—you know, like her cheerleader skirt totally doesn't cover it anymore."

"So?" Gina whispered back.

"Like her butt had to compensate for what her nose gave up, don't you see? That is freaky," said Rachel.

"Great, you guys, now all I'm going to do is look at this girl's nose," sighed Gina.

"Okay, enough—here goes," I said. "Myla!" I shouted. The crowd parted. Myla turned around. She cocked her head at us.

"Um . . ." I put my hand up. It's one thing for me to see one of them from a distance, but with her right in front of me, I got nervous.

"Who are you, again?" asked Myla with only half of her face visible, the half with her nose.

"We," said Gina, "are in charge of the memory album for Merry Jacobs, for Deerfield to supplement the yearbook?"

"Wait, didn't you guys get suspended?" said Myla.

"Yeah," I said, trying to be nonchalant.

"Oh, yeah, that was so cool," said Myla.

I became very conscious of the circle of girls who took a step closer to us, and now we were surrounded by sky-high status, popularity to the max.

"Only for the day," said Gina.

"That is really boss." Myla checked us out. "So why are you talking to me?"

"We're the memory album committee for Merry Jacobs. It's like a tribute." I looked at Myla holding my chin with my thumb and forefinger.

"That lip color is wild to the max," said Myla. "Memory album?"

"Well, it's part of yearbook, and I'm yearbook staff," Rachel explained, "and since we can't get an insert in the yearbook at this point, we need to do it this way. There'll be a picture of you, you know, your quote, a picture of Merry, and so on."

Myla sighed. The gold-like flecks dimmed in her brown eyes. She started to twirl a piece of her hair. The circle of girls waited for her to speak.

"Merry Jacobs. We were good friends. She was super, super talented. And she—she did make up these amazing routines, and we won at competition. Which was amazing. It's hard to—can you guys give me a minute—" It was like Myla was watching a movie or something in the back of her mind, like *Carrie* or *The Exorcist*, true horror. The circle of girls disbanded, and then it was just the three of us and Myla up against the backs of the popular people.

"You guys have no idea. Talking about her—it's just so confusing. I loved her. She was so with us, like we could do anything—"

"That's great." Rachel flipped the page on her clipboard and kept writing.

"Then she had to screw us over." Myla sniffed, such a sad sniff. With those really small nostrils.

"You're grieving; things get so mixed up," said Gina.

"Mixed emotions. Emotional. That's what the police called us, so we totally get you, Myla," I said.

"We might be the only ones who really understand," said Rachel.

"Maybe there's a reason Merry did that—like, you guys had a misunderstanding?" Gina asked.

"I mean, Lorelei couldn't lift a finger without asking Merry which one." Myla blinked.

"Yeah, we're looking for Lorelei," said Rachel.

"But why did Lorelei depend on Merry so much?" I asked.

"Because," said Myla crossing her arms, "the whole thing with her dad running for office. Lorelei had to turn into Miss Perfect-city. But no one can be totally perfect. She'd go crying to Merry, and Merry worked her magic. Then Lorelei would be perfect again."

"What did Lorelei do that was so *not* perfect?" asked Rachel.

"Breathe? I don't know. I just know that's all we heard from her. Have to be perfect. Merry was her best friend, so I guess that's why she went to Merry with her stuff. I heard Merry tell Lorelei she'd help Lorelei make it go away."

"What go away?" I asked. "A boy, a grade?"

"How should I know? Ask Lorelei." Myla turned away, her face in profile, hair over her eye.

"Right. We're cool. We get it," I said.

"Do you know where Lorelei is?" asked Rachel.

"No. Look, am I sorry Merry Jacobs is dead? Yes, I am truly, truly sorry." Myla turned to face us, pulling hair back for her full face to make a rare appearance. Her eyes teared up. "But when someone betrays you, you just don't get over it. Do I wish sometimes I could have pulled her eyes out and made her swallow them for ruining my life? Totally." She looked down, aware of what came out of her mouth. "I-I didn't mean that, I'm just, you guys are making me upset." The gold flecks in her eyes sharpened into knife points.

"Oh, sure, you're grieving. We totally get that. We understand," said Rachel.

"Hey, Myla, look." Someone pulled her away, and we raced down the stage steps.

"It doesn't make sense, does it?" said Gina. "I thought Merry was the perfect one."

"Well, who better to ask how to be perfect?" I said.

"But we have to find Lorelei," said Rachel.

CHAPTER 9

"You guys, that Myla's got *assassin* potential!" Gina yelled above the noise as we booked it past the cafeteria line that stretched out into the eating area of round orange tables and crazy lunch loudness. So much talking, people bouncing their quarters and dimes off the metal railing that separated the two cafeteria concession windows, the freshman girls at a table to the right, squealing at the freshman boys blowing up their paper lunch bags and popping them. The cement interior under the eaves echoed and sound bounced back and forth.

"I don't know," Rachel raised her voice, "but if *she* had to keep herself from getting back at Merry, what about the other three? Man, we need to watch our backs."

"None of them is strong enough to subdue Merry!" I yelled. "Can you see Lorelei?"

"No!" Gina yelled back. "But Myla looked like she could definitely track a wounded animal."

"I told you guys getting kicked off was super traumatic for them!" Rachel yelled.

"Okay." I nodded.

"Hey, over there!" Gina shouted. Rachel and I turned to see Lisa Black. Her signature yellow hair with bangs curled under made her look like one of those Egyptian hieroglyphs except blond. She also had this killer posture. Graceful. She stood talking to Joe Maldonado, her boyfriend, who sat with a group of jocks three tables to our left but still under the eaves. Joe was captain of the water polo team, and he and Lisa were Couple of the Year.

"They are so cute, aren't they," said Rachel.

It would have been nice if they really did look like newborn labrador puppies. But after our interview with Myla, I kept seeing tiger kittens before they learn to hunt.

"I kind of feel bad that she's still in Biology," I said. Just the other day I had seen Lisa coming out of Boatman's class. "Guess she just doesn't get evolution or photosynthesis or whatever." Biology was the science class you took your sophomore year, not your senior year.

"Addie, she's a teacher's aide for first period," said Rachel.

"Oh." Now I felt stupid underestimating a girl's intelligence.

"I have to eat," Rachel groaned and looked cross-eyed.

"Rae, we're talking life and death here. We can't lose our chance now." I ducked under the railing. We had to be able to make sacrifices like not waiting in the lunch line.

"But all this murder stuff makes me hungry," said Rachel. "Just some corn nuts, at least?" The noise at the cafeteria lines died out a little as we got closer to Lisa.

"Carlos Uribe is in jail, remember?" said Gina.

The minute we got close to Lisa's table, Joe and the other guys left. Lisa headed toward the quad, her back to us. We hurried to catch up to her. Rachel's Dr. Scholls clacked and Gina's rainbow sandals flumped on the concrete.

"Lisa!" I yelled. "Hey, can you talk a minute?" My voice echoed against the wall and the eaves in the tunnel between the lunch area and the sunlit grassy squares of the quad. Lisa stopped to face us. She looked surprised. Her eyebrows disappeared under her blond bangs.

"Hello?" Her voice was like powdered sugar.

"Hi, we're the memory book committee," I said. "For Merry Jacobs."

Lisa's thinly drawn eyebrows dropped back down as she inspected us. "I thought you guys got suspended."

"Just for the day," said Rachel.

Lisa had clear blue eyes that appeared to be staring at some combination of Loch-Ness-Sasquatch-man-eating shark monster right behind us. She backed herself up against a corner behind a pink stucco pillar next to the steps leading up to the outdoor stage area, where her friends could return her to her natural upper-esher habitat. We couldn't risk losing her.

"Oh, I don't know anything about it." Lisa lifted her shoulders up to her ears. She walked out of the shade, and we followed. She looked spooked, pale in the light. I noticed the purple cast on her eyelids when she blinked. She looked over her shoulder at the crowd of girls on the stage. They held each other's arms up to see who had the smallest wrist. She looked at us again, and I could see her trying not to shiver with her hands clasped together in front of her body to hold still. "What's on your lips?" She sounded as if she was a little short of breath.

"Gina, what's this color again?" I asked. "Cool, huh?"

"Very Berry."

"Oh, it's lipstick." Lisa relaxed and breathed a little deeper.

I looked at Rachel and noticed she had somehow smeared the gloss, so there were two big blobs of Very Berry goo at each corner of her mouth. In a certain light she might look like she had just eaten a really raw piece of steak. I nodded to Gina and she gave Rachel a hand motion to wipe both middle fingers at the sides of her mouth.

I explained the memory book.

Lisa looked down. "I just knew her from the squad, from being friends with Lorelei, but—" Lisa stopped and her lower lip trembled.

"Sorry, it's a real overload. But we get it, because we're the ones who found Merry," I said.

"Merry," said Lisa. "I mean she could be really nice. She really did want to help people. That's why it was so weird. Merry told me she was meeting Lorelei on Friday. Merry was going with her somewhere. Lorelei had been feeling lousy for a while. Bad about herself. I guess Lorelei's parents weren't listening to her because her dad is running for office. Anyway, Lorelei said she changed her mind, but Merry was still pushing her to go. I asked Lorelei if I could help, and she said no. I thought she and Merry were okay, but Merry didn't show up to Joey Ballard's party that Friday."

"Joey Ballard's party, the one on Friday night before they found Merry's body on Monday?" Gina asked.

"Lorelei said everything was fine." Lisa's voice sounded like a purr. She squinted. Looked down. Pawed at the little bow that tied the collar of her orange blouse.

"Loco!" We heard the smack of Jaycee's high-heel Candie's slides skidding on the cement behind us.

"Jayce," said Lisa. "These girls are interviewing me about Merry."

"Stellar." Jaycee shoved herself between us and Lisa. Jaycee's curly dark brown hair was held up above her ears by two plastic combs with yellow cloth flowers. She had peaches-and-cream skin, but a deeper, sexy voice that could grow into a growl in a second. Part girl-next-door, part Rottweiler.

"Didn't you guys get suspended?"

"Yes," I said. "We have to shake this whole school up! We have to turn the system upside down!"

Jaycee's dark brown eyes were almost black, like graveyard dirt at night. They got wider and wider. "Cool to the max. Why haven't I seen you guys before? Gnarly lips, by the way."

Lisa nodded.

"What is it going to take?" I said. "Merry Jacobs is dead, but not just dead, she got murdered, and they've got—"

"We have to make sure we get justice," said Gina. "The more we get people to open their eyes to what we've lost, we've done something good. Make up for all this lameness." Gina was on fire. "This lameness called school. We reject the status quo."

"Totally," said Jaycee.

"Yeah," said Rachel. "The status quo got Merry Jacobs murdered!"

"Jayce," said Lisa, bowing her head slightly.

"That is so majorly boss." Jaycee smiled up at the sky. "They get it, Loco. They get what we just went through. This school is trying to kill us too."

"Right," I said.

Gina looked at me as to whether or not I was joining the ex-cheer group. I could sort of see Jaycee's point. She had a brain, and not just about being captain of the ex-cheers.

"That's what you need to say, that this school is what killed Merry Jacobs. Am I right, Loco?" said Jaycee.

"Yes." Lisa had her arms crossed.

Rachel started writing. "Exactly how did the school kill her?"

"What any system does, man," said Jaycee. "It got into her brain and she started doing this stuff. It sucked her soul. Majorly. How else do you explain her getting us fired from the squad? Lorelei and Merry were friends from the beginning of time. They even competed last year to be the one junior on the cheerleading squad. But Merry pulled out, so Lorelei could win. Now, that's friendship. But this school just forces you to compete and fight and claw to the top. After Lorelei got on the squad, Merry started to joke with her about not being a 'dumb cheerleader,' stuff like that. Then it started with all of us this year, we're the seniors. Merry had to let us know she was better. She had to be number one. Being so powerful, she decided, 'now I'm going to push everyone, us, off a cliff.'"

"Really," said Lisa. "It did totally seem like that. Although, I'm sort of happy not being a cheerleader anymore."

"This place, it sucked her heart out too. Just ask Nick. I don't think Merry was so happy about dumping Nick. But you know who was really not so happy?" Jaycee asked. "I mean, how many times can you do that to a guy?"

"But Merry broke up with Nick all the time," I said. No duh, didn't I know. I'd heard it from the source, Nick, complaining behind me to whoever would listen. He should have complained to me. I could have solved it, and maybe Merry would still be alive.

"Wait," said Gina. "Are you saying Nick had something to do with Merry's murder?"

"I just know it bothered him enough to bother Merry. But I don't know any more than that. Fight the oppression." Jaycee held up her fingers in a peace sign.

The bell to end lunch sounded.

"Later days," said Jaycee, and then she and Lisa walked off together.

I noticed they wore identical khaki-colored flared pants. Even their creases were the same.

"Do you believe it?" asked Rachel.

"I was almost starting to like her," I said.

"She just totally faked us out," said Gina.

"Yep," I said.

"Because someone's in love with a guy who just got himself elected murderer," said Gina.

"Hey, I would believe it if it was true," I said.

"He's a guy, Addie," said Rachel. "That fits your criteria."

"Except that I'm not totally sure of that anymore," I said. "But Nick? Are you really falling for that?"

"Well, if they were making stuff up, at least they think we bought it," said Gina.

"But why should they play us?" I said. "We're cool with them."

"Why? Duh! We saw a cheerleader skirt with Merry's body. They are guilty of something," said Rachel.

"Well, we're still working our way into their inner circle," I said.

"How come they won't tell us where Lorelei is?" said Gina.

"I still haven't eaten," said Rachel.

"I've got some Pop-Tarts in my locker," said Gina.

We walked back toward the cafeteria area.

"How do we find Lorelei?" I asked.

"Try to get her class schedule," said Gina.

"Sure," said Rachel. "Plus, she's on ASB, Gina. Time to put your moves on Alex."

"Right. I was hoping that would be optional," Gina sighed.

"They used the whole 'pigs in power' thing against me," I said. "I am so lame."

"Get over it. The thing is, Carlos Uribe is not going get great representation, trust me," said Gina.

"He needs an amazing lawyer," said Rachel.

"How do we get him one?" I asked.

An almost empty milk carton sailed past my head and slapped into the pillar behind me. Heads turned. A group of boys behind us laughed and gave each other high-fives.

CHAPTER 10

All day long we'd questioned people and searched for Lorelei Miller, our missing ex-cheerleader link. I couldn't believe she'd vanished. To make things even more confusing, after school let out, I opened my locker and watched a mysterious page of yellow notebook paper fall to the ground. The paper was torn at the top and showed a stick figure whose head had long hair, so I assumed it was a girl. There was also a lightning bolt over her head with some stars. At least I think they were stars.

"Why are the eyes little *x*'s?" Gina asked me.

"I have no idea. I mean, it's like a cave painting—"

"It's *them*," said Rachel.

"Who?" I asked.

Two freshman boys bounced a small rubber ball against the pink pillar behind us. The ball ricocheted back across the grass of the quad, and the boys chased it. On the far side of the outdoor stage, the door to the music room was open and you could hear some horns and a drum.

"Duh," said Rachel. "This is from the ex-cheers."

"Are you serious?" Gina grabbed the piece of paper and studied it.

"Check it out," said Rachel. "They're trying to tell you something."

"Me?"

"What are *they* saying?" asked Gina.

"What do you think? It can't be good," said Rachel.

"I'm what? Going to be blinded?" I asked. I filled up my canvas book bag and shut my locker. Banks of brown book lockers lined the space between the windows and doors of the classrooms. I was happy to get one on the top row, so I didn't have to crouch down like a gopher to get my stuff like I had last year.

"You guys are the only ones who know this is my locker," I said.

"I'd say it's a warning," said Rachel.

"Please," said Gina, "you have to do better than that."

"Okay, go ahead, ignore the signs," said Rachel.

"Well, I'm not ignoring it. It's right here, and we're all looking at it," I said.

"It's not just a drawing," Rachel fumed. "It's a message—"

"Saying?" I asked.

"They're going to electrocute you. Dang, anyone can see that," said Rachel.

"I'm sorry, but these girls do not have the word 'electrocute' in their vocabulary," said Gina.

"Go ahead, be ignorant, just like the police. You really think Carlos killed Merry?" said Rachel.

I folded the paper in two and put it in my bag as we made our way around the corner and back to the lunch area. The corner classroom on our right was Mr. Boatman's, and his door was open. We could hear the hum of the aquarium, and the dim overhead light allowed us to barely make out the silhouette of the fish in the big tank. If only, I thought, I could just teach biology while underwater like Mr. Boatman, my life would be so much easier.

"Here's the thing, Rae," I said. "We just talked to the ex-cheers today." I felt stupid. Why had I even suggested we try to solve Merry's murder? All we had so far was a weird drawing that didn't make sense.

"I just know it's them," said Rachel.

"We've got a killer to find," said Gina.

"Wait a second." I stopped in my tracks. I could still hear the gurgle of the aquarium. "You guys, why didn't I think of it sooner? We have to go back to the scene of the crime."

"What?" said Gina.

"You're so right. We should have done that before," said Rachel.

"We've got no leads—we've just got all these suspects," I said.

"Which is why we have to go to the scene of the crime," said Rachel. "What were we thinking?"

"Up there?" Gina pointed to the group of three buildings that sat on the slope that went up to Calle Antonio. "But the police were all over it."

"Maybe they didn't find everything," I said. "Maybe they left the cheerleader skirt up there."

"Let's go," said Rachel.

We hurried past the back gates that led out to the basketball courts and headed north past the girls' locker room and up the slope to the outbuildings. We could hear the whistle from the soccer practice in the football field. It was late enough that the maintenance crew was gone, but the truck was there, an old white pickup with plywood sides. We tried the truck's doors, but they didn't budge.

Standing on this slope looking east, I could see most of Santa Raymunda. Calle Antonio went past the small Presbyterian church, a large home that had orange groves behind it, and some older houses before crossing the railroad tracks. The small city center branched north, with its stucco-and-clay-roofed buildings like City Hall, the more modern police station, then shops, offices, and the Mission Santa Raymunda. In the old days, Santa Raymunda hosted a couple of gunfights and bandits robbing stagecoaches. But most of the people back then had small family farms. On the hills and surrounding areas were large ranches owned by two or three people. Cattle ranches and orange groves, but the newer housing was pushing up against the ranch land.

"It was here," said Rachel. She walked in the area where we'd found Merry's body, and now I could see the bunch of old willow trees that grew near the warehouse building. There were still two small piles of dry leaves, gray chips of tree bark, and seeds with white tufts.

"Near these piles," said Gina.

It was easy to picture someone lying under the leaves, but whoever had tried to hide the body couldn't make it disappear. "See, they didn't have time to bury the body," said Rachel. "You guys, we'd better be careful."

"The police said she was killed between Friday evening and Saturday morning." Gina looked into the dark windows of the maintenance building that held an office.

Rachel pulled at the chained door to the warehouse building.

"Crazy, why would she be at school then?" I asked.

"On a Friday night?" said Gina.

"She never showed up at Joey Ballard's party," said Rachel.

"I bet it happened at night," Gina said.

I lay down on the ground, rested on my elbows, and tried to approximate Merry's body position the way we'd found her.

"Way," said Rachel. "Merry was right there."

The shade behind us covered everything in gray. The warehouse on the left and the other two buildings looked like they were sleeping.

"Cover me up," I said.

Rachel and Gina pushed leaves on me, and I put my hands over my face. "You guys see anything?"

"Dirt, tree roots," said Gina.

I heard them crunching in the leaves next to me. I took my hands off my face. I looked into the untouchable blue sky. I wondered if Merry felt that she'd been left all alone up here when she was still alive.

"Even if we could find a footprint . . ." said Rachel.

"Wait," said Gina.

"That's not a footprint," said Rachel.

"It's like—something," said Gina.

I sat up fast. Leaves, seeds, stems, and tiny bits of bark went everywhere.

"Oh, my God, you scared me," said Gina, flinching.

"These look like drag marks, maybe." Rachel pointed at the ground right by my feet.

I rolled on my side, trying not to disturb anything. Once I stood next to Rachel, I could make out the two thin trails of bare dirt that stopped right near where the feet of Merry's body would have been.

Gina bent down to inspect the exposed tracks. "Well, yeah, maybe they dragged her up here."

"From where?" I asked.

"It would only take one person to drag Merry," said Rachel.

"Or two," said Gina.

"If that's what those are," I said. "They could drive down from Calle Antonio and then drag the body down this way."

"But there's a chain across that driveway," said Rachel, pointing to the barrier that was several feet away from the garage. "Unless the chain wasn't there before."

"Or . . ." I looked around.

"They could have suffocated her closer to here and then dragged her," said Gina. "What's this?" She held up a thin triangle of paper.

"That looks like a label," said, Rachel taking the paper.

"Yeah, it looks like something from a jar or a bottle," I said. "It was ripped off the container, though."

"There's letters," said Rachel. "It has writing on it."

"What does it say?" asked Gina.

"Beats me," said Rachel. She handed it to me, and Gina and I looked at the faded half-word.

"Felinus." I tried to read the rest, but the paper had been torn from the back.

"Feline?" Gina asked.

"Latin," I said.

We looked down at the school. The athletic fields were empty. Only a few cars were parked in the lot.

"Let's get going," said Rachel.

We hurried back to the Pinto and drove toward town but got stopped at the train crossing. Our windows were down, and the roar of the freight engine flushed out all other sound.

"I don't know what the cat thing is, do you?" asked Rachel once the train had gone through.

The white crossing gates started to rise and the bells sounded for traffic to continue. On the right was the adobe city hall, with its trellis of orange and red bougainvillea and offices in back; a big square park with a large sycamore tree stood in the center. The tree had a trunk shaped like an elephant's belly, arches of branches, and green fuzzy leaves as big as hands. Next to the park was the deco police station, with a wide set of cascading stairs up to the entrance. Behind the police station was the jail, a smooth off-white box of a building with no windows or doors.

"Carlos is in there," said Rachel as we slowed for the stoplight.

"And we've got to get him out," said Gina.

"He needs a good lawyer," I said.

"You know it," said Gina. "Who's going to defend him? My mom says all he's got is some crazy public defender, and the longer he's in jail, the less chance he has of ~~not~~ getting out."

"Who's the public defender?" I asked driving in the slow pace of traffic.

"Watt," said Gina.

"Mr. Watt, piece of work!" said Rachel. Mr. Watt also taught Civics as a substitute teacher at our high school, and he would call anyone a hippie or a communist if they couldn't recite all fifty states in alphabetical order.

"He needs someone way better," I said. "Totally."

"Your mom got a divorce," said Rachel. "Didn't she have a lawyer?"

"Divorce and murder are two different things," I said.

"What about you?" said Gina.

"Oh, great, I'm Mexican, so I know someone?" asked Rachel. "Nice one."

"I can't imagine there's more than five lawyers in this town," said Gina.

I stopped at the red light.

"Mr. Watt doesn't even know the war in Vietnam is over," said Rachel.

The truck behind me honked because the light turned green, and I was still watching the police station. I continued through the intersection.

"How do you even hire a lawyer?" asked Gina.

"Stop the car, you guys, wait," said Rachel. She patted the top of my car seat.

"It's a green light," I said. We could see the front of the mission and the town bar, Los Buitres, just starting to fill up outside, with parked motorcycles and people in bandanas and cowboy hats talking.

"Make a U-turn, please," said Rachel.

"Okay, but why?" I turned on my signal, hammered the gas, and peeled around, barely missing a car on the other side.

"I know who we can get to defend Carlos," said Rachel. "His office is up there."

"Who is it?" I swung into a parking place on the street.

"David Diaz. He's sweet on my mom. And he speaks Spanish," said Rachel.

"Maybe he speaks Latin, too," said Gina.

"Very funny," said Rachel.

"So, where's his office?" I asked. We stood right in front of the Garcia Building, a three-story fortress with shops on the ground floor. The police station sat one block down across the street. Rachel studied the small wooden plaque with names for the offices on the second and third floors.

"Follow me." Rachel led the way up the wooden staircase.

"But how do we pay him?" said Gina. "With French fries?"

CHAPTER 11

David Diaz, Esquire, sat behind his spindly desk. A prehistoric rotating fan whirred on the floor next to a bare-bulb lamp. An old couch with thin upholstery sat pushed against the wall behind us. Two folding chairs occupied the space in front of his desk. The hot air inside the office didn't move at all. We watched Mr. Diaz inspect the ripped label with the Latin word for "cat" on it. We had already told him about the memory book and the ex-cheerleaders and the cheerleader skirt.

We were on the third floor of the faded white stucco Garcia Building with its green window shutters, one of the 150-year-old original architectural wonders of the town. It was the only building in Santa Raymunda with more than two floors. The third floor, we now realized, should have been condemned. Mr. Diaz appeared to be the only tenant. All of the windows that faced the walkway had newspapers pasted ~~in~~ on them instead of blinds, and the first three doors we passed had eviction notices on them.

Behind Diaz, a set of rickety French doors opened up to overlook the plaza below. I noticed some of the panes were missing. I stood on my tiptoes to see the plaza, which was kind of subterranean. This was because the Garcia building was on the street level but the plaza was a couple of floors lower. City officials ate at the old Mexican restaurant, El Pancho's, on the right side of the plaza. I'd never been inside it. I looked back at Mr. Diaz. It seemed like a long time to stand there. Gina nudged Rachel.

"Can you get him out, get Carlos out of jail?" Rachel stood with her hands clasped behind her back.

"Look, normally I handle civil cases," said Diaz. He had longish wavy black hair and a trimmed beard and mustache. Sort of like Al Pacino in *Serpico*.

We held our breath.

"Could you explain to me what I'm looking at?" he asked.

"It's a clue," said Gina.

"I'm not seeing how this absolves Mr. Uribe."

"Well, it's proof that the police didn't do their job," I said.

"Not really," said Mr. Diaz.

"Look, we know that Merry Jacobs was probably murdered by someone at the high school."

"You guys, murder is serious. It's not a game, OK?"

"We know that, but the police have the wrong person, wrong everything. We've got to stop them before whoever killed Merry kills someone else," I said.

"With *this*?" He held up the strip of paper. It was starting to look like a tired fortune from a tired fortune cookie.

"It means something," said Rachel. "See, it says 'cat.' It's off a bottle or a jar."

"Look, I admire the passion, I do. You guys are what? Modern-day Crusaders, Caped Crusaders—and I get it: truth, justice, and the American way, you know. But this—looks like a piece of trash." Diaz leaned back in his loosened tie and his rumpled white shirt, sleeves bunched up at the elbows.

"Fine, we gave you a chance—thank you. We'll go to the next lawyer," I said.

"Yeah," said Gina.

Diaz rubbed his chin. Then he folded his hands on the desk to contemplate. "Your mom knows you're doing this?" He looked at Rachel.

"Duh, of course," said Rachel. "Who do you think sent us to you? She's the one who said you would definitely be the person to take Carlos Uribe's case."

"Because I don't need to eat?" He looked at the three of us.

"No, because you're a good man," said Rachel.

Diaz took a deep breath. "Then I need real hard evidence," said Diaz. The sun was beginning to set behind the hills in the distance.

"But you'll do it?" said Rachel.

I took out the yellow notebook paper and handed it to him.

"Okay," said Diaz. "How do you get from two pieces of paper—one is handwritten and—"

"They're both handwritten," I said.

"These won't go anywhere in court," he sighed.

"But see?" said Rachel. "This one, that's got to be the cheerleaders. They know we have something on them."

"No." Diaz shook his head. "We need something concrete, a weapon."

"What about the missing cheerleader skirt? That would mean the police hid it, or destroyed it," said Gina.

"Or lost it," I said. "That shows the police are negligent."

"There's no proof," said Diaz.

Finally, the air inside started changing places with the air outside. You could hear the sounds of the cars on the street, the people walking on the sidewalk, the tables starting to fill up at El Pancho's down below, and the mariachis playing. On the other side of the office, the peel and halt of motorcycles and the Merle Haggard cover band from Los Buitres echoed from across the street.

"Merry had to be murdered by someone at school. That's the only thing that makes sense. But not by Carlos," said Rachel.

"Well, he doesn't have any witnesses to vouch for where he was on Friday night, which is when the police say the murder took place." Diaz pushed himself back from his desk, stood up, and rubbed the back of his neck with his hand. Now, it finally occurred to me that Diaz might be sleeping, eating, basically living in this office.

Swallows flitted in and out from their mud nests clustered under the eaves outside. Feeding time.

"What if the police are lying, what if the sheriff is lying?" said Rachel.

"Don't you think it's a little questionable that Uribe was arrested once before for something he didn't do, and then they arrest him for this?" said Gina.

"What happens when they charge an innocent person with murder?" I asked.

Diaz looked across the plaza, past Little Sunset, an older neighborhood on the other side of the railroad tracks. The hills above grew dark, violet colored. I started to see little dots of insects.

"Technically, you are innocent until proven guilty," said Diaz.

"But if he's innocent and he doesn't get a fair trial and he gets convicted?" I asked.

"Then he can face the death penalty," said Diaz.

"If the sheriff is lying, if the witnesses aren't telling the truth, then this can happen to anyone," said Gina.

Diaz paced in front of the open French doors. I looked behind us at the couch. There was a cardboard box next to it that looked like it held clothing. A suit jacket on its hanger hung on the side of a tall metal file cabinet. Diaz swung his arms forward and grabbed the back of his chair, which squeaked like it needed a year's worth of WD-40. "Okay. Find me proof."

"We will," I said. "We'll find everything."

"Hey, I want you guys to really watch yourselves." Diaz turned on his office lamp. He grabbed a business card and handed it to Rachel. "You need to be safe at all times. You call me the minute there's any kind of danger, okay?"

Rachel nodded.

"You won't regret this Mr. Diaz," I said.

We left Diaz in the shadows of his office and bounded down the rickety stairs in the dark until we got to the sidewalk, where a streetlight cast a pool of white. Across the street and down the block, the large concrete face of the police station sat with its wide front entrance doors like an open mouth and stone pillars at either side of the front entrance like rectangular sideburns. From here the jail had a trapezoid shape to it, a pyramid with its head lopped off, looming behind the station.

"I do not think Mr. Diaz likes us," I said.

"We have to find that skirt," said Rachel.

We walked past the shop fronts along the sidewalk on the way to the car. The street teemed with music booming from Los Buitres and the crowd of bikers smoking and showing off their motorcycles. On this side of the street, shadows of cars ran over us.

"Nice move there," I said to Rachel. "Using your mom."

"I know," said Rachel. "I just had to take a chance."

"Hope he doesn't ask your mom about recommending him for Uribe's defense," said Gina.

"He won't," said Rachel. "He is so shy. He doesn't even call my mom by her first name."

"Hey, that office of Diaz's," I said. "I think the guy lives in there."

"Man," said Rachel. "Those stairs to the third floor, dang—we could have fallen through it at any minute."

"Don't lawyers make some bucks?" asked Gina.

"I thought so." I paused to look in the shop window on the right. Even at night, I could see through the white gauze curtains and the gold lettering spelling out "Mission Souvenirs" a display with rows of little crosses, pictures of saints, and in the right-hand corner three bottles of holy water.

"What do you put in a bottle that has 'cat' on the label?" I asked.

"We have to find whatever that is too," said Gina.

Rachel walked to the next shop, Rancho Raymunda Real Estate, showing off its pictures of properties and houses for sale. She pointed at the largest one, advertising homes with their own personal stables, Casa Ridge. "I think Lorelei lives up in that area, you guys. We'd better find her before something happens."

CHAPTER 12

At morning break we met at Rachel's locker, across the quad almost directly opposite mine. Even though there was still a good month of school left, people were starting to act like summer vacation started next week. Girls smelled like coconut tanning oil and wore their bathing suits under their clothes to go to the beach after school, or after ditching fourth period.

"Gina, you cannot move back to Chicago now," I said.

"As long as my mom keeps her job," said Gina.

"She'll be fine. She can interview us," said Rachel.

"We would need something more than what we have for her to take us seriously," said Gina.

"No problema." Rachel kept rearranging her locker since books and folders kept falling out. "I will get you that information. I'm going to interview Nick." She shoved her sweater inside the locker to act like mortar between a binder and a box of charcoal for drawing.

"Wait a minute. I'm the best person to interview him," I said.

"Not on your life," said Gina. "You will be on your knees licking his toe-jam or something. Besides, you said we were going to find this missing Lorelei chick."

Rachel armed herself with her clipboard and paper, a pencil tucked behind her ear, her locker still open.

"Look," I said, "I will do the introductions. I am the one ~~that~~ who has an 'in' with Nick. Then you take over, Rae."

"Hey, if I need your assistance, I'll ask you." Rachel slammed her locker with one whap.

My friend was a lot of things: amazing artist, great cracker of jokes, also heavy-duty analyzer of information. Focused? No. Once Gina and I started hunting for Lorelei Miller, I knew Rachel would wait in line at the cafeteria window for her Cheez Whiz and crackers to fortify herself before cornering Nick. She'd get distracted without us, lose her chance, and have to start over.

"Come on," I said to Gina. "We'll make sure she actually gets near him."

Gina and I followed Rachel, and I saw Nick talking to two girls as he stood on the first step of the outdoor stage, right smack in the center.

God, he *was* pretty perfect. Talk about a babe-and-a-half . . . That smile, those priceless dimples, one on each side. Make me die now. Of course, he didn't see me, but that was a good thing. The girls were giggling at some story of his. You would think, hey, this guy's girlfriend was murdered, and he's got people laughing? But this was Nick Stanley. You were lucky to keep a thought in your head *and* look at him at the same time. I checked the corners of my mouth for drool. *Don't lose it.* His arms waved, his biceps flexed in the striped brown-and-white short sleeves of his rugby shirt.

"Hey!" Gina yelled to me as she saw me close in on Nick's little crowd.

"What?" said Nick.

I dove into his current, nudging one of the girls into the background. Nick's curly brown hair, his surfer-bleached saltwater sheen, his glossy dark brown eyes, almost midnight—you could see stars in there. *Careful.*

"Hi, Nick," said Rachel behind me, but she barely made any noise.

I opened my mouth.

"No." Gina grabbed my shirt collar from the back.

"Nick!" Rachel yelled in a super-high pitch. The girls around him turned their heads, their eyes focused on us with cattle-prod precision.

The three of us perched at the dividing line of the inner sanctum that the super-popular upper-esher students occupied. Oh, my God, face to face with Nick Stanley. Rachel kept her concentration. Jaycee and Alex's faces surfaced, but things just blurred when I looked at Nick. There were dragonflies buzzing around in my stomach. When was Rachel going to start asking questions? I looked at Gina. She held up her hands in a universal I-give-up sign.

Oh, I should have known he was going to try to flirt with Rachel, with all of us. What could you do? The guy needed constant attention. Okay, so I was distracted. I just had to trust Rachel to get answers, and that she wasn't going to be charmed out of her intelligence. Man, they were right. I was in love. Gag.

"Hey, Nick. Sorry to bug you. I'm Rachel Osario, and I'm part of the group that's—" She saw Gina and me right next to her. "Well, the three of us are doing this memory book for Merry Jacobs? The memory book committee." She rolled her eyes at me.

"Huh." His eyes lost their sparkle. Wait—a note of sadness, presumably dammed up and ready to burst forth. Burn, how could they not believe he was sad? "Okay, cool."

Rachel got his sole attention. Bingo. She took out her yellow legal pad. I could see the two damp marks from her hand sweat while gripping it. "Let's start off with a few questions. First, how would you describe Merry?"

"Well, she was—hey, do I know you?"

Gina elbowed me.

"We're the ones who found Merry's body," I said.

"What were you saying about Merry?" asked Rachel.

"We were together, you know, boyfriend and girlfriend, like that." He coughed and bent his head down. "Just really gets to me, you know, because I lost her. I'm still . . . still . . . you know." He cleared his throat and took a deep breath. "She was pretty. I mean if I go for a girl, she's got to be pretty much a fox, you know, which she was. She had nice eyes, big blue eyes, long brown hair. I liked that. A great shape."

He laughed. "Well, you know, total bod." He nodded at Rachel, so, not a revelation.

"Right," said Rachel. "What about her, her character, her personality?"

"Of course. Well, a lot of people thought she was bossy, you know, they reacted to that. But I mean, she just liked to be direct. She liked to take care of stuff then and there. Like, if something was wrong, she called you on it."

"She called me on my volleyball serves when I was a freshman," said Rachel. "Guess she thought yelling at me would make me a better athlete, but it didn't."

"Sports were killer. She loved that. She loved competition. I took her to the Cinco de Mayo fair last year, and we pitched softballs, and man, she was good. I missed *one,* and she just razzed me about it. But I could take that kind of talk. Not everyone can. You just had to give it right back to her. She didn't like people being passive. Like, wake up! If she felt you weren't telling the truth, she would make sure she got into your business about it. She was upset the cheerleaders got busted. I mean, she had opinions about the cheerleaders. She wanted them to be more athletic, not just clapping and stuff, but, like, the gymnastic stuff, flipping, handsprings. So, when they got busted—"

"What did she tell you about it?" asked Gina.

"Merry? She was totally outraged to the max," said Nick.

"But didn't Merry get those cheerleaders fired in the first place?" I said.

"That's the story we got," Rachel added, "from an informed source."

"No way," said Nick. "She felt so bad about it. She even said she could have maybe prevented it, because she knew Coach Stevens. Talked to the coach. No, man. She knew it was totally not fair. They all did it; they were all partying hard—athletes, ASB—why go after the cheerleaders, the seniors especially? Why make just them pay? She went to the advisors, and then Mr. Patrick, and Mr. Ennis." Mr. Patrick, our garrulous vice principal, taught American History and ran the Academic Marathon. He was the faculty patron saint of the brainerds.

"Really?" asked Rachel.

"Yeah. She was totally into it. You couldn't take her attitude as being rude; she just said and did what she thought was right. She wanted to be a lawyer, majorly. That was her dream. She would have been great . . ." His voice trailed off as he looked up at the outdoor stage, then back at us, his eyes almost watery. Then he forced a grin that peeled his lips apart. Like it hurt a little. "Yeah, she asked Alex if they could lobby the district, the school district, to get the school to reinstate the cheerleaders. She was friends with Lorelei, best friends. Merry didn't think cheerleading was right for Lorelei, but go figure. She didn't want Lorelei to be a bubblehead and stuff. She was going to fight for her, though, for Lorelei and the rest of them. Yeah, I mean, they really didn't do anything wrong."

"So, they were good friends? Lorelei and Merry?" Rachel continued.

"Oh, yeah. I mean—she should be in this thing. What's it called?"

"The memory book?" I should have let Rachel handle it.

"So, did you say why you guys broke up? I mean, you seem to have such respect for her and all." Rachel was good.

My stomach tensed. It was hard to stand there. Hard because, well, because he might just profess his love for Merry, or something. *Gag*. I looked at Gina, but she scowled at Nick.

"I did. I mean, still do. Wherever she's at . . . Yeah, she dumped me. Again." He looked up over our heads. "I loved her to the max, really."

He did say "love." I heard him say it. Heart-squash city.

"Did she give you a reason? Someone else in the picture?" asked Rachel.

"I thought they had the guy who murdered her." His eyes hardened to basalt. Okay, now, I definitely had my doubts about Nick's honesty.

"Well, it hasn't been proven yet," said Gina.

Nick gave her a look. "It's the janitor guy, right? That's who did it."

"Carlos Uribe," said Rachel.

He bowed his head and then raised his face up just quickly enough for me to see a sly expression; he was like a lion backing up slowly, ears pricked, perfectly attuned. "You know, I'm pretty sure he did do it."

"I don't think so." Rachel stood her ground. I felt sick, so many dragonfly carcasses piling up inside me. Gina nudged me, so I could see her smugness.

"Well, I'd seen him, the janitor guy, hanging around sometimes, when ASB went late on Fridays, when I was with Merry, before we broke up. See, I used to pick Merry up after the meeting. I'd see him waiting, like he was waiting for her. And then he didn't talk to anyone but her when they all came out to the student parking lot." What the hell was Nick talking about?

"You saw them walk together to the parking lot?" asked Gina.

"Yeah. But I didn't think about it until *that* Friday, when I didn't pick her up because we weren't together anymore. I mean, I've moved on." Nick seemed to relax again.

"Right," said Rachel.

Seriously eerie. I mean, believe me, I wanted to believe him. But no one could see all that. There's no way you can tell exactly where anyone has just been if they walked through that back entrance, whether separately or together. Plus, he told the police this? But he wasn't even there that Friday afternoon, and ASB got cancelled.

"But you weren't there, Nick. There wasn't any ASB meeting that day," I said.

"So, he didn't need to wait. This Carlos guy must have thought, 'Hey, nice young girl talks to me.' Thought she was interested, found out she could seriously fight back—I mean, she so could fight back." Nick clapped his hands together with a smack that made us all jump.

"But if she could fight back, then how did he take Merry down?" Rachel looked at him. Did he really think what he said made sense?

"Man, I'm so sorry, I really, really am. Seems like that's all I can say about it, about Merry. Broke my heart, and then—" He clapped his hands again with the same ferocity.

"You told the police this?" asked Rachel.

"Come again?"

"About Carlos? Waiting around?" asked Gina.

"Hell, yeah. I told them what I know. Hey, when does this book come out?"

"Last week of school. Actually, at graduation," I said, and then bit my tongue really hard.

The bell rang. Students flooded into their separate streams to get to classes. Nick disappeared.

"Change your mind, now?" Gina looked at me.

It took me a while before I realized what Nick had said.

"Hey," said Gina. "*This* is where I saw Lorelei and Merry talking that Friday at lunch."

"Did you ever tell the police that?" I asked her. My head was clearing.

"No." She shook her head.

"We should talk to someone who's with the police," I said.

"We have to tell them they arrested the wrong person," said Gina.

"Gross me out, you guys," said Rachel. "Nick lied to the police."

The backs of my knees felt weird, like I had stretched my muscles too hard. My tongue throbbed. It seemed so crazy, like a dream. Had he really tried to pin Carlos Uribe for the murder? Why would he do that? And then the police had believed him? Nick was definitely a charmer, so maybe the police couldn't help but believe him. I mean, I believed him about how much he cared about Merry. But the story about Uribe? We had to call Diaz, only it was all of ten o'clock. We'd miss class. We looked at each other. It would be such a long time before lunch.

"We can't wait," said Rachel.

Gina ran back to her locker for coins. Rachel and I took off to her locker for Diaz's card. We met back at the pay phone near the administration booth where the counselors and narcs smoked before going to their offices. We were all breathing hard.

"I can't believe he said that," I sighed, frustrated with this clammy, sweaty, crazy climb-Mt. Everest-and jump-off-the-top thing I had for him.

Gina put a dime in and Rachel dialed.

"Mr. Diaz, this is Rachel." She held out the phone's receiver so we could hear.

"Hey, Caped Crusader. What's going on?"

"I, we just got some information. We—" Rachel flipped back to the pages with her notes. "It's Nick Stanley. He's the one that gave the police the idea that Carlos Uribe killed Merry."

"Wait, what?" His phone voice muffled, then, "Who's Nick Stanley?"

"Her boyfriend. Merry's boyfriend." Gina looked at me.

"Correction: he's her *ex*-boyfriend, maybe jilted ex-boyfriend," said Rachel. "He's the one who told the police that Mr. Uribe did it, that he murdered Merry."

"You talked to him? This Nick?" asked Diaz.

"Yeah," said Rachel. "Just now."

I pictured what Diaz's face looked like through the round pitted receiver.

Gina grabbed the phone from Rachel. "He's lying about Friday, because there was no ASB meeting that afternoon. Alex Stapleton told me that, and he's the student body president."

"Okay." A door slammed in Diaz's office or something. "You guys, this is dangerous, didn't I say that? You need to be cautious. I don't want any of you getting hurt, or worse."

"But Mr. Diaz, you could use this," I said. "In court. That he lied to the police."

"I don't like the idea of you guys risking so much. We should talk about this," said Diaz.

"Yeah," said Rachel, "we don't know if he's—if Nick's—if he's the only witness." Rachel looked sick.

"Rachel got it all down," I said. "What he told us."

"It's this whole story we've never heard before," said Gina.

"We've got to have some clear lines here," Diaz sighed. "You're—this is a very important lead. Don't get me wrong. Can we meet? At lunch? I have a sit-down with the prosecutor this afternoon, and if he can go in with this, it might be the thing that gets Carlos Uribe off."

"Wicked to the max," said Gina.

"Can you meet us at Doheny Joe's?" asked Rachel. "Like, in ten minutes?"

"Great," said Diaz.

Rachel hung the receiver back in its cradle.

"It's Nick alright." Gina snapped her fingers.

"I don't know," I said. Would he do that? Give the police a complete bold-faced lie? How could I be wrong about Nick? But why in the world would he lie? What had Jaycee said, that Nick was unhappy when Merry broke up with him this last time?

We skittered through the crowds of people. Someone had launched a big beach ball in the quad and now people slapped at the bubble of bright green, yellow, and red stripes. I stubbed my toe on the sidewalk, and when I stopped moving for a second everything took on a strange, super-focused quality. I could see the light pencil markings on the pink pillars with people's names joined by plus signs inside unevenly drawn heart shapes. I could look down and see each square of the sidewalk under my feet with the space where grass grew in between. I could see the white sun-blast in the blue sky. Everything so clear. Too clear.

CHAPTER 13

"How are we getting out of here?" Gina shut her locker. "We can't be suspended for what we're wearing today."

I was still reeling over Nick. Why, why throw suspicion on Carlos Uribe? Why do that? I had strained my brain before, but not like this. Why the hell would Nick lie—didn't he want the murderer caught? He'd even said it: "I loved Merry." Really.

"We'd better move before we get in Nick's way," said Rachel.

"I've got an idea," I said. Time to pull the nitroglycerin option. Drastic, but it would get us gone with no questions asked.

"Where are you going?" asked Rachel.

"To forge us a note," I said. "I'll be right back."

"We don't have much time before break's over," said Gina.

"You guys, get your stuff. I'll be back in a flash."

"Okay," Rachel sighed. I heard her Dr. Scholls clomp on the cement while I raced toward the girls' locker room. I'd have to catch Coach Zamora. Yes, the door was still open. Into the dim and damp cement block I went. Down to the yellow counter in front of the cage where you got your towel or asked for feminine products or actually, on a rare occasion, bothered one of the two PE teachers.

"Ms. Zamora?" I saw her head of short black hair. She turned to face me and squinted. "Ms. Zamora."

"Class is starting. What do you need?" She stood up and turned the radio down. "Did you lose something?"

"I need—" Well, it had been a really good idea, but I had to make sure there was no one else around. You know, no one that would hear.

"Addie?" Zamora recognized me.

"I think I have . . ." I made a face. "They're down there, and they itch—you know, bites."

"Oh, my good God." She looked at me sorrowfully, which was perfect. She shook her head at me.

"They—" I was about to start going into more detail.

"You don't have to say another word." The whistle and keys on the chains around her neck swung and hit the edge of the desk; she plopped a pad of permission slips in front of me and wrote out a note. "Now, you see a doctor right away, and it'll be over and done, okay?"

I looked down. Yes, her signature was at the bottom, but I could fit Rachel's and Gina's names on the form too. I raced past the lockers. The bell rang and students laughed and high-fived on their way to class.

I got to the admin office window where you go for all those get-out-of-jail-free cards. The lady looked at me after she read Zamora's writing and shook her head. She filled out three forms, stamped them, and shoved them through the little opening.

I rejoined Rachel and Gina, and we headed toward the parking lot. The car was parked up on Antonio.

"See, you're getting the hang of this thing," said Gina. "Subterfuge. Way to go. Now, why can't the guy meet us at his office?"

"Don't ask me. DJ's popped into my mind." Rachel swung her book bag up and back as we walked.

"You guys, maybe this is it. Maybe Mr. Uribe goes back home in no time. I mean, a false statement—you know, that *has* to mean the police can't hold him." I felt for the car keys in my purse.

"What about that Lorelei," said Gina as we made our way onto the grass of the baseball field. "She's vanished?"

"Yeah, Addie," said Rachel. "What if she's victim number two?"

"That's the very next thing we do," I said. "Find that girl."

We climbed the stairs two at a time. Right at the top of Calle Antonio I saw a picture of Ron Miller, Lorelei's dad. It was one of his "Vote for Miller" signs. A drawing of his head was superimposed on an American flag. The thing was, I didn't think I'd seen any other candidate that was running for the state senate seat.

"Okay," said Gina. "We talk to him. He's her dad. He should know where she is."

"Deal," I said.

We threw our stuff in the car. You could taste just a hint of salt in the air coming from the ocean.

"Hey, Addie, how did you get us excused today?"

I wrestled the crumpled copy of our ticket to freedom out of my purse and into Gina's palm before I put the Pinto in drive.

"Gross me out," said Gina. "I give up."

"What?" Rachel whined from the backseat.

"Well," said Gina. "We have one foolproof excuse to get us out of pretty much any jam we come across now."

"Did you tell the school nurse you had the plague or something?" asked Rachel.

I checked the rearview mirror and waited for a car to pass us.

"Oh, no way, that's too easy—that would throw up some red flag and have a health official walk through the school. No, this is genius," said Gina.

"Okay," said Rachel, "I guess my next question is do I want to know?"

Gina balled up the pink form and tossed it overhead to Rachel in the backseat. I barely idled the Pinto before hauling it down to the Coast Highway. On the radio, Hot Chocolate was singing "You Sexy Thing."

CHAPTER 14

We sat at one of the outside tables at DJ's piled with cheeseburgers, shakes, and fries. All on Diaz's dime. This morning's paper ran the story that David A. Diaz was now the defense attorney for Carlos Uribe working pro bono, which meant for free. Which meant that he shouldn't have been paying for our lunch. The paper also reported that Diaz had only been practicing as an attorney for a little over two years. Diaz had been quoted as saying that he believed Uribe was innocent, and he intended to prove it.

Across the street from where we sat was the state beach entrance, with only surfer and beach traffic rolling in and out to the Coast Highway. Cars of tourists bunched up at the light and clogged the traffic. Two hotels sat on either side of the beach entrance. On the south corner was a decrepit hotel designed with the Swiss Alps or Shakespeare's England in mind but smaller. White stucco and broad black cross beams. It housed a bar called Villa Shores, which was also the name of the hotel. The only things that made it look tropical were the potted palms, the small sky-blue pool in front, and the hotel room doors painted yellow, pink, and orange.

The hotel on the other corner was Don Pedro's, with Spanish archways and a red tile roof. There was a gas station and little shops selling shells, swimsuits, swim masks, beach chairs, and soft-serve ice cream. A wood-shingled barbecue restaurant sat next to the gas station. Groups of people wandered up and down this small area of commerce, outfitted for the beach with towels and cameras. The men wore black sports socks and bright Hawaiian shirts and walked behind their wives in huge hats and sunglasses, pointing and waving. The nicer beaches were farther south, but only the locals knew where to go.

When we first sat down at DJ's, we were the only seated customers. Surfers came to get their meals to go. They filled up the parking lot with small pickup trucks, vans, and Volkswagen buses and then left to let the process start up again. Then a couple of guys sat one table away. Another group of four had decided to stay but had not sat down. They wore visors and straw hats. They didn't actually stare at Diaz, but they were definitely making a note of him in his tie and rumpled suit.

"Nick told the police Carlos had been talking to Merry after ASB," said Rachel. "But we know that's not true. There was no meeting on Friday."

"It was just Nick's idea of what happened," I said. "They had already broken up. He's telling the police about Carlos talking to Merry based on ASB meetings in the past, except Carlos probably never talked to her in the first place."

"Couldn't that lie be enough to get Carlos off?" asked Gina.

"Isn't there reasonable doubt?" said Rachel.

"We'll find out when we present in court," said Diaz.

"So, none of this stuff we found out helps?" I asked.

The group of four surfers finally sat down at a table all the way near the front by the street, and one guy waved at a white service truck that had stopped at the red light.

"Okay, people," said Diaz, "let's talk strategy. First," he wiped his mouth with a napkin, "what do we know?"

"The coroner said Merry was killed between three p.m. and nine p.m. on that Friday," said Gina.

"Merry was not at Joey Ballard's party later that night, but we saw all the ex-cheers there," I said.

"And Nick, Merry's ex-boyfriend," said Gina.

"What time did you see these people, and how long has he been her ex?" asked Diaz.

"We saw them around eight thirty," I said. "And Merry broke up with him right around the time the ex-cheers were kicked off the squad."

"What else do we know about that day, up to the murder time?" asked Diaz.

"Merry was supposed to meet Lorelei at the locker room after school," I said. "Which would be around three p.m.. They were meeting there to go someplace together."

"Why and where?" Diaz slurped his shake.

"We still have to ask Lorelei," I said.

"I saw Merry and Lorelei having an argument at lunch that day," said Gina.

"Don't forget, Merry took care of whatever Coach screwed up. Sort of her assistant, but to the point that Merry could influence the coach. And the coach has a violent streak," said Rachel.

"What's the reason Merry had so much power with the coach?" asked Diaz.

"Coach Stevens drinks," I said.

"Got it," said Diaz."

"Also," said Rachel, "Merry was Lorelei's best friend and Lorelei was under pressure from her dad. Not sure why, but she was talking to Merry about this. Merry was giving her advice about how to deal with that."

"Why's that?" asked Diaz.

"Lorelei's dad is Ron Miller, and it had something to do with him running for the state senate seat," said Gina. "They said Lorelei was worried about not being perfect."

"Well," said Diaz. "Carlos doesn't have anyone who can confirm his alibi for the time frame. He ran his kid over to baseball practice, dropped off a bicycle to be repaired. Went back to watch the end of the game. Ran the kid to the kid's friend's house for pizza. You would think I could find someone to say they saw him. But so far, nada. I could use some help on that," Diaz sighed. He threw some fries at the seagulls. "Do you guys know about Manuel Garza?"

"Yeah," said Rachel.

"We know Frank Garza," I said. "He's in our grade."

Frank Garza had five brothers and sisters. They lived in an older green farmhouse along Camino Raymunda. But there were other families of Garzas too. Those kids were older. They worked for their dad, who had a construction company or something.

"The Garzas have the orange grove along that back area across from the soccer field," said Diaz.

"It's a big family," said Rachel. "There's lots of Garzas."

"Manuel had a cement company, small but steady. About five years ago, he's set to pour slabs for some model homes over at Casa Ridge."

"That's where those homes are that have their own stables, right?" said Rachel.

Diaz nodded. "He got to work early one day to find two patrolmen there with a story about stolen property. He knew nothing. But when the cops came out to his yard there was a mixer, a generator, a truck. Like, they appeared overnight," said Diaz.

"What does this have to do with Carlos?" I asked.

"The stuff in Garza's cement yard belonged to Lloyd Griffin's brother-in-law," said Diaz.

"The sheriff's brother-in-law."

"Wait," said Rachel. "They arrested him, Manuel."

"Oh yeah, arrested. Convicted. He's got a ten-year sentence up in Tehachapi men's," said Diaz.

"Prison?" I said.

"I don't get it," said Rachel.

"Manuel showed up at his work to find stolen property. But he never stole anything. That stuff was planted there," said Diaz.

"But why?" I asked.

"Griffin's brother-in-law wanted *his* company to pour slabs," said Diaz.

"He was framed," said Gina. "I can totally see that. You guys in your perfect beach-bubble world."

Now, DJ's was crowded, and tourists were lining up to order. I noticed two local women in bathing suit tops and cutoff jeans ordering food at the window counter. Both of them were slim and tall.

One was barefoot; only locals walked around with feet that tough. She pulled her long, sun-streaked brown hair back. The other had dark hair and whispered into her friend's ear like a conspirator. They both laughed and smiled. They didn't seem to care that a murderer was on the loose.

"He was framed by the sheriff?" said Rachel.

"Of course, no way to prove it. Evidence is with the cops," said Diaz.

"So, now they're trying to frame Uribe by hiding the cheerleader skirt," said Gina.

"They arrested him before for stolen property," I said, remembering that part from the first newspaper article about his arrest.

"This time it's for murder," said Gina.

"But the sheriff," I said. "He's the law. I mean, he would do that?"

"Just because he has a badge doesn't mean he's a good guy," said Gina. "You told me he's got these illegitimate kids all over town."

"Four," said Rachel.

"Look, I don't think it's an accident that Uribe is in jail on this murder charge. It's history. It's a pattern," said Diaz.

"Well, what do we do now?" I asked.

"This will be a fight," said Diaz. "I could lose everything."

The shred of tomato hanging out of my burger looked like flesh.

"You guys have to understand—we have to have solid evidence," said Diaz. "I got an extension this morning, so I have more time to prepare. I meet with the prosecutor pretty soon—" He checked his watch. "Okay, I'd better get over to the courthouse. Maybe I can get the prosecutor to drop the charge on the basis of Nick's lie. Maybe. But in case that doesn't happen, I'm trying to get Max Walker to help me."

"Max Walker?" I said. "He's a city commissioner; you can't trust him either."

"It's a risk I take," said Diaz. "Proceed with caution."

We watched Diaz walk to the parking lot and drive off in his seven-year-old Plymouth Duster with primer on the passenger door.

My half-eaten burger's juice spilled from the wrapper. My fries looked like fingers. I didn't want to throw up. The tall giggling girls sauntered by, smelling of coconut oil and fries. The wind picked up and napkins blew past us. A woman in a halter dress and head scarf with a group of six children doled out paper-wrapped burgers.

"The Walker guy?" asked Gina.

"Max Walker's been a city commissioner for a million years. He always runs for mayor. He always loses. He always has some tax problem that you find out about later. He always has some cause. He had some lawsuit against one of the ranchers that went nowhere," said Rachel.

"Plus, he wears a white suit," I said. "He's just grody."

"Anyway," said Rachel. "Right now, we should go find Ron Miller, Lorelei's dad. He can tell us where she is."

"He's either at City Hall or his election office," I said.

"Let's go to the election office. Maybe Alex is there too. He said he volunteers for the campaign," said Gina.

"Stellar," I said.

Ron Miller's election headquarters was in the small office park across the street from City Hall. It was just one room with a glass front. There were red, white, and blue banners. More of those signs with Miller's head. His hair was very straight, like his nose, as well as his teeth, which were very large in a mouth that smiled from ear to ear.

"Are you here to pick up the flyers?" said a voice.

I looked around to see a mouse of a woman with blond hair teased back and big hoop earrings. She carried a bunch of mimeographed paper copies. Her dress was a lavender color with bell sleeves and a white collar.

"No," I said.

"We're looking for my friend Alex. He volunteers here?" said Gina.

"Oh, he's not here. I don't know where he is," the woman sighed. She set the copies down, and now I could see that they were advertising a fund-raiser.

"Okay," said Rachel. She looked at me and then up at the wall, and I could now see a framed picture of the Miller family. Beautiful Lorelei;

her dad; a brother, I guessed, who was taller than the dad, and this woman. She had to be his wife.

"Is Mr. Miller here?" I asked.

"No. Excuse me, but I have to get these distributed," said the woman.

"We were trying to find out about Lorelei; we needed to interview her for a thing at school," I said.

"She's been sick, poor thing. Stomach flu," said the woman. "I do need to leave, so I'll have to lock up now." She smiled, but she looked exhausted. Her makeup was smudged under her eyes.

"So, she's at home," I said.

"Yes, but she should be back at school tomorrow."

"We'll take some flyers," I said.

"Will you? Thank you so much." Mrs. Miller looked relieved.

"Let's make a note to check their home," I said as we got back in the car. I gave Rachel the flyers.

CHAPTER 15

At school the next afternoon I looked at Rachel. "You talked to Deerfield, right? About getting that memory album published?"

We were going to make the drive up to Casa Ridge, to Lorelei's house. Rachel had found the address for the Millers in the yellow pages last night.

"Not yet," said Rachel.

"Christ, if those ex-cheerleaders find out there's no book, you guys, they are going to give us a *makeover*," said Gina, implying epically nasty proportions.

"I will, I swear," said Rachel. "God, that means I've got to work on that scholarship thing for her."

"Whatever you have to do, the book *has* to be real," said Gina.

Our conversation echoed across the empty school grounds.

"And we have to find Lorelei," I said. "Man, I need to get my gym clothes. I think it's been three weeks now. Okay, then we go to Casa Ridge, and knock on her door."

"Majorly gross," said Gina. "Like, do you not understand hygiene?"

"Sometimes," Rachel answered for me.

"So, I forgot. We're on top of a murder investigation." I started toward the girls' locker room.

"Wait up," said Gina, falling into step with me. "Safety patrol, reporting for duty."

Rachel caught up to us. "If you think her *feet* stink—"

"Sounds like someone needs to learn how to use the washer and dryer," said Gina.

We stopped at the edge of the breezeway. Pieces of notebook paper rustled against a pillar and flapped from a locker. The open gate to the barren sports fields and basketball courts gave us an unobstructed view of the no-man's or no-woman's land. Granted, I had not been threatened with a falling power line, but I wanted my friends with me in that big, empty warehouse of girl sweat masked in Bonne Belle shower splash.

"Hey," said Rachel. She tugged my arm, and we all stopped walking. "Remember, it's *Friday*."

"So?" said Gina.

Rachel was right. Coach Stevens drank on Friday afternoons, hiding out in the girls' locker room. What was I thinking? Normally, Stevens conducted herself as part of the PE paramilitary. Her thick blond hair, all one unit, was held back with a wide headband, part of her uniform, in some pastel color that matched her cardigan, T-shirt, and shorts, mint green or peach, above all-weather tan legs, white tennis peds with little balls on them, and blinding white tennis shoes. She would stand at attention, clipboard up, whistle resting in her mouth, waiting for everyone to stand in their numbered spots on the asphalt for roll call. She'd bark about warm-ups, scores, and passing the push-up tests. Girls did not get to do "girl" push-ups.

But Coach Stevens, on Friday afternoons, knocked back some hard liquor. Like, a lot. Even before getting the freshman orientation packet, people knew about Coach Stevens. Yet she kept her job, and on the job, she was firm and serious. Everyone came on time, no slouching, no excused bench-warming no matter how badly needed, no ducking out of hitting the softball or serving in volleyball, which made the teams sigh in unison over consistent strikes and net-balls.

"In and out," I said. "I swear, you guys, just be my backup." I took a breath and squeezed the door handle, but before I could start to pull it open, the door shot forward, and we jumped back.

It was her. Lorelei. Lorelei Miller, who we'd been looking for. Her hair perfect, gold and almost bleached white in places, but her face was tear-stained, her eyes squinted.

"God, you guys scared me," Lorelei heaved. Tall and thin, her hair was almost heavier than she was.

We stepped back, and she stepped forward, and the door slammed behind her.

"Hey, Lorelei?" I said.

"Okay. You can get out of my way now."

"We've been looking for you," said Gina.

"Why? Look, if I were you, I wouldn't go in there. Stevens is plastered."

We kept pace with her as she walked away from the pink stucco wall of the building into a grassy area that led to the softball/baseball field. Then she stood near a large sycamore by some bleachers at the backstop.

"Unbelievable. And to think I spent so much time trying to please her in cheerleading." Lorelei looked down.

"So, what are you doing here?" I asked.

"She wanted to talk. And I thought she would, you know, stay on the wagon until I could see her. Wrong."

"What did she want to talk to *you* about?" asked Gina.

"Merry. What else?" said Lorelei. She stood in her platform sandals, one leg crossed behind the other. "She blames herself, for Merry's death, all that."

"Why?" asked Gina.

"Come on, you know. She kicked us off the squad. Totally wiped us off the map for no reason. Probably because she was like she is right now. Totally off her rocker. The thing is, if she hadn't been so harsh on us, maybe Merry would still be alive." Lorelei tightened her hold on her hobo bag, her bicep flexed. I noticed she had goose bumps even though it was hot. I mean, I was sweating a bunch. I would have given anything to be as tall and beautiful as Lorelei. But now she looked sad, even while flipping her hair, and somehow, I thought I knew that feeling. I'd felt like that. I'd lost someone. Lost trust in someone.

"Why haven't you been at school?" asked Rachel.

"Yeah, your mom said you were sick? What gives?" I said.

Why did the coach want to talk to Lorelei about blaming herself for Merry's death? My mind was racing. We'd totally forgotten the memory book, the questions, that Lorelei could be a suspect. Merry was killed on a Friday, later in the day, and Merry had been waiting for Lorelei to show up.

"You talked to my mom?" Lorelei's face colored pink suddenly. "Of all things." She looked down, punched the toe of her platform shoe into the crabgrass and dirt three times. "Why are you talking to *my mom*?"

"It's just that you weren't around, Lorelei, and we need to get this memory book done for Merry, and we need a quote from you," I said.

"Your mom said you were sick?" said Rachel.

"Yes, okay, I was sick, sick of all of this!" Lorelei raised her voice, then calmed back down and narrowed her eyes.

Rachel pulled out her legal pad. "Just a short statement, that's all. You were her best friend."

"Look, we understand, especially since you were the last person to see her alive," said Gina.

"Go ahead," said Rachel, "whatever you want to say."

"Merry was waiting for me in the locker room. We were supposed to leave together, but I told her I couldn't go. There was something for my dad's campaign that I had to do. So, I left, and then—that's the last time I saw her alive." Lorelei looked weak for a second, lost hold of her hobo bag, and as her arm hyperextended with all the weight, I could see it: three deep lines, scabbed, right at the bend of paler skin on the underside of her elbow. Whatever it was, it must have hurt. Bummer to the max, what had happened to her? And I wouldn't have been so boggled by it except this girl was so perfect. The scratches just didn't fit; they looked more like gouges. Then she pulled her bag up and held it tight in that crook of her arm where I'd seen the scratches. What the hell?

"No, I can't," said Lorelei. She shook her head, but when she combed her hair back from her face, I saw something else: three thin scratches at her temple. Thin and scabbed, and then at her nostril, a cut or nick at the base. Had she walked into a rosebush?

"Did a cat do that?" I pointed at her nose.

"What cat?" asked Lorelei, her eyes wide. Then she stepped back. "I don't have a cat, okay? I have to catch my ride. They're waiting for me."

"But this is about your best friend. She was murdered," said Gina.

"You think I don't care? Oh, my God." Lorelei blinked. Tears welled in her eyes. "I do want to say something. Ask me on Monday, okay?" she sniffed. "I'll totally do it. And it's nice of you, really, to do that for Merry." She turned, and then she turned back around. "Why exactly *you*? I mean, you didn't really know her."

"We found her," said Rachel.

"Oh," said Lorelei, "right."

"And because, well, Ms. Deerfield asked me since we couldn't get it into the yearbook," said Rachel.

"Okay." Lorelei nodded. "But, really, be careful in there." She nodded at the locker room. "Coach is, well, how she usually is." Lorelei walked away.

"Right on," said Rachel. "She's kind of nice."

"Sshh, you guys," I said.

Lorelei didn't go around the corner and through the middle of the school grounds, which would make sense if you were catching a ride in front. She walked through the student parking lot toward the long driveway that led down to the street. Gina tapped me on the shoulder. Then we heard the burning rubber. A bright red Mustang Mach 1 with a black stripe, going super-fast, braked at the empty parking lot, spun to go the other way, and stopped. Lorelei got in and the car and sped off.

"Burn, man, was that him?" asked Rachel.

"Who?" asked Gina.

"That's his car, Nick's car," I said.

"What do you know about that," said Gina.

CHAPTER 16

I opened the locker room door, and we went inside.

"I still don't get why Lorelei was here," I said.

"That's what I want to know. Like, she knows Stevens's routine better than us; why come by herself?" asked Gina.

"And why did Stevens want her to come?" I asked.

Man, we were making a racket. Now, I mean, I'd heard about Stevens, and I knew this Friday-afternoon thing with her wasn't good, and Lorelei had even warned us to be careful in here, and we were total jabber-jaws.

"Okay, keep it down," I whispered, putting my finger to my lips.

"What about the coach, you guys?" said Gina.

"Lorelei *and* Nick together?" said Rachel.

When we first entered, we were in regular bathroom territory, except for the chicken-wire door on the same side as the sinks. The wire door led into the actual locker room, with a cement floor and rows of aquamarine lockers. We heard the plunk of water from a shower-head not turned all the way off at the far left. We passed the equipment cage, the fenced-in far-right section that stored softball bats and mitts and bases, paddle balls and paddles, track posts, and whatever else went with sports. Then towels, then the two desks, Zamora's and Stevens's. A counter at the fence had a cutout. I'd just stood there a few days ago to get us an all-day excuse for crabs from Coach Zamora.

We were going all the way to the end, to my locker, and right now the only lights were back at the entrance. The radio played behind the teachers' desks, possibly from the laundry room. We heard a metal jangle, like keys, maybe on a key chain. I leaned over the counter and saw the coach; she had fallen asleep, I guess, on a pile of towels on the floor.

"Well, danger no more, I guess," I said.

The coach snorted, and we all ducked behind the counter.

"Why are we afraid?" asked Gina.

"I don't know," I said.

Rachel bopped up to check. "She's out."

We made it to the back, and I stuffed my PE shirt and shorts into my book bag.

"Let's get out of here," said Rachel.

We tiptoed past the counter. I leaned over just to make sure Stevens was still asleep. Dang. The towels were there, but not Stevens.

"She's gone," I said.

"Let's hope she's locked in," said Gina.

"OOUUUUTTT!!" The huge, deep bellow sounded like Stevens's voice.

"Jesus!" Gina shouted and then we ran, tumbling with book bags, and I heard the crash of an aluminum bat against the chicken-wire caging. I didn't know if it had launched from the cage side or not, and I wasn't looking.

"Wait up," I heard Rachel call behind us; those Dr. Scholls were not running shoes, and they were loud and echoing.

"Haul it!" Gina turned to get Rachel to go faster.

I got to the entrance and opened the door, stamping my feet for Gina and Rachel as if I could run for them.

"Noooo," I heard Rachel say and saw her waving at me behind Gina.

Gina ran past me, but Rachel stopped. "Back there," she said, her breathing heavy and uneven.

"Yeah, she's back there. Let's get out of here," I said and pushed her out, then slammed the door. I leaned against it, and then for some crazy reason I tried it. It was locked.

"My bag, Addie," said Rachel.

"What?" I asked.

"No, not today—we're not going back there. She threw that bat at us—the coach threw a bat! What makes you think she's not carrying a few more and coming for us?" Gina shook her head.

"But that's everything—all our notes, and—"

"Sorry, Rae," I said. "We have to go."

My car was parked up on Antonio, and we had to get through fields, track and football, and then up those stairs. I kept looking back. So far, no coach.

"Christ, first Nick, then Stevens. And Lorelei's scratches," I said.

We'd taken off our shoes and were on our way up the stairs.

"What are you talking about?" said Gina.

We could hear the traffic of passing cars.

"You didn't see? Lorelei, she had these three honking scratches, you guys, like, you know, like—a ditch-digging mission," I said.

"Like, she was in a fight?" asked Gina.

"We have to figure out if they match with Merry somehow," I said. "I mean, she got into something, and what about Nick, and Stevens?"

"Hey, what's this?" said Rachel. She pulled a sheet of yellow notebook paper off my windshield, held down by the passenger-side wiper blade.

"Better not be a traffic ticket," I said.

We hopped in the Pinto, and it was hot inside. A Jeep with a bunch of senior guys passed going the other way, yelling; the Jeep honked. Totally clueless.

"Oh, no," said Rachel. She showed me the drawing on the paper. The stick figure artist was at it again. This time it was a picture of three round heads with curled girl hair; the eyes were *x*'s but the faces had smiles with tongues sticking out and they were in a toilet bowel as far as I could see, either coming out of or going down. To the right of the picture were the words "Get Flushed!" in all caps.

"That is stupid," said Gina. "It's not even scary."

"Stevens's Jekyll-and-Hyde thing, that was scary—that was a baseball bat, you guys." I turned the ignition.

"We have got to talk to Diaz," said Rachel. "This is the second warning."

I punched the gas.

"You sure you saw scratches?" Gina turned to look at me.

"Yes," I said. "And it's not just her arm; she had them here," I raised my hand to my left temple, "and then one right here," I added, pointing my stubby pinky fingernail at my left nostril.

Rachel waved the yellow piece of paper. "We have to give this to Diaz."

"Stick it in my bag," I said.

I stopped at the light. In the yard of the corner house, kids belly-skidded across a rainbow-colored Slip 'N Slide. What was going on in this town?

"Too bizarre," said Gina.

The light turned green.

CHAPTER 17

Back in Diaz's stuffy office, we were all breathing hard.

"So, you definitely saw these wounds?" asked Diaz.

"Yeah, these scratches were deep, and the skin around them was red, could have been infected. Majorly gross," I said. "I mean they had to hurt, and she was trying to hide it, too, you know, definitely those ones on the inside of her arm."

"And Lorelei said the coach felt guilty about Merry's death, so what about that?" said Rachel.

"The coach threw a bat at us. Check it out, a bat!" said Gina.

"You guys have got to watch it," said Diaz.

"And Nick's totally lying," said Rachel. "He's responsible for Carlos Uribe being in jail right now."

"Okay, Crusaders, easy," said Diaz.

"If we could get into Merry's room, to see if there's something the police missed, maybe," I said.

"Or just talk to the parents?" said Rachel.

Diaz cleared his throat. "These parents have lost their child," he said.

"Okay," I said. "Here's what we do. We interview the Jacobses. We find out what they know about where Merry and Lorelei were supposed to go once they met at school at the locker room, like Lorelei said."

"And we ask them for a picture of Merry for the book," said Gina.

"That's an idea," said Diaz. "It's all taken care of, right?"

"What?" asked Gina.

"This memorial book thing," said Diaz.

I looked at Rachel. All those old notes, her clipboard, and everything she'd left in the locker room when we had to race out of there. We had to get that back, and who was going to open that locker room for us? On the weekend? Rachel said she had talked to Ms. Deerfield, but I didn't know if she had or not. She must have.

"Oh, yeah," said Rachel. "We just have to make sure we get it in by the deadline."

"Good," said Diaz. "Because if it's a totally made-up thing, we'll be in some trouble."

"No. I cleared it," said Rachel.

"Way to go," I said. Rachel didn't look at me.

"One more thing," said Diaz. "Have you had any more of these?" He held up the yellow notebook paper warning we had given to him.

"Yes." Rachel looked at me.

I dug into my book bag and handed him the new note.

"That's a problem," said Diaz.

"I thought you said it was trash," I said.

He took the paper from me. "No, I don't. Not after this. Not after someone's thrown a baseball bat at you."

"You guys," said Rachel. "It's five o'clock. If we're going to talk to Merry's parents, we should get going."

"Be careful. I mean it," Diaz barked after us on our way out of the office.

We hustled down the stairs to the street. The traffic was starting up. I had parked in the lot below the plaza, so we had a couple more flights of stairs to go, but I saw a car that looked familiar.

"Hey." I stopped. "Who has a yellow car?" I asked.

"Who cares?" said Rachel. "We've got to get to the Jacobses' house. Come on."

People were coming up to the plaza to sit near the fountain and at the outdoor tables at El Pancho's.

"We know where we're going?" asked Gina as I started the Pinto and cut up to head south through town.

"Over the creek, past the golf course," said Rachel.

The windows were rolled down, and I tried to rein my hair into a side ponytail. "Brick House" played on the radio.

"Hey," said Rachel perking up in the backseat, "here's an idea. Now I know it's going to sound like crazy city, but what if—"

"Hey," said Gina. "Do I not look like I'm open to totally crazy city?"

I saw the yellow car again. It was in the rearview mirror.

"See, I've been thinking. And it's just, you know, Merry and Lorelei," said Rachel. "They talked on Friday, right?"

"Right," said Gina.

I made the left turn over the bridge. The asphalt was always crumbling off the edge of this thing.

"So, it's totally psycho—it just popped into my head, and I can't not think about it—"

"So, spit it out," said Gina.

I could now make out the car following us. It was a yellow Karmann Ghia. A convertible. So boss. If I had a car like that, my life would be amazing.

"What if, like, you know, like, one of them was pregnant?" asked Rachel.

"What did you say?" I hit the brakes. Now everything was in slow motion. I felt like we were pitched into zero gravity, and then hit the atmosphere. I finally heard the screech of the tires behind me.

"Oh, my God, it's them," said Rachel.

They idled close to us: Jaycee, Lisa, and Myla. Their hair hadn't stopped blowing.

"Learn how to drive," said Myla. She was in the passenger's side of the yellow Karmann Ghia.

"We could have been killed," said Jaycee, who was driving.

"Think about it," said Myla. "Just think about that."

Lisa was wedged in the back, facing sideways. The car bucked into gear and sped off.

"Check it out," said Rachel. "It's them. How are we going to prove it's them?"

"Well, we're going to have to figure that out," said Gina. "Why did you stop in the middle of the road?"

"It just happened. I'm sorry, I got distracted," I said.

"Are you okay?" asked Rachel. "Are you worried about the second note? With the toilet?"

"I'm fine. I'm great. That wasn't a threat, okay? Now I know who owns that stupid car."

"We should look for falling power lines before killer toilets," said Gina.

"We can take them on," I said.

"I hope so," said Rachel. "Okay, here's my idea—stellar, crime of passion."

"This is where Nick comes in," said Gina.

I froze. I completely forgot where I was going, but the car was still moving. We could have been anywhere. *No. Not Nick.*

"Hey," said Gina. "Watch the road?"

I slowed down and turned the blinker on. You could hear the faint rub of the right tires against the curb. The golf course was to the left.

"Why not Nick and Lorelei?" asked Rachel. "Didn't he say he was playing the field?"

Oh, God. Not Nick *and* Lorelei. They were perfect. He was perfect. She was perfect. Why do they say "broken heart"? It's more like someone stuck a bazooka point blank at your chest cavity and fired away. Broken? No. Obliterated? They'd driven off in his car just a couple of hours ago from the high school parking lot, and now her friends were following us. They'd almost crashed into us. What was it going to take?

"It's possible, right?" asked Rachel.

I'd seriously thought I *was* over him, over Nick. "Anything's possible." I signaled to get back on the road. The cars looked like a sparse line of cockroaches. I had to accept it. I had to suck it down. That guy. Like, no matter how many answers I undressed for him to copy while he sat behind me in Calculus, no matter how many smiles he hypnotized me with, no matter how much my heart pounded in his presence—I served one, and only one, purpose for Nick Stanley. I was his ticket to keeping his GPA up, so he could be the sports scholarship king. And, so, yeah, maybe he did love Merry, and that had nothing to do with me. And maybe everything to do with Merry's murder. And now we were going to talk to her parents, Merry's parents. And even with all this, please, he just could not be a killer.

"You think Lorelei did it?" I asked.

"Except," said Gina, "she's not following us in her car, right?"

"Right, it's those other three we need to be on the lookout for," said Rachel. "Oh, my God. What if they live around here?"

"Great," said Gina.

"Hey," I said. "We are not scared of anyone."

"Did I say I was scared?" said Gina.

When we stood at the entrance of the Jacobs house, our three shadows cast across the double-door entry where a wrought-iron light fixture hung above our heads. We moved closer to the door, just in case. You could see the white chips of stucco that hadn't been swept out of the tile grooves; the "Welcome" on the rope doormat was faded, and so was the large brown butterfly that was part of the design. I wouldn't call it quiet; quiet had a way softer sound. Gina pushed the white doorbell button, and we heard the echo of it in this stagnant air that sucked us inside when Glenn Jacobs opened the front door.

All the drapes were drawn, so everything looked like it does when you wear sunglasses inside. Glenn brought us through the kitchen; our shoes slapped the tile floor. There was a dining room on the other side of the sink and cabinets, and you could see the sympathy flowers in vases. Then I noticed the food. In the kitchen every surface—counters, stool seats, the kitchen table—was covered in dishes, some foil covered, some plastic wrapped, and the others half uncovered and ready to be eaten, but not touched: enchilada casserole, brownies, sponge cake with strawberries and syrup; it was awful. Glenn motioned to the food, probably thinking he was offering us a snack of some kind, but he never actually voiced it, which was a good thing. In the large living room with sliding glass doors across the wall that fronted their backyard, Caroline Jacobs sat uncomfortably on the long orange living room couch with their little poodle, whose white pom-pom tail wagged up and down. Then it dug its nose under Caroline's hand.

There was no flashy artwork or quilts or crafts to distract us. I couldn't bring myself to look at Rachel or Gina, much less at Caroline or Glenn. Caroline tried to smile, but her red-rimmed blue eyes were unable to focus. All we could do was nod. I mean, what were we thinking trying to hit them up for our murder investigation? The six sons weren't physically at the house, Glenn explained, but there were those portraits, one of each of their children, all in gilt frames in a stepped procession across the wall above the fireplace. I recognized the one of Merry that was at the memorial. We did not sit down.

"Would you," Caroline put her hand at the base of her neck, "like something to eat?" Her voice was hoarse and grainy.

"No-no," said Rachel.

"We don't want to bother you, Mr. and Mrs. Jacobs; we just came to tell you that we are putting together a memory book, uh, for the high school," I said.

"Ahh." Glenn nodded.

"Mmm," said Caroline. She looked out past us into the distance, and I couldn't help but turn to see if something was going on in the backyard, but when I looked, there was just an old grimy barbecue with the lid up and a patio set, the chairs pulled far away from the table.

Glenn took Caroline's fingers in his hand to massage them. She slowly undid his gentle grip, smoothed her short, fine hair, and then left the couch and silently walked up the stairs.

This was nuts. What would Glenn Jacobs be able to tell us?

"So," I started. "We thought, and if it's too much, just tell us, but we were hoping you might have a picture that we could put in the book."

Glenn rubbed his thighs with his meaty hands. "Picture." He stood. "Picture, picture, picture." He wandered past us into the dining room, and rustled around in that pile of flowers and cards and, sadness to the max, we needed to get out of there.

"This was so wrong," Rachel whispered to me.

"You think?" Gina whispered back.

Glenn came in with a photo in each hand, but he was looking at them back and forth. "Well," he said. "I found these." He looked at them for another second. Then he handed one to Gina and one to Rachel. "Whichever one you think," he said, clasping his hands behind his back. He swallowed. I knew it was time to go. But we were only supposed to get one photo and someone had to give him one back. Rachel handed him her photo. Glenn shook his head. "No, take both."

"Thank you so much, sir," she said.

"We can see ourselves out," I said, backing toward the kitchen, Gina and Rachel doing the same. Glenn stood watching us go, and then we hurried through the kitchen. I looked straight ahead and pushed the door open into plain old outside air. Man! We made for the Pinto. We cut right through the geranium patch between the spindly trees. We must have killed ten flowers.

"Oh, my God." Rachel leaned against the passenger side of the car and took deep breaths.

"Well, we've got pictures." I fumbled with the keys and looked in the rearview mirror. No sign of the ex-cheers and the yellow car.

"Great, more school spirit shots." Gina waved her photo at me. I didn't get a good look.

"I still have to ask Deerfield about the book," said Rachel. "Hey, mine's a picture of Merry at an assembly. You know the one—Bright Futures. It was the Career Day one."

"Dang. Maybe that's what this is," said Gina.

Gina and Rachel shared their photos.

"See?" Rachel squeezed herself between the bucket seats to show Gina.

"Yeah," said Gina. "That must be it. The banner above them says 'Bright Futures.' I have the same one."

"Burn, you guys," I said. "They gave us two photos of the same thing?"

"No, it's—they're not the same. Look, Gina," said Rachel. "Yours has Lorelei in it. Mine's just her, just Merry. But I think we have something here."

"Well, what is it?" I yelled to Rachel and floored the gas pedal. I couldn't get us away from this dark, empty place fast enough.

CHAPTER 18

We sat in the Pinto in the lot below the plaza behind Diaz's building at dusk. Soon, people would start crowding into town, filling up the plaza and El Pancho's, and on the street level, walking past the shops, sitting on the benches in the park between the courthouse and the police station, and lining up for the live music at Los Buitres.

"Addie, what do you see?" Rachel flapped her photo of Merry like a wing in front of me.

The Pinto's engine ticked. We were looking at the two photos.

"Okay, show me again," I said.

The photos were similar. Merry and Lorelei in the first photo stood close to the stage at school. They were both smiling. Lorelei wore her cheerleader outfit, her blond waterfall hair shimmering. She held a small white sign that said "Future Financier" in dark blue bold marker. Merry's head tilted up to catch the sun. Her sign said "Future Lawyer." Bright Futures was Merry's idea for the career fair. She even got the mayor to come speak. She spoke too, making a big deal about how exciting the future was going to be.

"This was before the cheerleaders got kicked off the squad, right?"

"Yep," said Rachel. "Right before, because the party that night was the scene of the ex-cheers' so-called crime."

"Now, take a look at this one," said Gina. "In the background." Nick and Lorelei stood in the distance behind Merry, who stood alone in the foreground.

"Hey, Rae, can I see them both?" I asked.

"Sure." She held hers so both photos were side by side. "See?" said Rachel. "Nick's holding Lorelei's hand."

"Oh," I groaned. I felt my stomach drop like an empty safe, bummer to the max. "They're a couple."

"Merry must have seen them after this was taken," said Gina.

"But why kill Merry if Lorelei and Nick are together?" My heart had just crumbled into dust and blew across the Gobi Desert of my life.

"That's why Merry dumped him once and for all," said Rachel.

"Remember," said Gina, "Jaycee said he was unhappy about it, unhappy that Merry had dumped him."

"So, Lorelei was afraid he'd go back to Merry," said Gina.

"But how did Lorelei know she had to get rid of Merry?" I said.

"Yeah, and let's not forget," said Rachel, "Lorelei's probably got Nick's baby. I mean, she's been sick, missing school, with Nick. That's got to be it."

"What about those scratches on her face?" I said.

"I am definitely retracting my idea about Mr. Jacobs." Gina looked at me.

"Merry's parents," said Rachel. "God, you guys." Rachel leaned forward from the backseat and put one arm around me and one around Gina. "Those poor people."

Even when I could almost catch my breath, I felt this hollowness. I just kept seeing Mrs. Jacobs getting up and disappearing into thin air in her own house.

"Man, that food in the kitchen was paralyzed," said Gina.

Total bummer, we'd invaded these people's lives, we'd hurt them by going to their house; going inside, it was like going inside their skin.

"At least we got the photos," I said.

"We have to show them to Diaz," said Rachel.

"We've got to be on our guard for anything resembling a former cheerleader," said Gina.

"Come on," said Rachel, leading the way to Diaz's office. We were in the parking area behind the plaza, so we had to walk up one level of stairs just to get to the plaza behind Diaz's.

"I should have parked up on the street," I sighed.

"Crusaders!" Diaz greeted us at the landing by the fountain on the plaza level. Families were out, little boys and girls chasing each other across the terra-cotta tiling. The tiny lights strung around the plaza distorted faces in shadowy blips of blue, green, and red. "Hey, you guys okay?"

"Yes, absolutely. We have a clue," I said. "A really good one."

Rachel gave Diaz the photos.

"Note, boyfriend Nick is in the picture, and there," Gina said, pointing.

"Lorelei and Nick are a couple," I said.

"And Lorelei is pregnant," said Rachel.

"That's why she killed Merry," I said.

"Okay, wait a second. Let's review this at dinner. Max is joining us at El Pancho's," said Diaz.

"You seriously think he can help us?" I said.

"Max can definitely help us." Diaz tapped the photos while he looked at the restaurant entrance.

"See, it all makes sense—we know who the killer is," I said.

"And it's a cheerleader, ex-cheerleader," said Rachel. "Just like I said."

"Whoa—maybe, but this is still circumstantial. We'll go over it with Max. He got me interested in law, encouraged me—hell, helped me get a scholarship for law school. I—" He turned around and waved to somebody. We had to move closer to the fountain to let people up and down the plaza steps.

"I don't care what it takes," said Gina. "If he can help us, okay."

El Pancho's was definitely an institution. And old. Its open front faced the plaza. A sitting US vice president had actually eaten there, and some B movie stars. We followed Diaz and heard a mariachi band tuning up. Pretty soon the bar crowd at Los Buitres would echo onto the street across from Diaz's office building and fill the plaza with more sound. Their live music always blasted through town, and so did their infamous brawls. Some motorcyclist would make fun of some guy's cowboy hat, then bottles would be smashed and barstool legs snapped.

"Hey," said Diaz, "looks like Max beat us here."

"Hola, amigo." Walker waved, standing at a table with a multiple-fork place setting. He was a short pudge-ball of a man; his pants were hiked up to his middle, and his sports jacket served as drapery to frame a large stomach.

"The illustrious Crusaders, we finally meet." Walker bowed, showing off a shiny three-quarter pate with gray fringe. When he rose, you could barely see his eyes under gray tufts of eyebrows which were as thick as his mustache.

He looked like one of those merchants in old movies during wartime who help people get fake passports to get out of occupied countries. I looked at Diaz; this was going to take forever.

"Max," said Diaz quickly. "This is Addie, Rachel, and Gina."

The menus had that leather look with velvety tassels, as if what was inside were some parchment version of the Bill of Rights delivered on, like, horseback or something. They were so tall and wide, we couldn't really see each other unless we leaned back to look sideways.

Rachel whispered, "What do we order?"

"I don't know," I hissed back. What do you order when you're not quite sure if you're going to pay or someone else will?

"Pilar, looking forward to another delicious meal," said Walker to the waitress.

"You have quite a party here," said Pilar in her white ruffled blouse, long peasant skirt, and two large paper flowers spanning the upward sweep of her glossy black hair. She winked at Diaz, but he wasn't interested.

"What are you having?" Walker looked at us. I didn't see a soul our age here.

"I'll have . . ." I picked up the huge menu again.

"Do you have root beer?" I heard Gina ask.

"Oh, sure," said Pilar. "And to eat?"

Dang, I really hadn't even read past the appetizers.

"The chile relleno combo," said Gina. She was so suave. All that acting at the dinner theater in San Felipe probably. Or being from a big city like Chicago. She just knew how to do things.

"I'll do the same." Rachel closed her menu and passed it to the waitress.

"Me too." I watched the velvety tassel on my menu dip into a little custard dish of salsa.

"We'll do the usual." Walker nodded at Diaz. So, they had "the usual" together. But if Max Walker knew Diaz and knew he was on this case, what was his angle? A short while later, Pilar came with root beers for us and margaritas for Diaz and Max. "Have to enjoy life, David, when you're fighting the good fight." Walker smiled, threw some tortilla strips into his open mouth, and chewed with a menace.

After some shop-talk from Max about the prosecutor's office, Diaz listed what we had done at this point.

"So, the Crusaders are burning rubber here on tracking down the real murderer, and they are digging up some good information."

"Okay." Walker gulped his drink. "But you have no time to waste."

"Wait until you see what we got just now," said Gina. "Show him the pictures."

"What pictures are those?" asked Max.

"Hot plates, everyone," Pilar interrupted, laying down steaming platters of food. You wouldn't believe she could lift a fly, but she powered those plates like a longshoreman. The dish before me smelled spicy and sweet, and I was hungry. Pilar disappeared into the crowded restaurant, and when the mariachis strolled by, Max waved them off.

"These are pictures of the killer," I said.

"Case closed then?" said Max.

"Not exactly," said Diaz. "That's why I need your help."

"David was just like you," said Walker, looking intently at each of us.

"Max almost single-handedly got Andy Yamashito's farm back to his family. Did you know that?"

"No way, José," said Rachel. "That was a long time ago."

Yoshi Yamashito had been interned at Manzanar, and his farm, where our high school sat on the northwest corner, was confiscated and given to a white farmer until finally the land was returned to his son Andrew after a long fight. And now I remembered: Max Walker was at that ceremony. Huh. I must have been two. But I remember that picture. I think we studied that in our history class in fourth grade.

"Well, the pictures show why Lorelei killed Merry," I said.

"That is exceptional." Max shoveled enchilada into his mouth.

"Yeah, so how can you help us?" Gina asked. She spooned up some chile relleno combo. I did too. God, I'd never tasted something so good.

"Your mother? She's the *Gazette*'s new editor?" asked Max.

"Yeah," said Gina with her mouth full.

"It's a damn shame what Griffin's putting her through. A gag order," said Max. "I helped Lloyd become sheriff and now this—this is the stuff that makes an old man bitter to the core."

"Max, you old dog." A tall, lean man with blond hair and a three-piece suit clapped Max on the back and leaned in to our table.

"Ron Miller, a pleasure." Max turned to the man. "Your campaign causing you enough mortal pain at this point?"

Ron Miller—this was the guy running for state senate, with signs that had his face in black and white all over. Lorelei's dad. The man Lorelei had to be perfect for. And now she was the perfect murderer.

Ron threw his head back and laughed. "It's not painful when you are just doing the simple job of public service. Sorry, folks." He looked at us.

"You know David, don't you, Ron?" said Max.

"Of course, of course, wonderful," said Ron.

"We're working on a pro bono case. These young folks are interested in law, crusading for the truth, so here we are," said Max.

I thought I saw Mr. Miller wince just for a second. "Too bad business isn't booming for you, David. How long since you got your law office started?"

"Two years ago," said Diaz.

"Took you quite a while to pass the bar," said Ron.

"I had to do night school, work during the day for my dad's paint business. It's all worth it."

"Oh sure, but you can't pay your bills working for free. See, that's what I can bring to the state. Businesses have to make money. There's just too much free everything." Ron smiled.

"Not when you have an innocent man up on murder charges," said Max.

"Not my area. I stand by the law. Nice to make your acquaintance." Ron put his hand out.

"I'm Addie." I shook Mr. Miller's hand. It was a cold vice-grip. He shook Rachel's and Gina's hands too.

"So, not going to take one more second than I have to, Max, just letting you know. I'm giving a small speech at the Country Club. It's a fund-raiser, and if you could make it, it would mean the world to Darla and me."

"When is that, Ron?" Max looked off into the distance.

"That would be Sunday evening, and, like I said, Darla and the kids will be there, my daughter Lorelei and son Deacon. Great if you could, you know, just help with making it easier for them. They all love you, you know."

Max smacked his lips. "Well, then, I must clear my calendar. Time, Ron?"

"Oh, seven o'clock. Great, that is just great! Well, so nice to meet you all," said Mr. Miller. "Must be going." He walked up to a group of men heading up the stairs to the street from the plaza.

"That's Lorelei Miller's dad," said Rachel.

"That's the killer's dad," I said.

"He's all for himself. Anyway, what are we doing to find this hard evidence?" said Max.

"We have these two pictures," I said.

Diaz spread the photos in front of Walker, and we explained.

Max shook his head.

"Not enough?" said Gina.

"It makes sense, but we need *direct* evidence to challenge whatever the prosecutor is putting forward to sway the jury concerning Uribe," said Max.

"This Lorelei has scratches," said Diaz. "As though the victim put up a fight."

"We saw them on her face," said Rachel.

"Good, good support. But what you need is a big bombshell," said Max to Diaz. "Get another extension, petition, whatever you have to do."

"I don't know how much time I can buy," said Diaz.

"We need something that will tear through the walls of the courtroom," said Max.

"Like if Merry comes back from the dead," I said.

"In a manner of speaking," said Max.

"We could hold a séance," said Rachel.

"They don't allow that in court." Diaz didn't laugh.

"How about a good old-fashioned confession?" said Max. "Have we thought of that?"

"Sure, no sweat," said Gina.

"That's what will do it," said Max. "For the jury, and for this town."

"But how do we get someone—I mean, our suspect, our murderer—to say they murdered Merry?" asked Rachel.

"Good question. I don't think you will hit the jackpot like that. You might, but what you *can* get is something that nobody knows about that will make everybody come out of the woodwork."

"Dirt, you mean? So, if we get Nick to tell us that Lorelei's pregnant?" I said.

"That could do it!" said Max. He tossed his grimy white napkin on the table. "You get someone who's willing to tell you this secret and chances are your prime individual will spill their guts."

"We know she's pregnant; we get to Lorelei that way," I said.

"We need proof," said Diaz.

"That's why we have to go up to Lorelei's house," said Rachel.

"Wait, wait, wait," said Diaz. "No more house calls. Let's try the boyfriend. We already know he's lying."

"Good," said Max. He turned to Diaz. "You need a foolproof case, my friend. With what you have now, it will be a bloodbath. They are counting on you to fail and then to run you right out of town with your tail between your legs."

"Well, they'll have to do that literally, since my car's barely working," said Diaz.

"I'm telling you, you succeed on this case, you will have clients in droves." Max turned to us. "So, my friends, you three are going to have to shake something out of the trees, pronto!"

CHAPTER 19

We pulled up to Rachel's house to brainstorm after leaving Max and Diaz.

"How do we get Nick to say something about Lorelei?" said Rachel.

"This is classic, Rae. We get Nick to spill about Lorelei. I mean, we can tell him she told us he did it. He tells us she did it. We win. This is like out of the movies!" I couldn't wait for the action to start.

"Yeah, it's perfect, but I have to call my mom to tell her I'll be late," said Gina as we headed inside.

"By the way," said Rachel. "I talked to Deerfield, and she needs the memory book stuff typed and ready to go to the printer's on Monday."

"That only gives us two days," I said.

I liked Rachel's house. It was old, with little cabinet doors in the walls and a steep, creaky staircase that went up to Rachel's room in the attic. At my house it was just my mom and me, but Rachel had two brothers and fights and tension. We followed her into the kitchen. Rachel handed Gina the receiver.

"Baby? Rachel?" Rachel's mom practically flew at us in her nurse's outfit, a white polyester nightmare smock that zipped up the front with two patch pockets over pants with a huge hem. Rachel's mom was shorter than Rachel and had long black hair that she was twisting up and pinning as she moved around, opening the refrigerator. Her dark eyes were wide, and she had three bobby pins in her mouth. "Oh, *mi amor*, can you get Jamie his dinner? I'm so late."

"Sure, Mom," said Rachel. Jamie was Rachel's younger brother. Her older brother, Rigo, had moved out when he turned nineteen.

Rachel's mom stood on her toes to kiss Rachel on the forehead. "Adios. Hi, Gina. Hi, Addie. Off I go."

We watched from the kitchen window as her mom screeched the tires of her station wagon backing out of the carport—you could barely see her head above the dashboard—and then hauled it down the street.

"So, all we have to do is get this confession thing," I said.

"Yeah, Mom." Gina was trying to hang up.

Rachel pulled a note off the refrigerator with a vengeance, so the magnets holding it bounced on the floor, little green and yellow turtles and frogs. "Never again!" she swore as she tore the piece of paper into smaller and smaller pieces and threw them in the trash.

"What was that?" I asked.

"Perry's phone number! Ugh!" Perry was the senior boyfriend that never really seemed to be her boyfriend. Luckily, I never said that to Rachel.

"Don't you have that committed to memory?" I said.

"Perry? I don't know what you see in that guy," Gina said as she hung up the phone.

I looked at Gina. You could hear the faint sound of *The Three Stooges* that Jamie was watching upstairs on his little TV in his room. I thought it was lame that he was fourteen and Rachel had to make him dinner.

"It's called love." Rachel laid fish sticks on a cookie sheet as the oven warmed up.

"So, this confession thing," I said. Rachel handed me a can opener and a can of peas. Gina got the instant-mashed-potatoes job. We could at least be helpful.

"The thing is," Rachel leaned against the white tile counter, "how to get Nick away from people so we can talk to him."

"Plus, I don't think Nick is really ready to be a father," said Gina.

"Hey," I looked at Rachel, "you and Perry used—you, uh, took precautions?" I asked.

"You can't be serious," said Gina.

"Yes. We used a condom. Jeez." Rachel's face got redder and redder. "Jamie, dinner!" she yelled up to the ceiling. "The ones we got from the Women's Center."

"My mom sells all that stuff—condoms, the pill, diaphragms—to doctor's offices and clinics. It's her job," I said.

"*You* took her—" Gina looked shocked.

"For birth control," I said. "I'm her friend."

"But isn't your mom in nursing? I mean, going to school for an RN. Hasn't she told you about the birds and the bees?" said Gina.

"Uh, no," said Rachel.

"You and Perry," said Gina. "I mean, all the way?"

"Once," said Rachel. "Now, of course, he won't even talk to me."

"See, didn't that condom come in handy?" I asked.

"Wait, you guys do the nasty, and that's it, sayonara?" asked Gina.

"Yep." Rachel took the plastic wrap off the bowl of her mom's ambrosia and took bite after bite of the marshmallow-whip-and-canned-fruit mixture. "Want some?" She pulled two forks out the silverware drawer.

"That is so good." I forked down a big bite.

"That is just not right. Rae, Rae, Rae." Gina shook her head. "You deserve better."

"Can any man be better than that?" I asked.

"Yes!" said Gina. She'd dated a guy she met at the dinner theater three months ago. But she had broken it off.

"He really cared about you? After the dirty deed?" I asked.

"Yeah, believe it or not. Take it from me, Rae. You give a guy credit to be only a penis machine, you will only find those guys. But you give a guy some credit to be 3-D, you know, like, human, you will find them everywhere."

"One," I said. "You found one decent guy."

"I was only looking for one. Is there some sort of contest here?" Gina asked.

"So," said Rachel. "How do we get Nick to confess?"

"Right," I said. "Where do girls go who don't tell their mom or anyone about their sex life?"

"Interview the Women's Center for Merry Jacobs's memory book?" Rachel practically choked.

"Jesus," said Gina. "No way! You are crazy. I mean, seriously?"

"No. We're not going to *interview* people at the Women's Center. They have records," I said.

"How do we get the records?" said Gina.

I shrugged. "When we show Nick Lorelei's records, that will get a reaction."

"No, no. We are not breaking and entering. *That* I am so not doing," said Gina.

"Wait, think about it," I said.

"No, Addie, we'd never get the records," said Rachel.

"What happened to lying? We just tell Nick we have evidence that he and Lorelei murdered Merry," said Gina.

"No, he will totally shut down. We need something to go on, so that he takes us seriously enough to talk, unload," I said.

"Lorelei must have a diary, right?" said Rachel.

"We don't have her diary," said Gina.

"We have her address," I said.

"She would write about Nick, about, Merry," I said.

"Yeah!" said Rachel. "Lorelei would totally write about being pregnant."

"So, we get her diary," I started, "we commit it to memory. We get that into the gossip pipeline, people will talk about it. Nick will confirm it, and Lorelei will cave and confess."

"Wait, how do we get a hold of her diary?" asked Gina.

"Yeah, how do we do that?" said Rachel.

"Remember Casa Ridge?" I said.

"But how do we get into Lorelei's room when everyone's there?" said Rachel.

"No. I just told you, I am not breaking and entering," said Gina.

"Doing what?" asked Rachel.

"Go ahead, genius—tell her how we get a hold of the diary," said Gina.

I looked at Rachel.

"Well, if she carries it around in her purse," said Rachel, "we just divert her."

"Okay, sure. Are you carrying your diary around in your purse?" asked Gina.

"Well," Rachel sighed, then her eyes got big. "No."

"Rae, the stuff in the oven, it's going to burn," I said.

Rachel bent down and pulled the fish out. The kitchen filled with smoke and we opened the windows.

Just then, Jamie finally made his way downstairs into the kitchen and rummaged for food. His hair was so straight it stuck out in spikes, kind of like a sea urchin.

"Bummer, man, it's toast." He looked for the ambrosia. We had left two bites of it in the bowl. "What happened to mom's ambrosia?" He stood up close to Rachel, almost as tall as her. "You are *so* in trouble."

"You don't have to eat it," she said. We fanned the kitchen with dish towels.

"I swear." Jamie took the plate Rachel offered him and headed upstairs.

"You want us to steal a girl's diary? Out of her house?" Rachel's voice was loud, and we coughed as the smoke disappeared.

"It's the only way," I said.

CHAPTER 20

Saturday morning, we hiked up to Diaz's office, two and three stairs at a time. Now we knew that Lorelei had betrayed her best friend, had stolen her boyfriend, had proceeded to get pregnant with him, and then had engineered a careful plan to kill her friend.

"He's going to ask us for proof," said Gina softly behind me.

"We'll have it," I said before we stood at Diaz's office looking through the screen door, which didn't have much of a screen to it. We knocked, then pushed the door open, and it clapped against the door jamb with a whack.

"You tell him, Rachel," I said.

"So, this goes right to the crime-of-passion theory," Rachel explained. "Lorelei went after Merry to keep Nick, and she had motive to do that because she's going around carrying his baby."

"What are you talking about?" Diaz looked up. The air still full of old instant coffee, the overwatered spider plant on his floor in a pot, the congealed sweetness of several maple bars that looked like a third grader's Stonehenge diorama.

"We have a plan," I said.

"We find Lorelei's diary," said Rachel.

"I've got to keep my practice, guys. You can't go taking people's stuff."

"Whatever we do, it's not going to affect you," said Gina.

"Right," Diaz sighed. He plugged his hot plate in to boil water. "What about going after this Nick character? You just get him to confirm your suspicions about his relationship with Lorelei."

"Um, we are," I said.

Rachel looked at me with her eyes crossed.

"And? What's the strategy?" asked Diaz.

"We planned it all out last night," I said. "Nick needs to pass the Calculus final, so I tutor him, and he'll confide in me."

"Oh, no!" said Rachel. "My notes! They're still in the locker room."

The memory book, yeah. We still had to produce that thing. Rachel had dropped her notes when we freaked ourselves out thinking we were murder meat for Coach Stevens right after talking to Lorelei about Merry.

"No harm, no foul—we can get them," said Gina.

"But we only have until Monday; that's the deal with Deerfield," said Rachel.

"But you need that as your cover to talk to people," said Diaz.

"Yeah," I said. "Don't worry. We're totally, one hundred percent covered on that. Totally."

"Addie will totally get that little jock-itch Nick to cave," said Gina as we bailed out of Diaz's office.

"Crusaders," we could hear Diaz's voice follow us down the stairs.

I revved the Pinto, and we headed to DJ's. Man, those notes for the memory book. We needed to get our hands on those.

"Someone's got to let us in before Monday." Rachel squeezed her fourteenth packet of ketchup.

I was so excited I couldn't really eat. Too much was going on in my head. DJ's was crowded with the normal number of beachgoers and surfers. Coconut oil in the air. People talking. Someone tried to bank-shot a strawberry shake and it splattered the trash can pink.

"Let's just go and see if anybody is at school today to let us in," said Gina.

"Sure," said Rachel. "But who's going to be there on a Saturday?"

"Maybe we ask Phyllis?" I suggested. Our school secretary had actually thwarted the senior class from egging the gym; surely, she knew how to get the locker room open on a weekend.

"We have to meet that deadline. Type up all those notes. Deerfield was serious, you guys," said Rachel.

"Why not ask the gym teachers?" Gina shrugged.

"Hey, you're right," I said. "We need to talk to Coach Stevens anyway, right?

I noticed Val Muñoz was at the order window. Now she headed toward us. "You guys!" she shouted.

"Val, hey." Rachel stood up and waved. She swept everyone's stuff over to give Val a place.

I mean, I liked Val. She'd been Rachel's playground friend. No sign of Griffin's DNA in that girl. He must have learned to be evil, because this girl couldn't have had a mean thought in her head. And she was always ready to do a row of handsprings down the street. She plopped herself on the tabletop.

"So glad I ran into you," she said with a smile.

"Yeah, same here," said Rachel.

"I volunteered for the lunch run. A bunch of us are down near life-guard station ten if you want to come," said Val.

"Who?" asked Rachel.

"Alex is there, Gina." Val swished her ponytail. "He's got a crush on you."

"Well, he should call me," said Gina.

"Hey, are you guys still working on that memory book?" she asked.

"Pretty much done," I said.

"That is so boss," said Val. She switched gears. "You showing up to Martin Hellman's party tonight?"

"Gnarly." I opened a ketchup packet and it squirted in my fist. "He's good friends with Nick," I gushed. See, that fit totally with my tutoring plan. I could ask Nick at the party. "I know Martin."

"You know him or know of him?" asked Gina.

"Perry's down there, too, Rachel," said Val. "I'm sorry he's such a jerk. But it's so hard not to like him."

Rachel looked pale.

"We're there," I said. "Get Perry to come and make up with her." I looked at Rachel.

"Great. Martin's parents are, like, out of town. Everyone's going." You could hear the singsong in her voice; she jumped off the table.

"Cool." Rachel smiled.

"See you there." Val ran up to the take-out window and left with the lunch order for her and her friends, then turned around and saluted us before jay-walking across the street.

"That was a coincidence," said Gina.

"Is Val friends with Lorelei?" I asked.

"I don't know," said Rachel.

"I don't see a yellow Karmann Ghia," said Gina.

"Man, a party at Martin Hellman's?" said Rachel. "That's so A-list, check it out."

"Plus, I can ask Nick about tutoring," I said.

"And Perry," said Rachel, slurping her shake.

"And Alex." Gina shook her head.

"Man, can you say *too much* opportunity?" I smiled.

I picked Rachel up first that evening.

"I'm worried about that memory book, Addie," said Rachel. She had definitely dressed up to show Perry she was not crying over him. Her hair up, little curlicue spirals falling gracefully in front of her ears, an off-the-shoulder ruffled blouse. If Perry Littlejohn was there, he would so regret that he'd dumped Rachel.

"We just go to Coach Stevens tomorrow," I said.

"On a Sunday," said Rachel.

"I thought about it. She'll be over the hangover from Friday," I said. "Besides, we still need something from her to put in it, anyway."

Then we picked up Gina, who applied her royal-blue sparkly eye shadow and mascara with expert precision despite the patches of missing asphalt that the Pinto bounced across. Martin's house was a split-level on a really skinny road up from Antonio. You could see the lights of Santa Raymunda below and even San Felipe in the distance.

There were a ton of cars, so we drove pretty far down for a spot to park on Martin's street.

"You owe me," said Gina as we waited at the front door before a tall, angular girl with braces let us inside.

The house glowed with orange-yellow light. People danced in the sunken living room. The square modern couches were pushed back to the walls to fit in a ton of people. Hang Tens, cords, scoop T's, and wraparound pants for days. "I am the Walrus" echoed up to the high ceiling.

"Sorry, guys," I half-shouted into the music and chatter. "I have to find the bathroom."

I asked a girl who swayed to the music holding up a hallway corner where to go, and she motioned downstairs. I'm sure there was a bathroom right behind her, but down the stairs I went and just happened to catch Rachel's ex with—oh, my God—another girl. Christ, Rachel would have been mortified. Who would have thought? His buckteeth like two diving boards, watch for the splash, and his date, I guess, a pale, scraggy piece of Kleenex. Not that I cared. Then I heard the toilet flush, and Myla stepped out of the bathroom, her brown eyes with gold needle sharp glints. Where was Lorelei?

CHAPTER 21

I jet-propelled myself upstairs and saw Rachel wave at me. Aerosmith boomed on the stereo. Not everyone looked familiar. Martin must have invited kids from San Felipe High too. I pushed my way through a group of girls singing the lyrics to each other.

Rachel sat next to Val. Val was right. Everyone was here. "I saw Myla downstairs," I said. I pressed myself next to Val and a girl I noticed from French, who faced a girl on her left.

"Yeah," said Val. "Gang's all here."

"Ask her," said Rachel.

"Tell me the truth." Val looked me in the eye as she spoke. "About this memory book."

I wondered where Gina was. We couldn't get lost here. Now was not the time for small talk.

"That book for Merry Jacobs?" Val pressed.

"Yeah?" I said. We definitely had to get that stuff for the book out of the girls' locker room.

"What are you guys really trying to do with that book?" Val's dark, almost black eyes scoured my skull. *Busted.*

"What exactly do you mean?" I shot back, innocently. Why wasn't Rachel helping me out of this third degree? What did Val want?

"Addie." Rachel sounded like she might give up the whole charade.

"What do you want to know?" I said.

"I keep thinking you guys are using that, you know?"

"Look, I can't get the image of Merry's dead corpse out of my mind, so this helps," I said. Which was true, but also, I couldn't take the chance that Val might tell one of those ex-cheers, and then we would never get a confession from Nick.

"Finally." Gina shoved her way toward us with RC Cola cans. I grabbed one and watched Gina take a long sip from hers. Great, now we really weren't fitting in. Oh, well.

"Look, I don't buy Carlos Uribe as the murderer, do you?" Val came right out with it.

Gina must have just taken a gulp, because she spewed a mouthful.

"Man! Fuck! Freshmen!" The catcalls of the offended preceded an exodus of bodies. Hey, at least we could breathe a little.

Gina looked bummed. "Okay, okay, I'm going to clean it up," she said, turning to go in search of something to soak up the mess.

The stereo blasted "Give Up the Funk." Everybody started singing along loudly.

Val stared at me.

"We don't believe Carlos Uribe is the killer either," I said.

"You think it's one of the cheerleaders?" Val asked me.

"Maybe," I said.

"You know who you should talk to?" said Val. "Stevens. Merry was her right hand—you should know—"

"Hey, news flash." Gina was clutching a roll of paper towels.

"What?" I asked.

"I just saw Nick and Lorelei—massively making out."

Jackpot.

Val raised her right eyebrow. I looked at Rachel and nodded at Gina.

"Just a second—what about Stevens?" I asked Val, who looked like she'd just shown me some buried treasure that she would later come to collect.

"Merry had Stevens's key to the gym because Stevens—you know,"

Val tipped her head back and lifted a pretend bottle to her lips, "it takes her a while to get out of the locker room."

Strange impasse here. Our killers were making out like gangbusters, and, like, I felt like I owed Val some crumb, some acknowledgment that we, too, had not accepted the senseless arrest of Carlos Uribe.

"Val!" a girl in a pink gauze blouse yelled, standing next to a picture window and a door that went to the pool. "They're doing cannonballs!"

"Okay!" Val barked back at her friend and stood up but still eyed us. "Just—promise me something?"

"Yeah," said Rachel.

Val whispered in Rachel's ear.

Rachel opened her mouth wide, then closed it. "Okay." I saw Rachel tilt her head and look at Val.

Gina nudged me. I watched Val leave with the girl out to the pool and the night; you could hear the slap of someone's body hitting the water and then the slight delay of a group yelling and clapping.

"What did she say?" asked Gina.

Rachel looked around to check, but no one was in close range of us. "She said Coach Stevens has the ex-cheers' uniforms."

"What? But she said she didn't know about them before," I said.

"She doesn't want to tell the police." Rachel's brow furrowed. "She saw a laundry bag with the uniforms inside behind Stevens's desk. But the last time she looked for it, it wasn't at there. She couldn't find it or the uniforms."

"Why is she protecting Stevens?" asked Gina.

"She didn't think it meant anything until now," said Rachel.

"Now we really have to get to Stevens. We should go there now," I said.

"We can't get in," said Rachel. "We need her key."

"Hey, don't forget Lorelei." Gina nodded her head.

"Yeah? What? Where?" I hopped up. "Lead the way."

"Prepare yourself," said Gina as we followed her into the crowd around the sofa and the stereo.

God, Gina. No faith. I swear. She snaked between several bodies. I reached for her like I was drowning, but I got shoved by some guy backing into me.

"Hey!" I yelled, but he didn't even look. I glanced back. No Rachel.

"Hey, Chuck, I thought I saw you." I felt a hand on my shoulder. It was Nick. Why, God, why was he calling me Chuck?

"Nick?" *Okay, think fast. Ask. Don't freeze up. Don't.*

"You got me." He held his hands up and pointed to himself with his thumbs.

I had to go for it.

"Uh, believe it or not, I was hoping you'd be here," I said. *God, don't let my smile get too strained.*

"Well, kismet, right? Here I am." He grinned, his dimples deepening.

I could not lose my nerve. "I can help you out—uh, with calculus." There. That sounded completely harmless.

He looked dumbfounded. "Cal-cu-lus." He searched the floor for a second, then raised his head. He was high, but, God, even his knuckles were beautiful.

"First, I need some of Martin's killer bud," said Nick.

He steered us through the kitchen—loads of wood paneling, avocado-green appliances and orange countertops, a Danish modern table and chairs, the round space-age kind; it was like being in a *Star Trek* episode. Nick throttled me into the third eye of upper-echelon popularity. Standing behind Nick's empty seat at the table was Lorelei. She squinted down her perfect nose, her blue eyes cracked like ice cubes. Nick slid into his chair.

"What are *you* doing here?" She'd been out in the sun earlier, a pink glow under her tan, all her hair tumbling to the left, like her hair had its own undertow.

"I was, uh, just—" I mean, how did I forget to talk?

Martin, star quarterback Keith Slater, and Lisa's boyfriend, Joe, sat in the other three chairs. The crowd was all upper eschers, and right behind Lorelei were Lisa, Myla, and Jaycee.

"Come on, Marty." Keith leaned in, red-haired and freckled.

Marty lit up the joint and then passed it to Nick.

"You don't belong here, whatever your sad little name is." Lorelei's voice got nasally. It was like that burn from the sun had turned her into flesh-covered anger.

"This is Chuck," Nick inhaled, held his breath an impressively long time, "my pal from Math. And she's my tutor—is that boss?" The smoke and words came out at the same time.

"Chuck, seriously? Is that your name?" Lisa's boyfriend asked me.

"No, get it? She's not a *chick*, she's a *chuck*—like, I made it up." Nick folded his arms.

"She's not bad," said Lisa's boyfriend, "got that all-innocent act." Someone patted my butt, but I couldn't tell who.

"So, what's the plan, Chuck?" Nick asked.

I think the pot packed a wallop. No wonder everyone was so subdued, except for Lorelei.

"Yeah." Lorelei threw her arms around Nick from behind. "Go for it, genius. Tell us."

"Gnarly, man. If I can keep that scholarship." Nick wanted to high-five me, but there were a lot of arms, and I accidently brushed Lorelei's. She was livid.

"Did I say you could touch me?" She shivered.

"I didn't mean to—"

Nick passed the joint to Lorelei. "This is *math,* Lorelei. I need someone that's left bonehead geometry in the dust."

"You don't need the scholarship, Nick," said Lorelei.

"I can get you the answers to the final." I said it so fast I couldn't understand myself.

"Chuck, that is rad," said Nick, and then he started laughing.

Lorelei blew a giant cloud of smoke into my face.

"But we'd need to go over it. Monday." I started to cough.

"Okay, you're done here, little Miss Math," said Lorelei.

Instantly people parted for me to back out of the kitchen.

"Addie! Where have you been?" Rachel was concerned.

"You won't believe me," I said, pointing to Nick and Lorelei, barely visible through the silhouettes of bodies in front of us.

"Oh, my God, Addie. Did you ask him?"

"Yeah, but he's totally high," I answered.

"You were *there*." Her voice went up at the end.

"I have to grab him on Monday. God, I hope he remembers."

We headed toward the front entry. I saw Gina, and she saw us.

"She got him, Gina," said Rachel.

"Let's blow this taco stand," said Gina, opening the door.

Out in the night, I could fill my lungs with deep breaths; I took my shoes off as we walked at an angle across the lawn.

"She saw Lorelei, too," said Rachel. "Addie, what about Stevens?"

"We get Stevens's key to open the locker room."

"What about the missing uniforms?" asked Gina.

We heard the screech of brakes as we walked and saw the yellow Karmann Ghia convertible.

"Brother," said Gina. She put her hands on her hips and yelled out, "Too much beautiful for you?"

"Make me puke," said Jaycee.

"Let's just get to the car," said Rachel under her breath.

Down this far, only my Pinto sat under the circle of light cast by the streetlamp.

"You call that a car, Math Girl?" shouted Myla.

"For your information," I said, clutching my keys, "this is one wicked chariot!"

"Hey." Myla leaned over the passenger door. "Get this, genius. You stay away from Lorelei, and you stay away from Nick. You stay away, period."

Jaycee gunned the engine viciously. I could feel my heart thumping up into my esophagus.

I slammed the door and got the key into the ignition. The Karmann Ghia rolled slowly past.

Rev, die. Rev, die. Rev, die. *Dang.*

The Karmann Ghia came back the other way, then stopped.

"See you in auto shop, assholes!" Jaycee yelled above the Karmann Ghia's rpm throttling, and then the car screeched straight out of sight.

I decided I wasn't going to tell Rachel about seeing Perry with that girl.

"They know," said Rachel. "They know we know it's Lorelei."

CHAPTER 22

Sunday morning, I had hoped to cruise in silence to Rachel's. It's not that I was afraid of those ex-cheers. I just wanted to make sure they couldn't find us today. But the minute I started the Pinto, I knew my wish was not going to come true. The muffler rocked and rattled and left a skunk tail of smoke that I saw out the rearview mirror. Rachel must have heard me coming.

"I thought you got this thing fixed." She jumped in the front seat with two triangle slices of cinnamon toast and handed me one.

"I think it's okay for now," I said. I crunched down a bite of toast. "That is so good."

"We get those notes, and we start typing," said Rachel. "I am not, repeat, *not* showing up in front of Deerfield empty-handed."

"We'll get it done; don't worry." I punched on the gas as far as I dared. If I went at the speed of sound the cops would be following us, and that's the last thing we needed. We had less than twenty-four hours to get that memory book done. Actually, less than that, since we needed to get a hold of Lorelei's diary too.

We passed families walking down Camino Raymunda to the Mission Church for Sunday mass, and we got a few stares due to the black plume of muffler smoke. Then I turned right and drove up to

Gina's house. She was blowing bubbles on a patch of weedy lawn with her little sister Triana. Gina's mom was walking toward them, her dark hair pulled into a bun on top of her head. Gina had inherited her mother's dimples. She wore a white blouse and tan pants and huge platform sandals that made her even taller. Gina's mom definitely did not look like the dictatorial warlord that Gina described. Gina waved at us as we slowed to the curb.

"So, you and your mom are getting along?" I asked after Gina hugged her sister and waved to her mom.

"It's called diplomacy. Anyway, check it out—you're totally not going to believe the home address for Coach Stevens," said Gina.

I turned out of the cul-de-sac before Rachel had time to shut the passenger door.

"So, where does Stevens live?" Rachel asked above the motor's roar. I revved while we were stopped at the light on Camino Raymunda.

I looked in the rearview and noticed the exhaust smoke no longer looked so dark.

"At the end of San Marcos Street," said Gina.

San Marcos ran along the edge of the orange groves above Santa Raymunda Creek. It was out there.

"Dang, out by the Rodriguez stables?" Rachel asked.

"I guess," said Gina.

I took a left and a right and recognized the stables and the old Rodriguez farmhouse on the right, nestled in its overgrowth of bougainvillea and willow. The street pavement stopped just a few feet before their driveway. In front of us it turned into a bare dirt path. On our left was Santa Raymunda Creek. Bamboo, rushes, and grasses crowded both banks of the creek. When Rachel and I were younger we pretended we were on safari at the creek, sucked sour grass, and grossed each other out with catching the biggest bugs. On our right, the orange grove thickened, and we came to another farmhouse to the right in a clearing. An old fruit stand in front had been turned into a carport that housed a compact car and a pickup, but there was room for a couple more vehicles.

I parked off into the grass next to a fence between the carport and the house.

Oranges rotted on the ground. Insects whirred and buzzed around us.

"Okay, which one?" I asked. The farmhouse looked like it was divided into four units, two on the bottom and two on the second floor.

"Top unit on the left," said Gina, charging ahead of us.

Our flip-flops thwapped on the wooden stairs leading up to the second floor and the narrow deck in front of the door. A line of terra-cotta pots sat on top of a redwood bench shoved against the top railing with barely living spider plants, more spiderweb than plant, a couple of crisp geraniums, and some sort of ivy without leaves. A rusted TV tray balanced a hibachi barbecue in front of the drape-covered window. Gina nodded at me.

"Coach Stevens!" I yelled and pulled the squeaky screen door open. There were signs of the former gingerbread design accents of the house I remembered when we raided the groves for oranges as kids and then ran back down the bank to the creek and disappeared into the foliage. I had stood on the bank across from us now back when everyone watched the sheriff rescue the little boy from drowning a long time ago.

Layers of faded white paint covered the front door's three glass panels. Gina knocked. Rachel knocked.

"Coach!" I yelled again.

"Please, Coach," Rachel cried.

Gina knocked. *Dah-dah-dah. Dah-dah-dah.*

Nothing.

The heat and rush of sweat coated my skin.

"Come on, Stevens," I sighed.

We heard the slinks and chinks of multiple locks unlocking.

"Coach!" I yelled again.

"Good Lord, ladies," Coach Stevens's brown eyes blinked in the harsh sun. "It *is* Sunday. Am I wrong?" The cavern behind her doorway looked stacked to the gills with stuff.

"Yes, but it's very important," Rachel started.

"I see." Coach looked past us as if we'd brought reinforcements. She wore the same uniform for school but in white: T-shirt, tennis shorts, socks and sneakers, plus the wide headband holding back her hair. She steadied herself in the doorway. Underneath her tan, I could see red patches and where her makeup thinned, purplish skin under her eyes.

"Coach, we need your key, the key to the girls' locker room." I stood back.

"And why am I authorizing entry to school property for one, two, three people I hardly know?" She listed forward and then leaned against the door frame. She was a wreck, and we still needed a statement from her for the memory book.

"See, we left Merry's book, the manuscript, in there. By accident," said Gina.

Coach's eyebrows rose. "You have something of Merry's?"

"No, Coach, this is her—we're making a supplement to the yearbook," said Rachel. "A tribute to Merry."

"We need to get it turned in tomorrow by eight a.m.," I said.

"Please," Rachel begged.

Coach put her hands on her hips and studied the ground. "I just—" She shook her head. "I just wish it were all a bad dream." She took an unsure step forward. I leaned in for support but then caught a whiff. Whoof, man! She had definitely been drinking. And trying to cover it up with Cepacol. I felt like Dorothy when she finds the man behind the curtain in *The Wizard of Oz*.

Stevens sat herself down on the edge of the bench, pushed back the potted plants, and hunched over, her elbows on her knees, her hands loosely folded. She made a muffled snorting sound, then slowly raised her head up. She squinted at me. I could see her makeup slightly crack, its thick coating like mortar. I kept thinking about "The Cask of Amontillado." She looked trapped.

"I still don't believe it," Stevens sighed.

"Coach?" asked Rachel.

"I thought we were doing something really good with the squad. Everyone getting so good at competing. We won three awards at regionals. Lorelei and Merry were my world. Merry was so bright,

Lorelei just a sweetheart, then all the—the fighting, the yelling. It broke my heart. They were best friends!" Stevens dropped her head again.

"Coach?" Gina tried to dig Stevens out of her mourning state.

"I knew they were hurting each other." Stevens's whole body shivered.

"What? What do you mean, they fought? Physically?" asked Rachel.

"I know, I should have stopped them."

"Coach?" My voiced rasped with shock. Had she seen it?

Stevens snorted, straightened, took a deep breath, and wiped her nose. "Oh, God. Just despicable." She tried to rub away the mascara smudges under her eyes.

"Coach, did you see anyone? I mean, do you know who did it? The murder? The murderer?" Gina's questions were like pebbles that finally brought an avalanche.

"You said they were hurting each other?" Rachel asked.

"Who were you talking about?" I said.

Stevens wiped her face with her right arm, hooked her thumbs in her shorts pockets, and sat straight as a rod.

"Coach, we know Carlos Uribe didn't kill Merry," said Rachel.

"He was framed," said Gina.

"Who sent you? Who was it? It's the school, isn't it? They want to fire me, so they send you—"

"No way, Coach. I swear," I said.

"She made me do it, you know. I put my professional career on the line. Now, how is that going to look in front of the school board? But Merry insisted. She was just full of revenge. I—she ran all those practices, did so much hard work, helped me so much, and I felt I owed her, so I did it."

"What did you do?" asked Gina.

"I pulled the whole senior line." She spoke without emotion. "And then Merry hated me. I did what she wanted, but she changed her mind about it, realized how cruel it was. She was meeting Lorelei. I'd confiscated the uniforms, and Merry was going to give them back to Lorelei."

I looked at Rachel. Val had told Rachel at the party she had seen the uniforms in a laundry bag under Stevens's desk, and now we knew what happened to them, or at least why they'd disappeared.

"So, when they fought in the locker room, they hit each other?" I asked.

"They went outside. I thought I heard something, and I—well, I got myself outside, and I could see. Lorelei, all the other girls, they had Merry on the ground. I thought—it had to be a bad dream. This couldn't be happening."

"You left them there to gang up on Merry?" I asked.

"I can't be sure of what I saw," said Stevens. "You don't understand."

"You didn't stop it? Why didn't you stop it?" Gina demanded.

"You just let them fight? You just let Merry die?" Rachel almost cried.

"I know. I'll never be free of it. I failed her." Stevens got to her feet, but she didn't look at us. "I'll get you your key."

She disappeared into her apartment. The screen door banged against the door frame. I noticed it was missing its bottom hinges.

We waited.

"Stevens must have passed out, Rae," I said.

"That's no excuse," said Rachel.

"Well, she's in hell now," said Gina.

"We get the key, and we get out of here," said Rachel.

"I mean, what else is she capable of?" I asked.

The squeak of the screen door jarred me. Stevens looked like a ghost behind the screen mesh until she was out in the full sun. She held a jar close to her chest with her arm around it. There was something in the jar. A white thing. A bulb of ginger?

"What the—" I started to ask.

With her free hand she held out the key to me, and I grabbed it.

"I found it. Outside the locker room on Friday," said Stevens, looking at the jar with the floating thing in it.

"After the fight?" I asked. I felt the key in my fist.

"In the evening," she sniffed. "After everyone was gone. I found it in the grass." Coach held the jar out for Rachel to take it.

"Coach, you need to tell the police about this," I said.

Rachel held the jar up so she could look at what was inside. "Gross me out!" Rachel dropped the jar on the deck, but it didn't break.

Gina stopped it with her foot before it rolled down the stairs.

"But Coach." I looked at her. "What is it?"

"I don't know." Stevens looked at us with eyes like black holes in space.

Coach slammed the door, and we heard all the locks re-locking.

CHAPTER 23

"Let's get out of here," said Gina.

We charged down the steps of Stevens's apartment half in flight.

Once we hit the ground, we made it to the car, turning up dust clouds in our wake. "So now we know." I tried to catch my breath. "They really did it. Lorelei really did it!"

"And this!" Gina held up the jar.

"Grody-ness to the max," said Rachel. "I can't breathe."

"I think it's, like, a kitten," said Gina. "Looks like one of Mr. Boatman's famous formaldehyde life-forms."

"Puke city." Rachel cupped her hands over her mouth and took off toward the fence.

"It's in a jar, Rae. It's dead," I said, running after her.

Rachel leaned her head over the fence rail, catching her breath or trying to keep her cinnamon toast down.

"This is truly weird. Why did they have this thing?" Gina held the jar with both hands.

Rachel retched and we heard the soft splatter of vomit on the dirt.

"We've got to go, you guys." I patted Rachel on the back.

"Please." Rachel took some deep breaths. "Give me a second."

"What are we going to do?" asked Gina. "It sounds like Lorelei wasn't acting alone."

"Yeah, well, I don't see a yellow Karmann Ghia here yet," I said.

"We really have to watch it," said Gina.

"They are all in on it." Rachel lifted herself up. She looked pale.

Gina and I walked her to the car.

"That stuff normally doesn't gross me out," said Rachel.

I knew it wasn't really the cat that got her upset. It was Poor Merry Jacobs. Now we knew, really, really knew, that her killer was her best friend. Stevens had seen it happening and hadn't done anything to stop it. Awful on top of awful to the max.

"Let's go." Rachel crawled into the backseat. "We have to tell Diaz or the police about this."

"Diaz, yes," I said. "I don't think we tell the police."

I drove as fast as I could to the paved street. So much to do. Get all the notes from the gym, get that all typed, get over to the Millers' house and find Lorelei's diary.

"Hey." Gina studied the jar. "The label's torn. Says 'domesticus.'"

"That's the label we found at the crime scene," I said.

"It's hard to really see it—the cat, I mean." Gina held up the jar.

"Don't do that," said Rachel.

"You're in the backseat— you can't see anything," said Gina.

"What is up with the cat?" I asked.

"You think it's one of Boatman's?" asked Rachel.

"Oh, it totally is," said Gina. "He always threatens us in third period that we'll have to cut something like this up, you know, if we get all grossed out by planaria or those huge earthworms."

"But, what would they do with it? Either Merry or Lorelei—I mean, they're seniors; they don't do biology." I checked the small fifth pocket of my cutoffs and felt for the gym key. There and safe.

"God, Addie. Stevens! What did she do? What did she see?" asked Gina.

"She was there," said Rachel. "Go figure."

"We need her to talk to Diaz," I said.

"We need her sober," said Gina.

I slowed to stop at the red light.

"I swear to God, you guys, are we looking at a murder weapon?" said Rachel.

"Well this isn't the thing that killed her. She was suffocated," said Gina. "Just go."

The tires squealed, and we sped through the red light. My sweaty hands gripped the steering wheel. We still had to find a way to get into the Millers' house to get Lorelei's diary. We still had to fish all of Rachel's notes from the girls' locker room and type up three million pages for this memory book. We still needed proof positive that Lorelei Miller had killed Merry Jacobs.

CHAPTER 24

I admit I hadn't really thought it through, the whole sneak-in, sneak-out plan to get into Lorelei's house and get our hands on her diary while the Millers were out at the fund-raiser for Ron's campaign. We parked at dusk, two houses down from ground zero, and waited for it to get dark. The houses at Casa Ridge where the Millers lived were huge hacienda-style stucco-and-red-roof homes. They seemed massive and sprawling, gilt iron bars on the windows, palm trees and blue-tiled fountains in the front yards. The two-story houses had balconies in the front like something out of *Romeo and Juliet*. A horse trail had been put in beside the road going up the hill to the development because some people kept horses in private stables below the hillside crest where the homes were situated.

"Wow," said Rachel.

"I thought you said you had been here before?" I asked.

"No."

"Wait, what?" said Gina. "Uh, you said you knew the neighborhood. Do you not know the neighborhood?"

"I was thinking of Casa Arroyo—you know, that's closer to school," said Rachel.

"I really hope they don't have a dog," I said.

"Well, they don't have horses; I asked Val," said Rachel. "But she didn't know whether or not they had a dog."

Val had told Rachel the exact address of Lorelei's house. I felt a little nervous. The dry feeling at the back of my mouth. I knew people always kept a window or a door unlocked. My mom and I always left the back door unlocked, in case we forgot our house key. Okay, in case *I* forgot my house key.

"But I came prepared." Rachel pulled out a little baggie of dog treats from one pocket of her sweatshirt and a rawhide bone out of the other.

"I don't like dogs," said Gina.

"Well, I hope they don't have a cat," I said, "because I'm allergic."

"You are going in first," said Gina to Rachel.

"Mellow out—it's not my fault if they have a dog," said Rachel.

"You guys, quit fighting," I said.

The houses were set back from the street, and the driveways were long enough that we would definitely be successful getting to the Millers' house without being seen by the neighbors. I had the flashlight, but I wasn't going to turn it on until we were right at the house.

"Okay," said Rachel, "see that little statue at the second driveway? I say we run like hell across the street and get cover from that hedge, and then we'll just follow it to the statue thing."

In the pale streetlight, I could make out a figure atop a stone pillar. Possibly an angel.

"I swear to God," said Gina. "If anything bad happens, it's on you."

"Nothing bad is going to happen; there's nothing wrong with visiting the neighborhood," I said.

"Okay, let's go," said Rachel.

We bailed out of the car and managed to get across to the hedge. Luckily, there was enough light for me to follow Rachel, and Gina to follow me. We made it to the cement edge of the Millers' driveway behind the hedge.

"It's a horse," I said to Rachel now that I could see the little statue. Then something brushed against the back of my head. "What the—" I turned to look at Gina. "Why did you hit me?"

"That was not me." I saw Gina's eyes were wide with fear.

"Tell me it was a bird," I said.

"I don't know what it was," she said.

"You guys," said Rachel.

"Was it a bat?" I asked. I'd seen the little things before, mice with wings. If I thought about it too much, I would become paralyzed right there.

"Let's hope so," said Gina without any emotion. "Let's start thinking about that dog."

The Millers' house was a one-story as far as I could tell. Down the driveway, we realized the entry was around the side of the garage. Our best bet was to find an open window at the back of the house. Of course, we had to *find* the back of the house. Now we were at the edge of the planter near the walkway to the front door; little bugs and moths circled a light that hung at the entrance. The glare from the white stucco was blinding.

"Addie," Rachel whispered. "There's a dog."

"Great," said Gina.

"Hi, puppy dog," I heard Rae's high-pitched but soft baby voice.

The medium-size German shepherd was pacing slowly behind a wrought-iron fence that separated the front yard from the back.

"You're so cute," Rae's voice trailed off. Then I heard the tinkling of dog tags. I watched Rachel feed the dog out of the sandwich bag.

"Your genius is its own reward," I whispered.

"Okay, you guys, we have to get moving. You first." Gina looked at me.

"Rae, you have the treats," I said. "You pave the way."

At first the dog whined as we heaved Rae up to the top of the fence. Then he barked. Just once.

"Come on," said Rae as she dropped down over the other side and petted the dog.

"If that thing bites me," Gina looked at me, "I will never talk to you again." Gina flung her rainbow sandals over the fence and the dog barked. "I am not kidding." She placed her bare feet against the bend in one of the fence rods and in one motion leaped to the top of the fence rail.

"Just jump," said Rachel.

"This is totally insane," said Gina, and then she sailed to the ground.

"Hey, there's a latch right here." Rachel slid a metal piece back, and a gate that you couldn't see until it opened swung aside. "Duh," she said.

I went through, latched the gate, and saw Gina and Rachel and the dog well ahead of me.

"See?" Rachel pointed as I watched the dog run through a doggie door. "You can get through there."

I looked at Rachel. She handed me the plastic bag of doggie treats.

"Get through and let us in," said Gina.

"Why me?" I said.

"This was all your idea," she said.

It was not a smooth push, but an aggravated inching and then heavy-duty breathing until I got all the way inside.

"Let us in." I could hear Gina and Rachel outside the glass in the dark.

I was in the kitchen, and I just had to open the sliding glass door at the end of the living room. I put my hand over the end of the flashlight and turned it on. When I opened my fingers slightly, I could see more detail. I'd expected a tidier home, but I saw dishes in the sink, a box of cereal on the counter, and books and notebook paper on the dining room table, just like at my house. Right on—this was where Lorelei lived, breathed, possibly entertained Nick Stanley. I waved at Rachel and Gina, felt for the latch on the sliding glass, and realized the door wasn't locked and slid it back.

"Guess we should have tried this first," I said.

Gina walked right past me.

"Her room. Lorelei's room," said Rachel.

I pointed the flashlight at the floor.

"I found it," we heard Gina call from the tiled hallway.

"Hah-choo," I sneezed.

"Bless you," said Rae.

I caught the cat in the light as it rubbed against my shin.

"Oh, no." I felt a wet dribbling on my upper lip. I wiped at it with my arm and bolted down the hall, hoping the cat wouldn't follow me.

The light from the flashlight went everywhere until I caught my breath.

"Can you believe this?" I heard Gina in the room before I walked in.

Her arms were stretched out at both sides. There was a large four-poster bed like you see in Louis XIV pictures in European History, with swales of gauzy drapery tied to the middle of the posts like the bed was another room. The sheets were thrown back, and there was a pack of gum and about seven stuffed animals piled on one side—a hippo, a tiger, and a koala bear at the top. There were magazines, clothes, bathroom towels. There was a bureau with a mirror, another smaller one to the side, and then little boxes of tissue paper, and a picture of a real castle, and a picture of Lorelei with the dog, and then on the floor a picture of Lorelei and Merry, and Lorelei in her cheer-leading outfit.

"Okay, we each take a wall," I said.

"Think—if you want something to stay hidden, where do you put it?" said Gina.

"How long before the Millers come back?" asked Rachel.

"Hopefully, not for another hour," I said.

The cat jumped up on the larger bureau and walked to the edge to look out the window at the yard. I wondered if Lorelei looked at the moon from this window. The cat started licking its paws.

I panned the flashlight around. Rachel pulled a small lamp down from the other bureau and plugged it in.

"Maybe in a purse she doesn't use," she suggested.

"Or shoes," said Gina. "No one looks in shoes," and she opened the closet doors.

"Ha-choo," I sneezed, and started opening the drawers in the big bureau.

"Huh," said Rachel, "she has something under here." She reached under the bed.

"What is it?" said Gina, pulling the clothes back one hanger at a time, which made a clicking sound.

We had to be careful but thorough, not easy when searching for the tiniest thing or just a plain everyday thing that now held great significance. No one said anything for a while; the cat stretched. I started on the bottom drawer.

"Hey." Rachel dragged out a small canvas bag out from under the bed.

"Looks like laundry, Rae," I said.

There was a box at the bottom of the drawer I'd pulled out, a small jewelry box. I opened it, but it was empty, so I put it back, but then I felt something at the very back of the drawer. It was lodged between something. I pulled hard and the drawer crashed to the floor.

"Careful, Addie," said Rachel.

"Oh, my God. Look." I focused the flashlight on it. It was a book. With a maroon velvet cover. I opened it. "Mother lode," I squealed. "'My diary,'" I said, reading Lorelei's writing.

"No way!" Gina cried.

"Hey guys," said Rachel. "*Some* laundry." She pulled it out, and in the dim light we could see a cheerleader uniform. "There's more than one here," said Rachel.

"Yes," I said. "We take it."

"But—" Rachel started.

The dog started barking at the front of the house.

"Busted city—it's the cops," said Gina.

"Hurry," I whispered to Rachel.

She had unzipped her sweatshirt and then shoved the clothes inside and zipped it up like a hobo pack. I put the book under my blouse, trying to tuck the end into the top of my shorts.

"Where's the treats?" asked Gina.

"I gave them to Addie," said Rachel.

She had, but I didn't remember where I put them. Somewhere in the room.

"You guys, we have to get out of here," said Rachel.

My hands were shaking, the dog was barking at the front of the house, and then the doggie door banged and the dog was back with us. The cat freaked and sped toward me. Its claws punctured my arms and nose. *Burn, man.*

"Ha-choo, ha-choo, ha-ha-ha—" I sneezed.

Rachel opened the window, and I saw Gina hopping through it with her sandals in her hand.

"Where's the diary?" asked Rachel.

"In, *ha-choo,* my-*ha*-shirt-*choo—*" I turned off the flashlight.

We heard what sounded like a garage door.

"Come on." Gina tugged me out first, then Rachel.

We were in the backyard, which was a thin strip and then more fence, with open scrub behind. We had to try to get there. The dog was barking and following us.

"Up, you guys." I waved my hand. *"Ha—"* Rachel cupped her hand over my mouth and got a fistful of mucus.

"They're in the driveway," she said softly, and I could see the car's headlights—the Millers, if that was them, or a cop. We all ducked down. Then the headlights turned off.

"Now," said Gina, and we all climbed up the iron fence at the far back. Rachel threw the sweatshirt packed with uniforms. I felt the book jab into my stomach as I teetered over the fence rail.

I heard the dog and the voices.

"Ha-choo." I felt Rachel pushing me. The darkness and the whip of long grass and bushes and leaves. I tried to hold my breath. Now, we were running head first downhill, and you could see the lights from the houses up above. I didn't hear the dog anymore. Then I tripped, and as I went down, I knew I had to wrap myself around the book, and I remember balling myself up, nailing the prickly pear, and feeling all these little tiny pins.

CHAPTER 25

"You are lucky you fell backwards into the cactus," said Rachel.

"Ha-choo." I was miserable. Allergies plus human pincushion.

"I was right there," said Gina. "I was, like, *over here,* but no, you had to go the other way."

"I was confused. *Ha—*" I wanted to stop the sneeze because when I sneezed, instead of plucking the needles out, Rachel just pushed them in deeper.

It was midnight now, and we'd just snuck into Rachel's house. My mom was going to kill me. Gina's mom was going to kill her. Since Rachel's mom was on night shift, Rachel would be getting killed later.

Gina flipped through the diary.

"I swear," I said. "There's got to be something in there."

"Yeah, 'Life 101—a Portrait of a Young Woman as a—'" Gina sighed. "Who knows. Did you know that Lorelei dots her *i*'s with little open circles with faces?"

"Yeah, just because a handwriting expert would say this girl is not a murderer doesn't mean she doesn't have it in her," said Rachel.

"There's a lot of little rabbits in here," said Gina.

"Hold still. What do you mean, 'rabbits'?" Rachel plucked the thin, hair-like needles that made several little carpet patches on the back of my thigh, which I could only see at a weird angle with her mom's large handheld mirror. Some of the needles had actually come off with my shorts, thank God, but it all hurt a lot. Once I'd gone down in the prickly pear, I think I scared myself into a blackout. I barely remember Rachel and Gina shaking me, and the Miller family looking at us but unable to see us because the glare of the porch light served as a blind spot, and we were still behind the fence.

"She's got drawings of rabbits in here. It's her diary, so I assume she is the artist, ugh," said Gina.

"Okay," said Rachel. "I think they're all out."

"Your butt is inflamed to the max; I hope it doesn't hurt that much," said Gina.

"It hurts," I said. "Anything?"

Gina inspected a page.

"Earth to Gina," I said under a lake of mucus, and then tried to blow that out in one long, extended exhale.

"That is truly disgusting," said Gina. "Oh, well, another great rabbit drawing. It's a family and they're eating carrots."

"Lame," I said. "There has to be something. *Ha-choo*."

"What are we going to tell Diaz?" asked Rachel.

"Look, there's just got to be something here, and when we find it, he is going to thank his lucky stars, and us," said Gina. "What's this?" She unfolded some papers. "I hope it's not a permission slip."

"Hold still," said Rachel. "There's more needles."

"*Ha-choo*. Ouch," I said as I tried to sit on the couch next to Gina.

"They're not all out?" said Rachel. "Stand up."

"You got most of them out. They'll either work themselves out or dissolve." I stood up.

"And what do we do about Carlos Uribe, you guys? If we can't find the real killer, he's totally sunk." Rachel dropped her head. "I can't get out all the needles. We can't find any evidence. We'll never find the real killer—and all we've got is a criminal record in the making." Rachel looked at me. Exhausted, dirty, hurt, discouraged.

"No, Rae," I said.

"You guys, I found something," said Gina.

"What have you got?" asked Rachel.

"Yes, stellar," said Gina, waving the two pieces of paper that she had been reading. "It's here—you were totally right, Rae. Lorelei is pregnant."

"What?" squealed Rachel.

"Ha-choo."

Gina gave me a look.

"I told you I was allergic. What are you talking about?"

"Test results: Lorelei Miller is pregnant," said Gina, holding up a pink form and a receipt.

"No way, you've got it? We've got it!" I said. A rush of triumph, like standing under a waterfall of confetti.

"Just one thing," said Gina.

"What?" said Rachel.

"We still don't have anything that points directly to the murder," I said.

"Wait, this is evidence of why Merry and Lorelei were fighting," said Rachel.

I winced. An image of Nick and Lorelei and their adorable baby suddenly flashed through my mind. I looked at the form. Lorelei's name, and there it was: this little box that was checked, positive.

"Well, it's evidence she's pregnant," I said.

"We have her diary, and I'm sure that's where she mentions Nick. Plus, the results. That's it!" said Rachel.

"No, now we have enough to confront Nick." I waved the form.

"It is what we needed," said Gina.

"I get Nick alone and tell him to come clean about him being the father of Lorelei's baby," I said.

"We need to make sure you are not completely alone with him," said Gina. "Where are you going to do all this 'tutoring' stuff?"

"I'm thinking the library," I said.

"But he never goes to the library," said Rachel. "You've got to make sure none of the ex-cheers see you and him together, whatsoever!"

"I know," I said. "You guys are going to have to play sentry for me. Dang, we'll need some way for you to give me a warning if anyone, Lorelei or anyone else, comes waltzing into the library."

"We'll think of something," said Rachel. "Meanwhile, what do we do with this?" She untied the drawstring of the sweatshirt that she had carried back from the Millers' house with the ex-cheers' uniforms.

"I don't know," I said. "I mean, she's going to see they're missing."

"The uniforms," said Rachel. "This is gold."

"Totally," I said.

"But how does it point to murder?" asked Gina.

"Because, you guys," said Rachel. She unzipped the sweatshirt, and now you could see the thick yellow-gold band and the black square pleats of the cheerleading skirts. "We find the one outfit that doesn't have the matching skirt."

"But anyone could have choked Merry with a skirt," I said.

"It's a start," said Rachel.

"But it's a good point: why did Lorelei hang on to all these uniforms?" said Gina.

"Because she's guilty," I said. "Remember, Stevens said she gave the bag with the uniforms to Merry and Merry was supposed to give them to Lorelei, like a peace offering."

"Maybe they have something that's incriminating on them," said Rachel. "Why put them where they aren't going to get washed? Plus, they don't belong to her. Is there blood or something?"

"Well, there wasn't any blood, but maybe something else." I tried to think of what was significant about a pile of cheerleading uniforms.

"You guys," said Gina. "I'm just going to say it. We have less than seven hours to get that memory book stuff typed and back to Deerfield. And if we want to get there early to talk to Stevens, we have less time than that."

Rachel pulled out one of the uniform skirts and examined the tag.

"What are you doing?" I asked.

"I thought Val said they sew their names into the uniforms," said Rachel. "This is Jaycee's; no surprise there."

"We already know who they belong to," said Gina.

"Okay," said Rachel, but she pulled out another skirt.

"We've got to get that memory book going," I said.

"We can't type in my room," said Rachel. "We'll wake Jamie up."

"What about down here?" said Gina.

"Yeah," said Rachel. "Let's use the kitchen table."

"What time is your mom coming home?" asked Gina.

"Six thirty," said Rachel.

"Oh, we can get it done way before that." I cracked my knuckles to get ready for the fastest typing job of my life.

CHAPTER 26

"We need to talk to Diaz, asap," said Rachel as we walked to the school from the parking lot near the basketball and tennis courts. The sun seemed brutally bright that morning. Probably due to the lack of sleep. I could still hear the typewriter keys clicking.

"I can't believe we got it done," Gina sighed.

"Yeah, we did it," said Rachel.

"I am getting Nick's confession," I said. "We'll talk to Diaz after that."

We were definitely early. Early enough to park in the student parking lot, early enough that hardly a soul was on campus. The sky was a flame blue. I felt kind of dizzy, and my eyeballs were itchy.

"I want some sleep so, so bad," I said.

"Look, you have got to get Nick to tell you that Lorelei killed Merry and that he will testify to that. Otherwise, Uribe is going to go to prison," said Gina.

"You guys, trust me," I said. "I will bring water back from the desert."

"That is total swami talk, right there," said Gina.

"That's a surprise to you?" said Rachel.

"I can feel us getting closer; we just, you know, hang in there," I said. "Between Stevens and Nick, today, we'll be set. We'll have all the proof Diaz needs."

"And if we don't?" asked Rachel.

"You know, you can stop working on this anytime," I said.

"Oh, what, because you are in charge? Because you are not in charge." Rachel looked at me.

"Hey, mellow out. We have to get that key to Stevens, you guys," said Gina.

My head was throbbing from lack of sleep. I couldn't concentrate on anything because that would require patience, and none of us was able to exercise patience.

"Okay, then, move it or lose it," I said.

"Fine," said Rachel, who marched ahead of me and Gina.

A wooden doorstop kept the girls' locker room door open. The lights were on, and we could hear those sorry first-period freshmen suiting up. We got to the cage. Zamora's and Stevens's desks sat empty. I looked at the large clock on the wall. Seven twenty on the dot. Class started at eight.

"Coach?" Rachel yelled into the cage.

Stevens appeared from behind the equipment shelves in a matching salmon-pink T-shirt, shorts, headband, and cardigan.

"Ladies." Stevens held a pile of folded white towels. She cleared her throat. "Down at the end." She darted her eyes left to the towel drop-bin, away from all the talking and banging locker doors. Once we got down there, Stevens moved the piece of plywood that covered up the opening in the fencing where you could also get equipment, like if you lost a softball or something.

"Here's the key." I fished into my purse and handed it to her. She easily joined it back onto her circular key chain with a major amount of keys and whistles, not to mention a rabbit's foot, and a Minnie Mouse figurine dangling down.

"Look, we need you to tell us or the police what exactly was going on with Merry and Lorelei," said Rachel. "If you don't, we are going to watch an innocent man go to prison or worse!"

Stevens stared back at us and then leaned into the fencing. "I told you everything I know."

Rachel leaned in closer to the coach's face. "We are working with a lawyer on this, so he can just call you as a witness, and you can repeat it all word for word."

"In court," I said.

"In front of the sheriff, and the principal, and the reporters," said Gina.

"And Mr. Uribe's family," said Rachel.

"Okay," Stevens sighed.

Behind us, a large group of girls trooped through to the bathroom to stand outside for roll, so we waited.

"That night," said Stevens, her eyes still bloodshot and puffy like maybe she had been crying.

"Tell us, please," I said, trying not to get impatient.

Stevens licked her lips. "I don't remember it clearly, but it looked like, it looked like the cheerleaders I let go from the squad. They had a hold of Merry. They were calling her names. I wanted to do something."

"It wasn't just Lorelei; was it the others, the other ex-cheerleaders?" I asked.

Stevens nodded.

"What did you say to the cops?" said Gina.

"Nothing." Stevens looked down.

"But she's dead, Coach. Merry's dead," I said.

"You don't think I don't know what I've done?" Stevens grabbed the metal chicken wire between us. Her knuckles turned white. She breathed in and out three times and then swallowed. "I have a class out there right now. There's nothing more I can tell you."

"But—" I said.

"That's all I have, and that cat-thing, so there, do something with that." She stood back.

We nodded.

"Okay, ladies," she barked in usual Stevens fashion. "That's all. You've done your duty for the day." She walked back down to her desk.

We headed from the locker room back out into the stun-gun blast of sun.

"We have to get to Diaz," said Rachel. "Like, yesterday."

"I know," I said. We stopped at my locker so I could unload my book bag. "Huh." I reached for a piece of folded yellow notebook paper. I opened it. The drawing was similar to the ones before. Three stick people were standing on a hill, only they didn't have heads. The hill had little trees, and then I saw three heads with that weird girl hair were rolling down the hill between the trees. Above the picture someone had written, "Lose your head and lose your mind. You choose."

CHAPTER 27

We stood frozen for a second in the breezeway with my locker door open, the school grounds still relatively silent. This was the third one. The third threat.

"The ex-cheers strike again. Too much!" said Gina.

"Their artistic ability hasn't improved," said Rachel, looking at the drawing. "But," she dropped her voice lower, "it's pretty clear they know we are on to them."

"Okay, let's be on the lookout." I folded up the paper.

"We have to tell Diaz, Addie," said Rachel, her arms wrapped around the memory book draft.

"I know. When we see him later today," I said.

"Right now, it's over to Deerfield's," said Gina.

We arrived at Deerfield's studio classroom feeling only slightly groggy. I'd forgotten the room's slanted high ceiling was all windows. One minute we were underground troglodytes in the girls' locker room, and the next minute we were going blind with the sunlight in here. True, in the wintertime this place got a little drafty, and you'd have to get a bucket or two when the window seals leaked. But today, we needed sunglasses.

The students were setting up for work. Rachel knew Deerfield would be at the back of the class, so we made our way to her as chairs skidded and tables got dragged out of the way. Next to a large easel close to the supply cabinet, Deerfield painted away. She wore an old kimono with paint splatter and a bandana scarf to hold back her wild brown curly hair. People said she was weird. She painted abstract work, wore Birkenstocks and no makeup, and we were lucky she thought Rachel was exceptionally talented. Otherwise, we'd never have been able to do this memory-album yearbook insert for Merry Jacobs.

"Ms. Deerfield," said Rachel. "We got the book done!"

We watched the kimono sleeves drop, and her face appeared from behind her canvas. She held a palette knife in one hand, palette in the other, and in her mouth, a large horsehair brush.

"Not enough hands," she said with the brush handle still in her teeth.

"Here." Rachel held the manuscript out to her. We had divided it into three sections: Merry as a student, as an athlete, and as a young leader. That was our genius at three thirty a.m., anyway.

Deerfield put the knife and palette down and took the brush out of her mouth. She wiped her hands down her front and motioned to Rachel to put the stack on the end of the table, next to her easel. "Okay, let's see." She scrutinized the type, wording, and margins. She nodded at Rachel to flip the first page and then another.

"Very promising," she sighed, and rested her hands on her hips with her elbows out, her arms like wings. She nodded for Rachel to continue turning the pages. She looked up at each of us and clicked her tongue.

"We only have a couple of pictures of her," said Rachel.

"Oh, we must have some in stock. Give the yearbook folks something to do." Deerfield had a stripe of white on her face near her ear.

"You can get it in on time?" said Rachel.

"The delivery service comes at two," said Deerfield, nodding. Her brown eyes were glossy. "I still need to make corrections if there are any. Had to make sure you guys got it to me in time. *You,*" Deerfield frowned at Rachel, "still owe me that scholarship application. You can't turn your back on free money."

"I will," Rachel groaned. "I'll get it in. We just had to get this finished first."

"Rachel, this memory book was inspired. Very thoughtful. Very sophisticated. Nicely done, people." She thrust her arms out and gave us two thumbs up.

"Thanks," said Rachel. "So, this will get passed out at graduation?"

"Oh, yeah," said Deerfield. "And I don't mind saying, much better than that cheer-thing at the memorial. Okay, I have a class to teach. 'Bye."

"Man, I am so relieved," I said as we headed down the breezeway.

"We did it!" Rachel jumped up and down.

"I can't believe you have that kind of energy," I said with a yawn.

"It's victory coursing through my veins, man," said Rachel. "Except for the head rush."

We dragged ourselves into pre-first-period student traffic.

"We don't have all day to get to class," said Gina, looking at her watch.

"Wait," said Rachel. "I need to check something."

She slipped into the bathroom, and Gina and I followed. Rachel put her book bag down and stood leaning over the sink closest to the door, studying her forehead in the mirror.

Gina flung her head back. "Make it fast."

"You don't have to watch me," said Rachel.

"Oh, no way, José," I said. "You cannot start this week's zit harvest."

"Puke city! You guys! Man, we can't fool around," said Gina.

"Rae, you're not thinking clearly. You're going to wait and do this at home. We have to make it through class. I have to get that confession from Nick."

Rachel moved herself closer to the mirror, her arms resting on the shelf. Her fingers went in for triage right between her eyebrows.

"You just get him there," she said, squeezing. "Of course, he's totally not the person of interest anymore," then she pinched her zit. Something landed on the mirror.

"Gross me out," said Gina. "You are so immature." She ran to the nearest stall and grabbed some toilet paper.

"Cu-uh-glccchhh!"

The sound came from behind the one stall that had the door closed, four down from where we stood. We all looked at each other.

"Who is that?" Gina whispered.

I went down and knocked on the door. "Are you okay?"

"Ach-cuh." Pause. The vomit plopped in the toilet bowl.

"That doesn't sound okay." Rachel stood behind me with a tuft of tissue stuck between her eyes.

"So much better." I looked at Rachel.

"Should we call the nurse?" Gina asked through the door.

"Nuh-uh. Go away," the voice managed to answer.

"We just don't want you to die in there," I said.

Then, *whoosh!* The toilet flushed. We waited. Still nobody. The door stayed closed. Gina shrugged her shoulders. The bell rang. I wondered who was sick as a dog in that stall.

"Let's blow this taco stand," said Rachel, picking up her books.

Just as we opened the bathroom door to go, we heard movement down at the end. I craned my neck around to see. A girl stepped out.

"It's Lorelei," I whispered.

The sounds of the passing students seeped past us as Gina held the door ajar.

"Who is it?" Gina asked, tightening her grip on her purse straps.

"Lorelei. I'm going to see if she's okay," I said.

"Be careful." Rachel looked at me and waved the flat of her hand under her chin to remind me of the drawing from the ex-cheers with those rolling heads.

"She's upchucking a storm—" I started.

"She's—you know." Gina rubbed her stomach.

"Oh. Right." I nodded.

But I couldn't stop myself from turning around, and then I saw Lorelei cupping water at the sink, her face a kind of yellow-green, her hair almost greasy and sticking to her face. She looked up to see me.

"Go away, creep. Leave me alone," she said, and then she cupped more water and tried to throw it at me.

"Addie," I heard Gina calling me.

That was all it took. I booked it past Gina and Rachel outside. The three of us hurried back toward the grassy quad to make it to class.

"She's coughing up her guts all right," I said.

"So majorly gross," said Rachel.

"Just so you know, you still have toilet paper on your 'operation,'" I said.

"Oh, no." Rachel felt her forehead and pulled the tuft off.

When I turned to look forward again, two guys crossed us at a diagonal. I couldn't believe my luck. Nick was one of them.

"Hey, Nick." I reached my hand up high to get his attention, but the weight of my book bag kind of threw me forward, and I grazed his armpit with my chin. My adrenaline was so high it didn't matter.

"The hell—?" Nick moved away from me.

"Tutoring for the exam? Calculus? Remember, I sit right in front of you?" I was breathing way too fast, starting to feel light-headed. I saw Gina and Rachel ready to grab me.

"Yeah, so?" He studied me up and down.

"It's me, Chuck, you know, 'not a chick'?" I had no shame.

"Oh-ho, now I got you," he started, nodding his head up and down. Yes, recognition. "What do you want, again?"

"Passing the exam, but you have to score—"

"Look, not right now, Chuck. I got class."

"I know *that*." I tightened my grip on my book bag.

"Easy, okay?" He was being a dick.

Rachel looked like she was holding her breath. I tried to walk around Nick. Rachel and Gina were right there. What if he didn't meet me? Then I felt his hand on my shoulder.

"Chuck, hey, don't go sucking your thumb like a baby on me, now."

"I'm not," I whined.

"Come on." He smiled. "Where're we meeting?"

Majorly rad. Don't lose it. "Library," I swallowed. "Today, sixth period. Meet me there."

"Nah," he said. "No can do today. Tomorrow, maybe?"

"Um, sure, of course, okay." My mouth was so dry, I was afraid dust was coming out of it.

CHAPTER 28

After the long day at school, we staggered up the stairs to Diaz's office. I wasn't sure how we were going to break it to him that we didn't have Nick's confession about Lorelei being guilty of murder yet, but we figured we would totally majorly impress him with the haul from Lorelei's room. We opened Diaz's screen door into a wash of paper: fanned out on the floor, in piles on his desk, and then a series taped all along the back wall above the worn couch.

A thick black time-line ran through the middle of the sheets taped to the wall with times and days and pictures and pieces of paper. On Friday, the day of the murder, there were notes for the ten a.m. ASB meeting that was cancelled; noon lunch period, where Gina saw Lorelei and Merry fighting; and four p.m., when Nick lied about the ASB meeting and seeing Uribe talking to Merry. There was a blank between four and eight p.m., when Joey's party started and where we saw the ex-cheers and Nick; and nine p.m. was highlighted in bold. The autopsy had concluded Merry was killed sometime between four and nine p.m. Saturday and Sunday were marked-out black squares. The next entry was eight a.m. Monday, when Rachel, Gina, and I had found Merry. Diaz kneeled on the couch tapping his finger on the blank spot between four and eight p.m. His hair was smashed here, sticking out there.

"You have no idea what we've got for you," I said, holding Lorelei's diary tight in my hand so I didn't lose the pink form with test results from the clinic that validated her pregnancy.

Rachel set her sweatshirt still stuffed with ex-cheer uniforms on the unsteady coffee table. I hadn't noticed Diaz filling up his office with furniture, but I thought it might be a good sign. That, or he really was living here permanently.

Diaz backed up from the couch, staring intently at his taped sheets of paper, and scratched his head with the hand that held a felt marker.

"Hey, watch that thing," said Gina. "You don't have the top on—you'll write all over yourself." She held the cat in the jar.

"Okay, where's that confession about the murder, you guys?" Diaz turned around. "My timeline," he beamed. I had never seen him look so positive. He was almost smiling.

"Oh, I get it," I said.

"If we just go over what this Nick says and fill in this gap here . . ." He turned to face the wall again.

"Um," said Rachel, "we don't have the confession yet."

"What does that mean?" said Diaz, spinning back around.

"We have all this!" said Gina.

"We're getting the confession *tomorrow*," I said.

"You guys, you can't—I need to prep the guy to take the stand. This is the real thing—court, jury, judge, no joking around." He grabbed at his tie and pulled at the loosened knot, which loosened more.

"Tomorrow," I said. "I promise."

"Meanwhile," said Rachel as she unpacked the treasure trove, pulling out the uniforms, skirts, and sweaters, black and gold. They smelled a little. "Check it out: more reasonable doubt than you can count on your fingers and toes."

"Why do I need that?" Diaz asked.

"Why?" I said. "Because it's everything."

Diaz pointed to the cat in the jar. "What am I supposed to do with this?"

"Remember the label that was torn?" I said. "It came from this jar."

"I don't understand," said Diaz.

"Stevens found it outside the locker room," I said.

"Remember, we found the other half of the label where Merry's body was?" said Rachel.

"Merry must have torn the label, at some point," said Gina.

"Stevens told us today that on Friday night, when she left the locker room, she saw the ex-cheers holding Merry down," I said. "They were shoving that pickled cat in her face."

Diaz took a breath, clasping his hands behind his head. "When was that?"

"The night of the murder," said Rachel. She pointed to a section in the timeline between when Merry was supposed to meet Lorelei and when her body was found.

"Merry was supposed to give Lorelei the uniforms that the coach had kept in her office at the gym," I said.

"They must have killed her there," said Gina. "Then dragged her body up near those buildings."

"And tried to bury Merry under all those leaves," said Rachel.

"Oh," I said. "We found this, too." I took the pink test form out of Lorelei's diary.

"What in the name of—" Diaz stared at the cat in the jar of formaldehyde.

"We got it, and we're still getting the confession; it's just one day off. Even without it, all of this is solid."

"Wait a second." Diaz gave us a look. "Where did you get your hands on this girl's diary?"

"Found it," I said.

"Where?" said Diaz.

"Well . . ." Rachel looked up. Sweat formed just above the zit we'd watched her pop this morning.

"On second thought . . ." Diaz shook his head. He covered his eyes with the heels of this hands. "If you guys stole any of this—"

"Who says its stolen?" I said.

"This cat belongs to the school. We're just, eventually, getting it back to the rightful owner," said Gina.

Diaz took his hands off his eyes. "How does that help us?" He stared at the animal again.

Gina pointed to the timeline. "There are four hours between when those ex-cheers got Merry on the ground and shoved this thing in her face, and when they were at the party, right?"

"Okay." Diaz melted into the couch.

"They took their prank too far, but then they didn't say anything," I said.

"The diary?" said Gina. "The diary is the whole thing. It proves Lorelei is pregnant."

"Yeah, I have this now. Her test. She's pregnant. Nick's going to cough up every crumb in his gut," I said.

"Lorelei's been hanging onto these uniforms because she couldn't give them back to Merry and she couldn't give them to the police," said Rachel.

"Why didn't she try to get rid of them?" said Diaz.

"She did. They were under her bed, and we had to really dig under there—" Rachel stopped and cupped her mouth to keep anything else from coming out.

"Don't—" Diaz put his hands on his ears. "I did not hear that last part."

"But you need all of this, we need all of this—we had to go the extra mile. And we—" I protested.

"You are going to take it back," said Diaz.

"Wait," said Rachel. "The police have arrested the wrong man, with no evidence, a bold-faced lie, oh, and, meanwhile, they lost the evidence and—"

"And they still won't go public with the details of the murder—does that sound like *they* are following the letter of the law at all?" asked Gina.

"Yes, you're right. They're not—but if we play it their way, we're sure to lose. I'll be disbarred. Is that how you want it to go down?"

"Man, virtue is a such a bummer," said Rachel.

"I didn't say *when* you had to take this back to—wherever you found it," said Diaz.

"The cat is ours," said Gina, putting it in Diaz's hands.

"And we got another one of these." I took out the note from the ex-cheers.

"Third one," said Rachel.

Diaz looked at the note. "These are *girls* doing this?" Diaz turned the jar in his hands and watched the cat slowly swirl. "*This* is part of their game these days? What is the world coming to?"

"Don't lose that guy," said Gina.

"You, Crusaders, have to lay low." Diaz got up, put the jar on his desk, and looked out the open French doors warped with age. He hung his head and took a deep breath. I'd never heard him sound like that, like my mom does when she burns dinner, and we don't have anything else, and she makes me run over to the neighbors next door and ask for two slices of bread, and then wait and run to the other neighbors down the street for two eggs. It's the worst sound. Oh, man. Maybe we'd really crossed the line. What if he didn't want us working for him anymore?

"So, you're not mad. We're still working on this?" I said.

"See," said Rachel, "if we hadn't got this, there'd still be that gap between four and eight, and now you have something to fill the gap."

He turned around. "I do not want to argue with you."

"So, we did good?" I asked.

"Legally?" He shook his head.

"Look, we just made a bit of a detour," said Rachel. "We'll put the diary back, for real, totally."

"I didn't tell you to ransack the Miller house, did I?"

"We didn't 'ransack,'" I said. "That's so not accurate."

"*Steal*, I think, is the word," said Diaz.

"These are just visual aids," said Gina.

Diaz held his chin on his fist, but then I could see the tiniest smile. He stopped smiling and crossed his arms. "Very funny."

"See, this helps, doesn't it?" said Rachel.

"I'm counting to three." Diaz looked into the coffee cup on his desk, picked it up, walked over to the trash can behind his desk, and turned the cup upside down. The dregs dripped from the cup. "Okay . . . one."

"We're going," I said. I grabbed a bunch of the uniforms and helped Rachel stuff them back into the sweatshirt. Gina pushed the diary in too.

"We go to court in four days." He looked at us, then turned on the hot plate to boil the leftover water that was in the little dented pot.

"We?" asked Rachel.

"I go to court with my client, who I am defending," said Diaz.

"But you need us there," I said.

"Yeah," he said. "But what I really need is that young man's confession. The lie about the ASB meeting, the murder, the history of his two girlfriends, everything. By tomorrow. And bring me Coach Stevens, too."

"There is this thing about Stevens," I said.

"What's that?" he asked.

"She might be a little—inebriated," said Gina.

"You figure that out," said Diaz. "She's *your* job."

"Okay, we'll get her," said Gina.

We stumbled down the stairs to the car.

"I am beat," said Rachel.

"You guys, we have to go over the plan for meeting with Nick, sorry to say."

"No, I get it," said Gina. "If we don't win this case—"

"You cannot *even* say that," I said.

"If we don't," Rachel sighed, "those ex-cheers will make our lives misery city."

CHAPTER 29

The library was definitely not in Nick's orbit. Not exactly the place to hold court, entertain the minions, that sort of thing. But the library's soft darkness seemed romantic to me. The air totally still, maybe because it was air from 1921 when they built this part of the school. I kind of loved it: the shadowy recesses with built-in shelves and ragged old volumes, the yellowing pages with old handwriting from previous owners.

The small lounge windows at the front offered the only sunlight. In the rest of the library, you were, like, Jonah in the whale. With the energy crisis, they'd stopped using a third of the overhead lighting, and you could get lost due to the deep-sea visibility. For me, the library was the safest place ever. I could come in here when things were seriously tanking. I could be insulated by all the words and stories and the old maps that depicted the state of California as an island. Now, all I had to do was not screw up this meeting with Nick.

Gina, Rachel, and I left fifth period early, and I sat at one of the big oak tables in the back, prepared with scratch paper, the textbook, and exam review sheets from previous tests of yore. I wasn't sure what I was going to do, how I was going to start. Then I heard him walk in, and the murmurs of other students, mostly girls, rippled all the way back to me through the library's mine shaft. I had to get from integrations to murder like *that*, but a smooth *that*. I didn't have time to think beyond that because now he stood this close to my table.

"Hey." Nick towered above me, his keys skidding on the table, one of twelve in rows spanning like ribs. He'd managed to turn his book into a short rolled-up carpet. I guess it made carrying in his back pocket easier.

"Great," I said. I wanted to say more, but I was trying to think ahead.

"This place is like a morgue," he said full-voiced. Some heads behind us popped up.

"We should be a little bit quieter," I whispered.

"Oh, you bet," he whispered loudly, saluted, then dropped in the chair opposite me.

I glanced at the reference section near the checkout desk, where Rachel had stationed herself, and then at Gina in the lounge, flipping through a magazine. I really didn't think we'd see the ex-cheers, but just in case, we had our lines of defense ready.

"So, Chuck, *can* I get up to an A on this thing?" asked Nick. He wore a Hang Ten shirt, striped and faded. He tugged at the stretched collar. I didn't quite know how to switch the focus to Merry's murder, but we needed a whole lot in exchange for his math grade.

"Well," I said, going for pleasant *and* breathy, "what gives you the *most* trouble?"

He leaned forward in his chair, eyed me for what seemed like a full minute, then he gave a hollow laugh, more of a cough. "Oh, man, Chuck," he said, and he dropped his head.

"Nick, I have to tell you . . ." I could still only see the salt-watered brown curls of his hair.

"Look, okay. If you don't think I can make any kind of progress—I guess, I guess I knew it was too much to expect—"

"Nick! Man, listen to me!"

His mouth opened.

"I'm not talking about math, okay? I'm talking about your future, your life!"

"Hey, Chuck—"

"Don't be a dick. I'm talking about you and Lorelei and Merry's murder. You're—you're like a total prime suspect."

"Mellow out, I did not—she was *my* girlfriend."

"Uh, yeah, 'was' is the operative word."

"What the hell is this? Who are you with? Listen, I went along with the—No." He shook his head, pushed his chair back, and stood up.

"Wait!"

"What?"

I looked at him, trying to say something, scraping at the gray matter for, like, one lousy syllable, but it wasn't coming.

He turned his back to me.

"I'm *trying* to help you."

His shoulders tensed, but he didn't turn around.

"I—I don't think *you* killed her."

It took a while to break through his dense ego casing of lead.

He swooped around and leaned on the table, his hands in fists. "So help me," he said, his voice low and tense, "if you say one more word about me killing anyone, I *will* hurt you." His lower jaw pushed out. I saw the look. The look I'd seen when he wanted to convince us that Carlos Uribe was the obvious murderer.

"Nick, I'm on your side. I want to help you. Why do you think I asked to help you?"

He exhaled a breath that had been buried alive.

"Just sit down, hear me out," I said.

This time he slumped into the chair, hunched, his eyes darting. My tutoring props seemed ridiculous; I plowed a space of bare table between us.

"My friends." I nodded toward Rachel and Gina. Nick glanced over his shoulder in their direction. "We know David Diaz, Carlos Uribe's defense attorney, and it's pretty clear that someone in that group of ex-cheerleaders murdered Merry. Was it Lorelei?"

He held up his middle finger to me.

"Come on, Nick. What do you know?" I realized how loud and whiney my voice sounded.

"I already told you what I saw." Nick's voice had a bit of a rasp now.

"That is a lie, and you know it. You weren't even there Friday afternoon."

"Look, I don't know why you're harshing on me."

"It just doesn't look good, because what you said didn't really happen."

"Who the hell are you, man?" When his mouth opened, I could see a string of spit, then watched it fall and pool.

"Nick?" Okay, now I felt bad.

"You." It was the quietest thing, word, sentiment, as thin as a moth wing.

"Nick, come on. I'm asking why you'd tell such a big, humongous lie."

He laid his head on the desk. "Man, I'm in so deep now."

"Please, you're not that deep into anything."

He looked up at me, and now I saw his eyes like wells, his lower lids puffy, totally exhausted.

"I'm sorry." Sad to the max, he was going to make me cry. "Anyway," I swallowed it down, "you *can* get yourself out of this. You tell the truth, and you have nothing to worry about."

"No way, Chuck. Not even. Not humanly possible."

"Why?"

"Lorelei's dad is—he says jump, and I—I go into the stratosphere."

"What are you saying?"

"Man, what do you think? Think I walk around pulling stuff on innocent people? Like, that's how I get off!" His voice rose and pushed the dust motes up like a volcano propels lava.

"Nick," I whispered. "Mellow out."

"Mellow out?" His voice fell into a whisper and he shook his head.

"Okay, if you don't get off on lying about people, Carlos Uribe, for one, why in the hell don't you just go tell the police—"

"Who do you think made me lie in the first place!?"

"They made you lie? So, like, what? I thought you said Lorelei's dad—"

He pulled his sleeve up to his eyes and snorted some mucus. I could feel my stomach simmering. He looked up into the arc of the ceiling, then at me, but not really at me, at whatever was in front of him. Whatever was doing this to him. He cleared his throat.

"So, here's the story." He snorted again, folded himself over the desk, and held his arms in a kind of circle where some big action was going to take place. "I got to school on Monday, you know, when they found her, Merry." He swallowed, looked away to halt whatever cry was trying to come out; we both waited for it to ebb, then he came back to the story. "And I'm on my way back to the parking lot after they dismiss everyone, you know, no school because of this 'emergency,' and I don't even know why, right? I hear people talking, but I can't believe—anyway, I'm going out," he planted an index finger on the table, "and I see right in front of me, it's Griffin, you know, the sheriff." He planted his other index finger ahead of the one already planted.

"The sheriff told you—"

"Can I tell my freaking story, Chuck?"

"Sorry," I said.

"Anyway, I'm, like, what is this? I take a step back. So, you know, I'm not going anywhere. Griffin says there's something *he* wants me to take a look at." He stops, shuts his eyes for a second. "And it's *her*."

"No way, Nick, why? I mean, how do you go from there to Uribe being the murderer?"

"That was *his* line, about the connection. He told me he thought it was Uribe, then he suggested maybe I saw Uribe acting weird, to help him, help Griffin, since there was this other stuff. I mean, it didn't even look like her anymore when I saw her. I let her down, and that's freaking awful."

"Nick."

"Except if you want me to tell on myself, I'm screwed. Griffin was right there, so—and you have no idea what else is going on." He sighed and let his head rest on the chair back.

"Nick, Diaz can help you if you testify on Uribe's behalf in court—Griffin can't get away with this."

"You are totally naïve, Chuck. This thing—I took money from him, like everyone else, and the police." He picked up a stray rubber band and began stretching it.

"Who? Who did you take money from?"

"Ron, Lorelei's dad, when he called me into his office. I mean, I sat there like a turd, and he's telling me, you know, I knocked up his little girl, so I'm part of the family, and things are going to change, and this is how it's going to be. He gives out these white envelopes. With money. Now, I get one. I mean, at first, I thought, this is nuts. I didn't even get to talk to Lorelei. She just blurted it out, like, she's pregnant, and then she walks off. Like, tag, you're it. Next thing I know, I'm sitting in Ron's office getting the lecture. I take the money and a job in his business or be accused of rape and locked away."

"You took money?"

"It's to—I don't know, that's all the guy does. We were in his city council office where he runs his campaign. I'm in this thing deep, Chuck. After that Monday when the police showed me Merry's body? That wasn't all. Later, I get picked up by Griffin and driven over to the city council office. I hear them, Ron and Griffin, talking about if it wasn't for Lorelei there wouldn't be such a mess. Then they walk in and tell me to be really clear about Uribe being the murderer, right? Because the prosecution is just a little unsure since I was Merry's boyfriend, and they tell me it would be a real shame if I get pegged for the murder. So, if I don't want to play ball all the way with them, I get to change places with Uribe." His voice faded.

"Could Lorelei have killed Merry?"

"No—I mean, I don't know. I just know my future is, like, gone." He shot the rubber band behind me.

I heard it hit something.

"Look, I don't move unless he tells me—I shouldn't even be here, much less trying to get some help on Calc. I better go."

"No, you can't, don't. I told you, you can get out of this thing. What are you doing after this?"

"This? What do you think? Show up for my job at Ron's office for whatever the hell he needs."

"We're due at Diaz's as soon as we leave here. I want you to come."

"Forget it, Chuck."

"Look, do you want to say good-bye to your future or do you want a chance to salvage something worth living for? You showed up here.

Your life's over, but you follow some dweeb to the library, a place you'd never be caught dead in? You want to be Ron Miller's lifelong ass-licker?"

"*You*, Chuck? You're offering me what?"

"You said you let Merry down. Well, now you have a chance to make it up to her. Better late than never, right?"

He covered his eyes with his palm, the muscles in his arm flexing.

Then it just flowed out of my mouth: "What would Merry want you to do?" I asked him, my voice finally calm and measured.

He slowly peeled his hand away from his face. "Yeah, okay." He nodded.

"You will so not regret this," I said, trying not to hyperventilate.

"I hope so." He slapped both hands on the tabletop. Then he looked at me. "*You* want to breathe into a paper bag or something?"

"No, no, I'm fine." I could feel my face turn a blazing maraschino red. "Just follow me, follow us. We're in the lot—are you in the lot?" I swept up the papers and books into my book bag.

"Yeah, Chuck, I'm in the lot." He readjusted the book-bag strap that fell off my shoulder.

"Then just follow us. Diaz's office is on Camino Raymunda, third floor above the old candy store."

So, now, everything was upside down. The sheriff and Ron Miller? And Lorelei? Really? What was the story? If Nick just made it to Diaz's — the bell rang announcing the end of the day. We still had to navigate to the parking lot. I tugged at Rachel's arm and she grabbed Gina on the way out of the library. I glanced over my shoulder to see Nick still bathed in shadow as he kept pace behind us.

CHAPTER 30

The three of us fell in step on our way to the parking lot.

"What did he say?" Gina asked me.

I looked behind us. Nick was talking to Keith Slater at the second-to-last pillar. Was he playing it cool now, or was he going to go back to Ron and screw us over into three stages of reincarnation?

"I couldn't get him to name anyone, *yet*, as the murderer." I looked back again. I didn't want to lose Nick. *Please, he can't be shining me.*

"Say what?" said Gina.

"But, he said Ron Miller and Griffin told him to make that stuff up about Uribe," I said.

"Burn, man," said Rachel.

"Play it cool, you guys. He's following us to Diaz's."

"Oh, I knew he was lying. But now, what, the whole town is in on it?" said Gina.

We joined the crowd streaming toward the exit gates; groups of kids trooped through the basketball courts. I turned to check on Nick's progress behind us. I stopped because I couldn't tell where he was, and then we saw her.

"No way, José." Rachel looked at me.

Lorelei had cleaned herself up a little since her morning sickness scene in the bathroom. She trailed behind Myla, with Jaycee and Lisa on either side. Still stunning. Her hair floated on the breeze behind her, whether it was a little greasy or not. She wore mirrored sunglasses with white frames and carried a straw bag, so cool, like a beach bag, which said, "I have better things to do than school." In her other hand she carried a paper folder and one textbook, down low at her hip, you know, like you'd carry a surfboard. Then she disappeared into a vortex of teenagers climbing into adjoining cars, laughing while flip-flops got thrown in the air. Upper eshers could do that, throw people's shoes, and it was rad. We all watched Lorelei, a shooting star.

"See that?" I shook my head.

"See it? More like, breathe it," said Gina.

I saw Nick's face finally about three people deep away from us, still talking to Keith.

"That chick is living on totally borrowed time, but how does she get to look like that?" said Rachel.

"Because," I said, "she thinks she's getting away with it."

"Just wait," said Gina.

"We bring Nick in to testify," I said, "we blow the trial and this town wide open."

"Maybe there won't even be a trial, right?" Rachel held up her hand for a high-five.

"Oh, no. I can't believe this," Gina said in a raised voice as we stopped at my car.

My Pinto was now a huge Etch A Sketch mess. "Neutered girls." "Come and eat me." "Do the world a favor and kill yourself." And that was just on *this* side of the car. As we walked around it, we saw strange drawings—cartoons, I think—trying to depict girl genitals, but they looked more like third-grade rainbows. Then there were three girls' faces with *x*'s over their eyes, a picture of a cat, and some writing that had tried to be insulting but had been smudged out. At this angle, the red lipstick—at least I hoped it was lipstick—on the blue paint gave the car a kind of paisley design.

A short shriek of brakes and skidding tires made us all turn around. It was Jaycee driving the yellow Karmann Ghia, top down, with

Lorelei in the passenger seat, and Lisa and Myla squeezed into the shelf behind them.

"Great paint job, guys," said Jaycee, grinning. Lorelei turned to face us with her mirrored glasses. She looked like a bug.

"What are you guys doing? It's a great day. Get to the beach! Like, get a tan." Lorelei pretended to be demanding.

"Maybe you should get your car washed first," suggested Myla.

"No, keep it," said Jaycee. "You want everyone to know the truth, right?"

"Are you kidding? I love it," I said. "I certainly don't want to ruin this."

"Artwork," said Rachel. "It's very, uh, representational."

"Yeah, representational of lug-heads," said Gina.

"You must be deaf!" Jaycee yelled.

"Not unless it's important, but maybe if you could speak up!" Rachel yelled back. I was impressed.

I opened the car door and swung my bag and purse inside, while Rachel and Gina followed my lead.

I watched the Karmann Ghia come closer and closer to where Gina stood with the passenger door of the Pinto open.

They really wanted us to fight? Like, physically. Were they really, like, really like that? Hair pullers, scratchers, biters? Practiced in the arts of drawing and quartering a cat and spreading it across the hood of someone's blue Pinto? Well, whatever their problem was, I didn't want to have to tell Diaz about why the four of *them* landed in intensive care.

"*This* is the supreme creep," said Lorelei, kneeling on the seat so she could look at me. "Look, you little full-of-it creep show, your friends, here? They bug me."

Jaycee gunned the engine. I looked around at the half-amused kids in groups dispersed to the far corners of the parking lot. I didn't see Nick.

"Well, you know," I said yelling above the noise, "too bad for you! Your friends bug me even more!"

Jaycee took her foot off the gas.

"See, the trouble with bottom-feeders like these," said Myla to Lorelei, "is that they don't understand plain English."

"They are total, supreme grody-ness, and they don't even know it," said Jaycee.

"What did we tell you, huh?" asked Myla. "We said to stay away from her and—"

"Hey, you're the ones that can't get enough of us. You did it Saturday; here you are again," I said.

"Burn it, man, let's get out of here." Lorelei looked straight ahead, the back of the school reflecting in her sunglass lenses.

"I'm so bummed out," said Gina with false sadness.

"You're so full of it," said Jaycee.

"So are you," said Rachel.

"Be careful," said Myla, her incisors visible for just a second.

I think we were in a stare-down. The three of us. The four of them. Locked in mortal retinal combat.

"Jayce." Lorelei sounded like she might be getting another dose of nausea.

"You are walking puke!" Jaycee snarled at us, her car door coming this close. And then in slow motion I heard the scraping-scratching, the metal grating, and then a *shnee-ipe* sound.

"Oh, no," said Rachel. "Addie, they just thrashed your car."

"Oh, you *do* want to fight," I said.

"Like it would even be a fight," said Myla.

"You are going down," said Gina.

"No, you are." Myla flipped us the bird.

Gina opened her passenger door to get out.

The Karmann Ghia took off. Lisa leaned over the back. *She* hadn't said a word. Was she totally comatose?

Clumps of people who had been looking in our direction went back to clumping.

"Hey, Chuck." Nick appeared out of thin air. "*That* is wicked." He pointed at my car.

We had to get going, but I couldn't seem to move. All I could do was watch Nick inspect my car, crouching down at the back, I guess, to read the timeless inscriptions. I had the steering wheel in a death grip.

Gina stood with the passenger door open, drumming her fingers on the roof of the car and looking down at the scratch.

"That scratch, that's what your friends just did," said Gina.

"That's not a scratch, that's a dent," said Nick. "Ouch."

"I'm getting it fixed," I said really fast. "We're due at Diaz's like yesterday."

"Right," he said. "I'm over there." He looked in the direction of the red Mach 1 parked in front of two other cars, then looked back at me and smiled.

"So, you know where we're going?" Gina seated herself and slammed the door as Nick walked away.

"Oh, yeah." He cocked his head over his shoulder. "I got the lowdown."

"Addie, come on," sighed Rachel.

"I sure hope Prince Charming isn't setting us up," said Gina to no one.

We sped in Nick's direction. I was still trying not to shake too much, and while I aimed for a quick hop to stop beside his driver's side, it was a bit more bucking bronco. He wore mirrored sunglasses like Lorelei's, so all I could really see was me and Gina and Rachel in miniature.

"So, follow us," I said.

"Yeah," he gave us a thumbs-up and put his car in gear. "Hey, Chuck?"

I leaned too far forward taking him in, and my elbow hit the horn.

"Really?" said Gina.

"Ladies first," said Nick above the sound of his booming engine and my spastic exhaust. Then he raised his hand at us and turned his palm up.

"Really?" said Gina. "Really?"

"You don't have to like him," I said. We drove out of the parking lot with plenty of students finger-pointing, howling, and yelling in our wake.

"Addie, we're supposed to lay low," said Rachel.

The radio played "Hotel California." The light changed to red, and we slowed down next to a school bus waiting to make the left turn at the light.

"Lesbos! Lesbos!" a crew of boys who probably couldn't tell the difference between pus and sperm shouted out the windows before I could make the right.

"Well, this is fun." Gina threw her head back while her right arm rode the air drafts out the window.

"Those ex-cheers must have seen you, Addie, talking to Nick," said Rachel.

"They weren't anywhere near the library," said Gina.

"Maybe they had a spy," said Rachel.

"Rae, they can't really do anything," I said. The Pinto picked up speed as we rounded the bend and stopped at the next light. A suit-and-tied gentleman on the sidewalk to our right tried to read the car.

"Need a translation?" Gina called out to him, and he quickly lowered his head.

"But Addie, what if Lorelei is—what if she knows we know about *her*?" said Rachel.

"What can she know, Rae?" I revved the gas while we idled. I looked into the side-view mirror and saw Nick's car two cars behind us. I grabbed the steering wheel with all my might. The light changed, and my arms pulsed with adrenaline.

"Come on, Lorelei!" I shouted through the windshield. "You just try and choke me with a cheerleader skirt. I will so be ready." I floored the Pinto into flying mode with Gina and Rachel screeching like blasting after-burners.

CHAPTER 31

I pulled a quick U-turn, and we parked my girl-graffitied car at street level right below Diaz's office. I didn't care who saw my car at this point. Half the school already had an eyeful, and if people found it entertaining, well, that might be the highlight of their year. They might even learn something.

"Addie," Rachel protested. "This thing will draw a serious crowd."

People slowed down to looky-loo.

"Rae." I set the brake and opened my door. "Face it. We can't let those ex-cheers bully us. Or anyone else."

"It's offensive," said Rachel.

"So is murder," said Gina.

Someone honked. Cars crawled down our side of the street even though the light was green. Yeah, I loved my town. Don't get disturbed or distracted over a murdered teenager or a trial set to convict an innocent man or a corrupt police department, but, by all means, make sure you get your fill of X-rated teenage graffiti angst.

"I thought Nick was following us to Diaz's?" Rachel demanded as we got out of the car.

"He will," I said.

"He'd better," said Gina.

We raced up the building's rickety stairs.

We paused on the second-floor landing to look for Nick. Nothing. Okay, so maybe he wouldn't show up after all. That would really torch us with Diaz.

"Nick lied before," Gina sighed.

"There's a reason for that," I said. "You'll see the whole thing."

Inside Diaz's office the air was thick and hot like my mom's macaroni casserole, even with the French doors opened all the way. Diaz was talking on the phone, his back to us, as we crossed over the snake of phone cord. Max Walker sat in one of the chairs near Diaz's desk, inspecting the cat in the jar. When he saw us come in, he smiled. His white linen suit looked like it had more wrinkles than fabric.

"Good to see you, Crusaders," he said, his voice low. "Interesting specimen." He nodded at the cat.

The Iron Age fan hurdy-gurdied back and forth on high. Empty donut boxes towered on Diaz's desk. A package of white T-shirts sat on top of the file cabinet. More piles of paper were stacked near the couch. The timeline on the wall above the couch was starting to peel off in places where the tape wasn't sticking anymore. Diaz turned, saw us, and waved his hand.

Gina looked at me with concern. "You're sure Nick knows to come *here*?"

I took a deep breath.

"Crusaders." Diaz nodded after hanging up the phone.

"Nick's on his way," said Rachel.

"He's right behind us," I said.

"*Who* are you talking about?" Max raised his furry brows.

"Lorelei's boyfriend," said Gina, dropping to the couch, where she realized that most of her body was trapped because the cushion was more like a sling. "Before that he was Merry's boyfriend."

"Got it," said Max.

"His testimony can raise doubts about Uribe," said Diaz.

"And he's indicated that the Miller girl is involved as well?" asked Max.

"He's way involved with helping the police and Ron Miller cover up for Lorelei," I said.

"He said that?" said Diaz.

"That and more," I said. "Wait until he tells you the whole story."

"How does this fit in?" Max held up the cat in the jar.

"Stevens gave it to us," said Rachel. "She found it. Outside the girls' locker room."

"After she witnessed the ex-cheers pretty much torturing Merry Jacobs," said Gina.

"Lorelei must have murdered Merry then," I said. "It fits into the timeline between when Stevens saw the ex-cheers with Merry and when everyone but Merry showed up at Joey Ballard's party on Friday night."

"That has to add up to reasonable doubt," said Diaz. "Plus, testimony from this boyfriend, Nick, will describe to the jury the inner workings of this romantic triangle."

"It's way more than that. Nick's being blackmailed—" I said, but I couldn't finish.

The screen door screeched open with a violent rush. It was Nick. "Chuck?" His deep voice sounded so weird. His chest rose and fell, so I guess he'd covered the stairs at a run, but why? Was he running from the ex-cheers?

"Hey, I thought we lost you," I answered. Phew, total relief. I didn't want to doubt him, but I had been nervous. Finally, Nick was in Diaz's constellation. I'll skip the part about the glow around his body. That was just plain daylight.

"Come in." Diaz stood behind his desk and looked up and down at Nick and offered to shake Nick's hand.

Nick took a few steps and introduced himself but then retreated to stand with his back pressing on the screen door.

Rachel grabbed my arm and sucked in her breath.

Why wasn't he coming inside Diaz's office to join us?

"We're going over what you just told me." I looked back at him. "At the library."

Nick shrugged, still standing in the doorway.

"You said the sheriff asked you to lie, to frame Carlos Uribe," I said.

"That is extremely important information," said Diaz. "When was this? We need all the details." Diaz took up a yellow notepad and flipped some pages over as he leaned on the front of his desk, almost knocking off the cat jar.

"And the whole thing about the money? Nick?" I looked at him and then at Diaz, who nodded and kept writing.

"David, this is an incredible turn of events," said Max.

"Money?" Gina shook her head.

"He—I swear to God, I just wanted to talk to Lorelei, just talk about her and me—" Nick tapped the door jamb.

"You *would* take money." Gina turned her head to stop looking at him.

"Wait, *why* are you taking money?" Rachel asked.

"Go on," said Diaz, treating Nick like a horse that's backed itself into a corner in the stable and might just bolt through the wall instead of through the barn door that's already open.

"The deal is I go along with what Ron Miller wants," said Nick.

"But why is Miller paying you? And how does this relate to the sheriff?" asked Diaz.

"Griffin told me he was sure Uribe had killed Merry. He needed help to arrest Uribe. Before I know it, I'm in Miller's office, and he pushes this cash to me in an envelope, and that's it. Griffin's right there, his cuffs out, like—" Nick hung his head.

Diaz frowned at his notes, then looked at Nick. "I need you to be very specific. Did Ron Miller indicate in any way that he was involved with the murder?"

"He said we had to protect Lorelei," said Nick.

"But why did the sheriff tell you that Uribe was the murderer?" asked Diaz.

"It's a cover-up for Lorelei," I said. "Because why else would Ron Miller be in on it?"

I looked at Nick.

"Lloyd Griffin doesn't do anything for anyone unless it serves him," said Max. "David, you still have enough to show a jury that Uribe isn't the murderer. Especially if this young man will testify."

Nick shook his head. "No, I can't do it."

"If you don't testify, that's not going to work for Uribe," said Diaz.

"Give the law a chance," said Max.

"I can ride all the legal arguments from here to Timbuktu. I can cite the law all I want, but in that courtroom in downtown Santa Raymunda, my client will go to prison unless it gets really clear really fast who murdered Merry Jacobs." Diaz turned to look at me and Gina and Rachel. "The sheriff asked him to lie, I've got maybe one, two, three people, if that, who will buy that Griffin isn't this close to God. Miller pays him to do so on behalf of his daughter?"

"If I testify, I look like the bad guy," said Nick. "Lorelei and I—we were involved, and now she's going to have a baby. That's why she—she could have gone after Merry."

"I can't make you say or do anything you don't want to do, but this is about murder," said Diaz.

I looked at Nick. "Come on."

"She had a cheerleader skirt stuffed in her mouth." Rachel looked at Nick.

"No, please don't talk about it." Nick slumped in the doorway now, the screen resting on his shoulder.

Gina shook her head at him.

"I just want out," Nick sighed.

"If you testify, you'll save a life!" I said.

No one said anything. We heard a honk and the occasional cry from outside.

"Okay," said Nick, gulping on the word, "I'll do it."

Even though it seemed like we'd just had this amazing victory, I felt sad. But I was right, after all: he was a good guy. He was doing the right thing.

CHAPTER 32

We stood in the quiet of Diaz's office. The fan whirred. Nick's life was going to be over after he testified to taking a bribe to cover up for his girlfriend who had murdered his ex-girlfriend, and who was going to have his baby. I needed to remember all that before I started falling even more in love with him.

"That's right," a man outside shouted, "take it away!"

I heard the clanging and reeling of chain from a tow truck.

"Nooooo!" I freaked. I don't know why, but with everything else going on, I couldn't have anything worse happen to my car. I ran out of Diaz's office and hit the wooden railing, forgetting that we were up three floors. The front end of my car had been tied up to the back of the tow truck, I guess, to carry it away.

"Hey!" I yelled down to the tow truck driver. He looked under the front of my car to hook the tow chain.

I waved wildly. I had to get down there, and then I felt myself going down, falling over the rail, for real.

"Hold it!" I felt a strong grip at my waist, like maybe God, except when I looked back, it was Nick. No wonder he was the star running back. He could catch anything.

"Thanks." I could barely find my voice.

"Addie," Gina gasped behind me, "what's going on?"

"They're towing my car," I sighed.

"No way, José," said Rachel.

Diaz and Max stood behind Nick. How was I going to explain, you know, the artwork on my car? To anybody?

"Excuse me!" Max bellowed to the tow truck driver. "That is a legal parking space."

"This piece of junk is an abomination!" a man in a business shirt yelled in disgust. "Do you want to look at this—this pornography? I don't."

"We'll figure this out. Stay here," Max wheezed. He trudged down the stairs.

Max buttonholed the tow truck driver and eventually got him to reverse the pulley and lower my car to sit level on all four tires. But I was now staring at the roof of my car. Burn City! I hadn't seen the roof. The sides, yes; the back below the rear window where the whole third-grade approach to female genitalia gave pause. But the roof of the car had this crazy cat-person drawn to look, I swear, as if it was going to be drawn and quartered. It had a cat head but a person's body, in clothing and shoes. The head had whiskers and ears, and the legs and arms spread out eerily like the way we pulled apart those frogs in the dissection tray. Those ex-cheers, they had put all that on there to frame us! As if we had tortured Merry Jacobs with a dead cat. How totally gross to the max can you get?

"Why is there a cat on the roof of your car?" Diaz held onto the railing to lean over to see.

I swear to God, I did open my mouth, but nothing came out.

"It's those ex-cheers," I finally breathed. "We are taking them down!"

"What did I tell you about being safe?" Diaz looked fortress-like with his arms crossed.

Max waved to us from below. "All clear. Got a meeting. See you later." He walked toward City Hall.

"It was those stuck-up ex-cheers," said Rachel. "They did all that to Addie's car."

"Please," said Gina. "They are trying to frame us for the murder. They are so asking for it!"

"You know anything about this?" I looked at Nick.

"No." He shook his head. "But it looks like they *are* setting you up."

"It's Lorelei," I said. "She doesn't even know who she's playing with."

"Okay," said Diaz, "everyone inside."

Back in Diaz's office, things had cooled down except for my temper.

"That's it," I said. "I've had it. Now we have the perfect reason."

"Reason for what?" said Gina.

"A fight," I said. "We are taking them down."

"But there's only three of us," said Rachel.

"Us? A physical fight?" said Gina.

"Yeah, it's perfect," I said. "They've threatened us enough. They think we won't come back at them. But they are going to have the surprise of their lives!"

"They've stepped it up to vandalism. I can't let you guys put yourself into any more danger," said Diaz.

"We're already in the danger zone. They scratched the passenger side while we were in the car," said Gina.

I looked at Nick. I'd melted when he'd had his arms around me pulling me back over the railing. Now, he looked distracted.

"There's a dent," said Rachel. "He even said so," she added, pointing to Nick.

"Just think." I looked at Diaz. "We challenge them to a fight. The exact thing they've been wanting."

"Wait, wait, wait," said Diaz.

"Nick will help us," I said.

"He could be our lookout," said Rachel.

"We get Stevens, too," I said.

"She's not entirely reliable," said Diaz. "Plus, there are four of them, and one of them is a murderer, so how do you defend yourselves against all that?"

"We'll take the risk. If we wind up like Merry Jacobs, it proves their guilt," I said.

"Once they've started down that path, we'll get them to tell us how they killed her," said Rachel.

"It's too risky," said Diaz.

"I'll make sure nothing happens to them," said Nick.

Now, I really was in love.

"We really *can* take care of ourselves," said Gina. "You haven't seen us in action."

"Besides," said Rachel. "If anything goes wrong, we'll call the police." She laughed.

"That's not funny," said Diaz.

"We have the element of surprise," said Gina.

"The only thing they have going for them is to band together against us. Divided, they are toast," said Rachel.

"We'll fight them at school, we'll be on school grounds, and we'll get Stevens to help," I said.

"Awfully creative," said Diaz. "If it goes wrong? No, it's just too dangerous."

"What? Oh, we're girls, so we'll just blow away like dandelions? Please," said Gina. She stood up.

"We are going to get those ex-cheers to spill their guts," said Rachel.

"Only figuratively speaking," I said.

Diaz folded his arms across his chest. "No."

"What do you mean, 'no'?" said Gina.

"When I said I wanted you guys to lay low, I didn't mean to end up like Merry Jacobs," said Diaz. "I can't give you permission to go rounds with a murderer. Period. I need you guys to stay alive."

We stood in the stagnant air.

"Okay," I said. "Have it your way."

Rachel nodded to me and Gina was already out the door. We rushed down the stairs, Nick following. The sun was setting. The bikers and the cowboys were congregating outside Los Buitres across the street. I looked at the police department a block down.

"Hey, that sucks," said Nick as we got into the Pinto.

"Yeah, got to wash it before I pull into the driveway or my mom will have a cow," I said.

"We could hose it at my house," said Rachel.

"No," said Nick. "About your whole taking-down-the-ex-cheers plan."

"What are you talking about?" Gina laughed.

"Well, he totally thrashed the idea, right?" said Nick.

"Yeah," I said. "He did." I slammed my door shut and looked up into his dark brown eyes.

"So, I'm just saying sorry," said Nick.

"Nah, don't bother," said Rachel. "We just need to know if you're still in?"

"You mean, you're still going to do it, challenge them to a fight?" said Nick.

"Challenge, fight, and win, total-victory city," I said.

"Okay, yeah," said Nick.

"Good, we'll be in touch," I said.

"When she has a plan," said Rachel.

"Nothing stops her," said Gina.

I gunned the engine, made a wide U-turn, caught the stares of the crowd outside the bar, then sped through town.

CHAPTER 33

I was in bed the next morning, and I guess because we'd pulled that all-nighter the night before last, and because we'd used up all our adrenaline last night to set up our plan of attack to surprise-fight the ex-cheers, when I went to sleep I really slept, and slept in so much, my mom took a big chunk right out of me just as I woke up.

"Get up, so I can put you on restriction!" she yelled, standing in the doorway of my bedroom, which she'd opened with a typhoon force because the loose things in my room floated in midair for a second and then floated back down to their respective surfaces. She was not smiling, standing there in her light blue jacket and skirt, her arms folded.

"Mom!" I collapsed face first and felt the drool on my pillow. Not a good sign.

"The *alarm,*" she said, putting her hands over her ears.

I realized why she was yelling. I turned my head to see my alarm clock hopping up and down on the nightstand.

"Okay! Crazy-city, I overslept." I reached to hit the alarm clock OFF button, but the clock jumped to the floor.

"You do this to yourself." My mom sighed, shut her eyes, and counted to ten. She wore pale pink frosted lipstick. She was always doing some kind of yoga or Zen thing. I assumed because of me.

I somersaulted out of bed to grab the alarm clock and push the pin back in.

"It's eight?" I held the alarm clock up to see. "Why are you still here?"

She opened her eyes and took a deep breath. "Catching you." She combed her hand through her short brown hair.

"I'm working this case," I said.

"As long as it doesn't interfere with schoolwork." Her voice went up a note higher than normal.

"It's not."

"And what is it with that car? Why does it have smears on it?"

"Trust me, it's all under control."

"Hey, you are not an adult—do not pull that crap with me."

I took a deep breath. We were both late. I was late. And I needed a note from her for this. "Yes. Okay, Mom. You're right."

"Rachel already called, so she is not happy, and *her* mom is worried about you, so you've got to fix that too, and you are on restriction."

"Wait, Mom, I'll land in detention if you don't give me a note. Please, please, please!"

"Oh, now *we* need me, now we're going to be nice to me."

When she got onto the "royal we" part, it was death march time, very little negotiating. "Okay, I swear, whatever you want, whatever."

"You're smart, you think of something, and we'll see."

"But you have to give me a note and—Gina and Rachel too—and I still need to pick up Gina." I was pulling on clothes and brushing my teeth, except I sort of brushed my hair with my toothbrush.

"You do because Gina is at Rachel's, and you have to make peace with both of them."

"Mom, please, please, please."

"I'm going to do this today, but tomorrow you may not have a car." She clicked her ballpoint pen clicker.

"Mom! No, we have way too much to do." I could not lose the car.

~

After school we trekked to the awful cement-sweat swamp of the girls' locker room. I called out for Coach Stevens, but Zamora was the only one at her desk. She raised her eyebrows and said the coach was out sick, so we headed to the coach's house, but she wasn't there either.

"She could be at the doctor? Hospital?" said Rachel.

"Or," I said, "it's early, but she likes her whiskey."

"Addie, we can't go into a bar. You have to be twenty-one," said Rachel.

"They won't kick us out, Rae. No one gets kicked out of Los Buitres," I said.

"Seriously," said Gina. "Even I know we can't go into that place without a vaccination."

"What do you mean?" asked Rachel.

"That bar is low-life city," said Gina.

"Well, we can go to the doctor's office, but that's on the other side of town. And something tells me she's at the bar."

We zoomed up Camino Raymunda. Past the mission, past Wild Mustang Molly's diner, past the souvenir shop, and there it was, Los Buitres, The Vultures. Right across the street from Diaz's office building. It had two tiny windows above the sign in the brick shop-front that had blackened in a way that made you think they were cross-eyed.

"She might not even be in a state to say anything," said Gina as I made a left, then a right. You had to hand it to the city planners. The police station and the courthouse were one block down.

"We go in through the kitchen," I said.

"It's a bar," said Rachel.

"With food," I said.

Sure enough, the back door was kept open by a dishrag stuffed at the bottom between the door and the jamb.

"How do you know all this?" said Gina.

"Because once upon a time when my mom actually dated, she had this biker boyfriend, and he spent a lot of time here." I pulled the door open; the place was packed and loud. But it was dark. Luckily, no one was back here where the dishes got washed and the glasses got stacked in green plastic crates. The music was super loud, all that sad cheating-heart twang—how did people listen to that? We heard beer mugs slam on the bar top. People were arm wrestling, howling like wolves at the moon, and throwing darts, sometimes at the dartboards.

"Come on." I looked over my shoulder at Gina and Rachel.

"We're going to get arrested," said Rachel.

"No, we're not," said Gina.

"You don't have to come," I said.

"This is you and your crazy ideas, Addie, I swear," said Rachel.

"If we don't do this," said Gina, "the killer gets off scot-free."

"Hey, I said I was sorry about sleeping in, what do you want? The Nobel Prize or something?"

"You guys," said Rachel.

One more step and we would be right at the cash register. And I was right on two counts. No one gave us so much as a glance, and Stevens was there. I could see her hair. She was at the bar, wedged between a man and a woman. Granted, there were very few women here.

"You're kidding, right?" said Gina. She pointed to a large picture behind the bar of a naked woman lying on a bearskin rug, with parts of her body sectioned off like they do to identify parts of the cow for cuts of meat.

I hung my head. "I swear," I tried to grab Gina by the arm, "I didn't think they still had that thing."

"It's not a *thing*," said Gina. "I'm complaining."

"This is a freak show and a half. Addie, you go get Stevens," said Rachel. "And make it fast."

The day was turning into complete toilet city.

"Hey, shortstop." The bartender waved his towel at us. He wore a bandana tied back on his head and a leather patch over one eye.

Great, the bartender recognized me from years ago when I'd come looking for my mom's boyfriend.

"We're here on business," I said.

"That's so funny I forgot to laugh," said the bartender, snapping the little towel.

"That is really ugly," said Gina, pointing to the painting.

"Don't say bad things about my girl," said a drunk falling over the bar three stools down from us.

All we had to do was get Coach Stevens out of here, only she was at the other end of the bar, rapt in conversation.

"We'll say what we want," said Rachel. "It's a free country."

"Hey, Glor-i-a Steinem." The bartender stared me down with his good eye, possibly, only eye. "You have ten seconds before I call the cops. That," he pointed to the painting, "is a work of art."

I swallowed hard. "We're here to get Coach Stevens."

"Then get her," he hissed.

"What a lug-head," said Rachel.

"Why is the floor greasy?" said Gina.

"Let's stay focused," I said.

We marched down to the end of the bar. The noise was deafening with the music, the people yelling over a pool game gone bad, and everybody else's conversations trying to compete.

"Hey, Coach," I said.

"I beg your pardon?" She crunched her ice.

"We need your help."

"What?" She had a weird easygoing quality now.

"Something's come up with Merry's murder!" I yelled in her ear.

She gulped her drink and got to her feet.

"Out the back way," I said.

I steered her to the light from the open back door. Rachel and Gina walked ahead to the car in the lot.

"What's this got to do with Merry?" said Coach. She looked sad in the daylight, and her eyes got hard and filmy again.

"We have to set a trap," I said.

"And we need you to help us," said Rachel.

"Why, who?" Coach wobbled a little; her tennis shorts were creased and there was a stain on her cardigan.

"There's a whole cover-up," said Gina.

"The police," said Rachel. "They're covering up for the real murderer."

"And the ex-cheers," I said. "They're involved, and Lorelei is the killer."

"No," said Coach. She steadied herself with her hands on the roof of the car.

"We don't have a lot of time." I said. "You've got to help us."

CHAPTER 34

The next afternoon we staked ourselves out in the girls' locker room. You could smell the bleach and the foot odor all at the same time. Stevens had the radio tuned to KSFE, the San Felipe station. They played Hall and Oates's "Rich Girl." I know what you're thinking. What were we doing with the radio playing and the lights on? How did that square with the ambush idea? We needed the lights on to build our trap for the ex-cheers. This consisted of six volleyball nets that we tied together by knotting the anchor ropes at each side. Rachel would hold one side, I'd hold up the middle, and Gina would hold the end.

But then we needed some height off the ground, so we didn't tangle ourselves up in a mess. At first, we thought we could just stand on the bench between the lockers at the back. But this eliminated the element of surprise. Luckily, we could climb up onto the equipment shelf above where they stored things like gymnastic mats and safety cushions, basketballs, track starting blocks, poles, and tennis rackets. Here we would hide in the dark, well-positioned behind the wire cage, and especially obscured once Stevens turned the lights out. We would have to jump a bit off the shelf, crawl on the floor, not snag the nets on anything, pause at the doorway of the coaches' office, not bang into the desks in the dark, surprise the ex-cheers from behind, and capture them.

"You guys better be ready!" Nick yelled at us from other side of the cage, checking the time.

"We are," said Gina.

"Turning out the lights now," said Stevens from the coaches' office area, farther down toward the back of the building.

The lights dimmed. The radio went dead.

Right when the morning school break started, we didn't pull any punches. Once the bell sounded, we broke through the cafeteria lines, marched up to the ex-cheers at their table, and brought the battle down. You should have seen Jaycee's eyeballs, like, practically pop out of her head, roll around on her face, and then hop back in—I mean, I don't think they had any clue that we'd make the first move, and just because we'd blasted the upper-esher territory with dweebness, all those people shrank back after I said, "We are ready to fight."

"Fight what?" Jaycee fumbled, and Myla jerked back.

"You want attention? You trashed my car—so, yeah, you got our attention. So, okay, we'll take you on, but we pick the place." My eyes bored into the Mr. Bubble Bath she had for brains.

"You'll take us on?" Jaycee coughed.

"Oh, my God, it's the Chuck!" Myla jumped on top of her seat like she'd seen a spider.

"We don't have all day," said Rachel.

"You're not chicken, are you?" I asked. I thought I was in a dream for a second.

"Yeah, okay—you name the place, we're there," said Myla.

"Locker room, after school," said Rachel.

"How are we supposed to fight in there?" Jaycee whined.

Gina clucked, *"Bluuuckk-bluck-bluck!"*

"Hey, we'll be there. You just be ready to be one with the sidewalk," Myla snarled.

~

So, now we waited in the dark. With Nick out there, the ex-cheers would think they had someone in their corner. The final bell of the day sounded, and the clock on the far wall of the cage buzzed loudly. Stevens had dragged the phone out as far as it would go, and gently placed it on the floor. We watched the receiver cord stretch out of sight. We would call Diaz after we got the ex-cheers hog-tied at the end of the showdown.

Click, whoogg, chee-eech. That, without a doubt, was the door. We all took a collective inhale. Footsteps and voices. I got used to the darkness and started to see where Rachel and Gina sat very close to me. Finally, we could see each other. We couldn't move until we were completely ready, since all we'd really done was shove the supplies on this shelf of first aid stuff. If we accidentally shoved a box of Band-Aids on the floor, the jig was up. Not to mention we could not make a sound. I was hoping no one could hear my heart beating. I had to press one of my palms to the center of my chest just so it wouldn't pop up into my mouth, and keep my other hand holding the netting, otherwise I would wind up getting snared in my own trap.

"Hey." I heard Nick from the back of the building, and then the sound of his cords as he walked past me to the restroom near the entrance to the locker room. I blinked at Rachel and Gina in the semi-darkness.

"Whoa, what the hell?" said Jaycee.

"Like, what are *you* doing here?" Lorelei asked. *Oh, Lorelei.*

"No, I just heard you had some fight set up, so I"—he was so cas—"thought I'd make sure nothing bad happened to you guys, you know, just in case."

"Crap," said Myla, "so those assholes aren't even here?"

"I'm wondering where Stevens is." Nick sounded concerned.

"Please," said Lorelei, "she's totally passed out by this time of day." I winced.

"Yeah, she tends to disappear when it's just her and her thermos," said Jaycee.

"Oh, no, I'm going to be sick." *Slap-Slap. Wha-clang.* It sounded like

Lorelei running to a bathroom stall near the entrance. Great. We'd have to handle her with kid gloves. We heard everyone scramble after her.

"What if she leaves?" I whispered.

Rachel patted me on the back.

"Okay, let's get you cleaned up," we could hear Nick say, his voice peanut-butter smooth.

We heard the sink running and a frantic up-and-down friction, someone whirling out paper towels. Rachel accidentally leaned into me, and I looked up.

"Better?" Nick's voice echoed along the tile. We heard footsteps getting louder.

"Well, where are they?" Myla complained. "They're supposed to be here by now."

"They *are* sophomores, guys. I mean, you can't really expect a whole lot. I wonder if you should move further back here, and then when they do get here, you can scare their sorry asses back to junior high," said Nick.

"*That* is a plan," said Jaycee.

"Totally gnarly, Nick," said Myla.

"You're so amazing, *baw-hup,*" Lorelei burped. The thumps and clops of the ex-cheers walking toward us got closer and louder, and then less so as they passed by.

Suddenly, I saw Stevens's silhouette as she barely leaned out from the laundry room. I really hoped she wouldn't forget that she was supposed to call Diaz. Rachel raised her edge of the green netting and held it up until I could follow the thin white vinyl strip to the corner, where it was knotted to the other anchor rope of the next net. I saw her tug at the knot to check it. I nodded, but I didn't want to get distracted from the conversation of the ex-cheers and how Nick was moving them farther to the back and past us. He was supposed to help keep them cornered.

"Hey, stupid Stevens," Myla's singsong voice rang out.

Gina whispered, "We have to get as close to them as possible and then wrap them up like lunch meat."

"Okay," I whispered back.

"Lasso one?" asked Gina.

"Check," said Rachel.

"Lasso two?" said Gina.

"Check," I answered.

"Lasso three?" Stevens asked. *Phew*, Stevens was still with us.

Now, I could hear their footsteps fading. This was it. We carefully hopped down to the floor and crouched.

"What was that sound?" asked Myla.

"I feel sick," Lorelei sighed.

"Lorelei, keep it down," said Jaycee.

"I didn't hear anything," said Nick. "Give it one more second."

We crawled on our hands and knees, keeping the netting tight in one hand. Rachel rose, and I could see the doorway into the office and Rachel with the net she held. It had somehow got up behind her on her head a little, which was weird, but to the ex-cheers, hopefully, it would be scary. I stood next to Rachel, and Gina was behind me. The ex-cheers weren't visible. We tiptoed, letting the nets stretch out, and got to the back just before the very first row of lockers. They had to be around the corner. This was even better, since it would take no time at all to crowd them in and wrap them up.

"This is over—they couldn't even show up," said Jaycee.

Rachel looked back at me. I nodded.

"Hey, guys." Rachel darted fast around to the area where the ex-cheers stood with Nick.

"Great, what is with that getup?" said Myla. "Where's the rest of your gang?"

"Right here!" Gina and I yelled together, and with Rachel's voice joining, we launched a major banshee wail. Man, you should have seen those girls. They didn't just turn white, they went translucent, like, human-anatomy-diagram clear except for Lorelei's gray-green sheen.

But their reflexes were quicker than I thought. I made the wrong move up on the bench, which gave them a way to race around. So, we chased them around the bench. They banged into lockers. Nick was supposed to keep them back for us, but I couldn't see him now. They couldn't get away. They got out to the long strip of a walkway but made the mistake of stopping to look at us. And we just hauled it, like a wave, like a tsunami.

"Haaaaahhhhh!" yelled Rachel in the lead.

The ex-cheers froze in a line up against the cage, their mouths wide open. Then they made a run for it.

"Heeeehhhhh!" I yelled.

"Ahhhh!" Gina yelled.

The adrenaline was on our side, and we ran right smack into them. We were like big game hunters, rushing and jumbling amid flapping wraparound pants, skirts, and striped scoop-neck T's.

I pinned someone's arm to the floor. It was Lisa.

"Okay, you got me." She turned around, saw me, shut her eyes, and crouched into a ball, except she had one arm around Lorelei's leg, and Lorelei was barely making any movement.

"Lisa, no," Lorelei wailed. "Let me go."

Lisa was still holding on to Lorelei's leg, and I crawled closer to Lorelei, threw my net over her, and then got up and pushed Lisa closer, and folded her under the net, so I could stand with one foot on one edge and one on the other and help Rachel. She had pulled Myla down to her knees under her end of the net.

"Come around, Rae," I said, taking deep breaths. "Push her closer to me."

"Stop it," Myla whined, almost crying.

"Not until we take all of you," said Rachel.

She dragged Myla in a sideways sling up to Lorelei and Lisa, who were bunched up. We watched Myla and Lisa and Lorelei jab their elbows and knees out as much as they could for a couple of seconds in their confined cocoon.

"Here!" Gina hefted Jaycee over.

Jaycee stuck her middle fingers out from one of the openings at us.

"You guys," said Rachel. "Just lie straight. You're only going to hurt yourselves."

Lorelei sighed.

"You didn't even try, Lorelei," said Jaycee.

Rachel and I grabbed their feet and Gina managed to twist enough of the rest of the extra-long net under them twice, and rolled them up like fish in wax paper. Their heads and feet were free, their wedge sandals clacking.

"Here." I took off the nylon rope that I had been wearing like a necklace. We used the rope to tie them up around their arms and legs but not squeezed super tight. They looked like quadruplets.

"You wanted a fight? You got a fight," I said, breathing hard.

"This is what it looks like when you lose," said Rachel.

"We wouldn't lose if it was fair," said Myla.

"Oh, right. By the way, you guys are lousy artists," said Gina.

"You are crazy," said Jaycee. "Let us out of here."

"We're calling the police," said Myla.

"So, we can tell them you killed Merry," I said.

"I don't know what you're talking about," said Jaycee.

"Sure, you don't," said Rachel.

"What about this?" I said. I held the jar with the cat above Myla's head.

"Oh, my God, they know," said Lisa.

"You did it, you did it!" said Rachel.

"And then you let an innocent man take the blame?" said Gina.

"They told me to get it, to scare Merry." Lisa sounded like she was crying, and I felt worse.

"You took the cat from Boatman, didn't you?" said Gina.

"Nothing bad was supposed to happen," said Lisa.

"Oh, man, what did you do?" I said.

"Stop it, stop talking," ordered Lorelei.

Lisa moved her head in quick movements from side to side. I could see the tears making stripes across her face. "Then we couldn't put it back," she sobbed.

"Loco, shut up." Jaycee tried to raise her head. "See what you've done?"

"No," I said. "It's what *you've* done. You made her do it." I looked into Lorelei's eyes, which were iceberg lettuce cold. "We know about how you trapped Nick. First comes love, then comes marriage, then comes baby in a baby carriage."

"How do you know that?"

"It's so obvious," I said.

"Lorelei, just be quiet," said Myla.

"You creeps." Lorelei struggled in the nets. "You are so in trouble. I'm calling the police."

"Right," said Gina, "because they are the ones saving your guilty necks."

"I didn't mean it," said Lisa. "I didn't mean for anything bad to happen."

"What did they make you do?" I stared at her.

"Lisa," Jaycee warned.

"See, she just admitted it," said Rachel.

"I took the cat," said Lisa.

"Why?" said Gina.

"Don't say anything," said Lorelei.

"Because," Lisa sighed, letting her head fall slowly back onto the concrete flooring. "We were going to scare—"

"Shut up, *now*," said Jaycee.

"Merry—" said Lisa.

"But you didn't just scare her, did you?" said Gina.

"No," said Lisa.

"No," I said. "No, because you wound up killing her."

"See?" Rachel was taking big gulps of air.

"I swear," Lisa's voice got smaller, "she was alive, she was—"

"You're going to tell that to a judge." My voice was shaking; I was shaking. "We've got you."

We heard the slam of the bathroom door and dress shoes clopping on the tile flooring. Good—Diaz was finally here, and he could hear Lisa firsthand.

CHAPTER 35

Gina and Rachel and I were still in semidarkness and out of breath in the middle of the girls' locker room. We made a barricade facing the captured ex-cheers wrapped in volleyball netting. They looked like moray eels ensnared in seaweed and lying lengthwise across the cement walkway.

"Who's there? Lorelei?"

That was definitely the voice of Ron Miller. It was the voice he used when he wasn't interested in getting people to vote for him.

"Dad?" Lorelei moaned.

Vote for 'R' Guy, Ron Miller! That was his stupid campaign slogan. Stevens had called him for the second half of our plan. We weren't just going to get Lorelei to admit her guilt, we were going to get her to admit it right in front of her father and the sheriff and Diaz. But first, Miller had to come to Lorelei's rescue. He made his way to us halfway between the locker room entrance and the back of the building, his dress shoes making a carving sound that echoed. He was outraged.

"You! You untie my daughter this instant!" said Miller. "What do you think you are playing at here? I'll have you arrested."

"No, Mr. Miller. The one who's going to be arrested is your daughter," I said.

"You will regret this. I'm warning you!" Miller yelled.

"Calm down, Ron." Nick appeared behind us as if he'd just come out of Stevens's office.

"What is this, Nick? How could you let this happen to my little girl?" Miller bent down to try to untie Lorelei and the rest of the ex-cheers, who struggled like little anchovies in the netting.

"Please, Dad, please," Lorelei whimpered.

"Please, Mr. Miller, these girls are crazy," said Jaycee.

"Just get us out of here," said Myla.

"SERRRRRVICE!" We heard the long, drawn-out bellow of Coach Stevens.

"What the— " Miller stood up.

The tennis ball shot like a meteor leaving a gleam of yellow past us, and then it hit, made a sound, *pock*, and then we saw Miller hold his crotch and hit the ground.

"Nut shot," said Gina. "That was gnarly."

Miller had a delayed reaction, then he let out a moan like a squealing mule.

"You are—going to jail." He shut his eyes and breathed hard.

"Look, Ron." I stepped over the ex-cheers as they let out little puffs of panic. "We know you are paying people to frame Carlos Uribe and cover up the fact that your daughter Lorelei murdered Merry Jacobs."

The locker room entrance door clanged again.

"Crusaders." We heard Diaz's voice echo toward us and the speed of his footsteps.

"David, be careful." We heard Max approach at a much slower pace.

"SERRRRRRVICE!" Stevens was back on point, but we still couldn't see her.

"Wait, Coach!" Rachel yelled to Stevens.

Another tennis ball soared past all of us, but it hit the top of the last row of lockers and then ricocheted back to where it came from.

"Hold fire!" shouted Gina, and she took off running back toward Stevens. Somehow, the ex-cheers had found a way to loosen the nets enough to free their arms.

"What are you doing?" Diaz raised his hands above his head at us and his suit jacket winged out.

"They're trying to kill us," Lorelei wailed.

"It's true," said Miller. He tried to sit up, resting his head against the bench seat between the aqua-colored lockers, his knees tight together in front of him. "These young girls are out of their minds, Diaz. You need to call the cops."

"Dad." Lorelei tried to console her father, reaching her arms out to him.

"We know they did it," I said. "Your daughter, Lorelei, killed Merry, and they all helped her."

"She just told us." Rachel pointed at Lisa, who turned her head to the side.

"I can't believe this." Miller dropped his head.

"It's true," said Rachel.

"And they thought they were going to get away with it," said Gina.

"These girls," Miller coughed and squinted at me, "are going to jail. I've been attacked, for God sakes! And God knows what they've done to my daughter and her friends."

"You have no idea what they've been doing to us," said Rachel.

"We're just making sure nobody else gets killed like Merry Jacobs," I said.

Diaz looked at me, his dark brown eyes wide; he was still trying to assess the whole situation.

"You're a pig, Miller," said Max.

"Are you behind this, Walker? If you are, you are going to pay for this," said Miller.

We heard one more slam of the front entrance door to the locker room and the distinct crackle of Sheriff Griffin's black patent-leather oxford shoes. Everyone froze as the sheriff filled the hallway opening, blocking whatever residual daylight there was from the high bathroom windows.

"Well." Griffin took off his sunglasses. "What do we have here?"

"These girls tried to kill us," said Jaycee.

"Yeah," said Myla.

"Arrest them, Lloyd," said Miller.

By now the ex-cheers had crawled out of the nets to their knees. I felt like I had on three layers of sweat.

"Okay," said Griffin. Then he looked in the direction of Coach Stevens's office and yelled, "What in God's name is going on? LaVonne?"

"LaVonne?" I whispered to Rachel and Gina.

We looked back toward the PE cage to see Coach Stevens gripping her tennis racket in front of her face; in her other hand she tossed a tennis ball up and caught it three times.

"That woman has paralyzed me," said Miller.

"I'm not sure what I am looking at here," said Griffin.

"Arrest these girls," said Miller.

"They tortured us," said Myla.

"They almost killed us." Jaycee pointed to me.

"That is a lie," said Gina.

"Don't just stand there, arrest them," said Lorelei.

Griffin looked down at the ex-cheers. When he turned and looked at us, his pants and shoes squeaked.

"Go ahead," said Rachel.

"Arrest us," I said.

"You just try," said Gina.

"But you know you can't," I said. "Because you will have to arrest them too."

"Well," said Griffin, "why don't you tell me what happened. I got Stevens's call that there was an emergency situation out here, and that I might want to call a SWAT team once I come and see."

"You are trying to frame Carlos Uribe, and we know all about it," I said.

"And you did it to take the heat off *them*," said Rachel.

"Because they are the ones who killed Merry," said Gina.

Griffin squatted down and put his hand on Miller's shoulder.

"Where's Nick?" Miller winced. "He's already told the police about the Mexican."

"That's a lie," said Nick.

"See," I said, "you've already lost. Nick's on our side."

"We have Nick, we have this girl telling us that you ex-cheers were out to get Merry," said Rachel, nodding at Lisa, who bowed her head.

"The only killers in the Merry Jacobs case are these girls," said Gina.

"Well," Griffin put one meaty hand against the lockers and one hand on Nick's shoulder, "you're switching sides?"

"Lloyd, if you are going to arrest someone, do it and get out of here," said Max.

"If you do change your story now," Griffin continued talking to Nick, "you are a liar. And that just won't hold up in court either way."

"He's just trying to intimidate you." I looked at Nick.

"I've had enough out of you and your little vigilante circus," said Griffin.

"Don't you say one more word to her," said Coach Stevens.

"LaVonne," said Griffin, "put the racket down, or I'll haul you in for being intoxicated on school property."

"I am protecting these young women," said Stevens. "I only wish I'd done more to protect Merry."

"You are full of it, Coach," said Lorelei.

"Am I?" Stevens raised one eyebrow. "I saw all of you there, tormenting Merry."

"You don't even know what you're talking about," said Myla.

"You choked Merry Jacobs with a cheerleader skirt, and she died," said Gina.

"And that's murder," I said. "And that's on you no matter what."

"Hey, Junior League." Griffin snapped his fingers. "That's enough. You." He wagged a finger at me. "You are done with your citizen's arrest act. Untie these girls."

"Hey," said Diaz, "they're just making a point. They've been harassed for the umpteenth time. They just want these ex-cheerleaders to back off. Looks like they got the result they wanted."

"That better be all that this is." Griffin's dark eyes were full of lightning.

Rachel and I tugged off the nylon rope around the ex-cheers' ankles, and Gina stripped the netting away, shoving mounds of it under the bench.

"I don't know what you think you are pulling with these little groupies of yours," said Griffin, "but whatever they think they heard from these girls, or this young man," he looked at Nick, "or Ron or anyone else, is complete horse shit." He turned, positioned his hands on his holster, and stared at Gina and Rachel and me.

"You may think you can intimidate people," Max told him, "but you are dead wrong."

"Are you threatening me, Walker?" The handcuffs on Griffin's belt jangled.

"We'll see you in court," said Diaz, straightening his tie pin.

"Oh, I can't wait. You haven't even got a case. The judge won't let you get past your opening argument. Listen, I'm the law and order in this town, and I know a guilty man when I see him."

"Then you must be looking in the mirror a lot these days," said Diaz.

Griffin stood stock still, his hand resting on his pistol handle; his sheriff's star pinned on the front of his uniform gleamed.

I looked at the sheriff. What had happened to this man who had seemed so good and honorable back when I was a little girl? Or had he always been this way? It didn't make sense. I couldn't believe he'd always been like this.

"They're guilty of murder," I said. "And you know it."

"Walk it off!" Griffin growled at me.

We trooped back outside and watched Griffin escort Miller and the ex-cheers to Miller's blue sedan, parked in the middle of the basketball court. Miller limped and leaned on Lorelei. It looked like Griffin was saying something to him as Miller took the wheel.

Griffin turned around and waved at us standing there. No one waved back. Diaz scuffed his shoe on the concrete and put on his sunglasses. Stevens tapped the tennis racket. Nick rubbed the back of his neck. Max wiped his forehead with his threadbare handkerchief. The sheriff's car made a lazy circle and drove off behind Miller. There was a long silence.

"I don't know what you guys were thinking," said Diaz.

"It's that girl, Lisa," said Rachel.

"She's the weak link," said Gina.

"Call her to testify, and she'll describe the whole thing," I said.

"Got to hand it to you." Max couldn't help smiling just a bit. "Brave maneuver."

"I would call it an insane maneuver," said Diaz. "Do not, I repeat, do *not* try that malarkey again." He paused. "I will see you all at the courthouse tomorrow at eight a.m., sharp."

Dang. We were going to get justice. For real.

CHAPTER 36

People came out of the woodwork for the murder trial. The noise in the tiled hallway outside the courtroom sounded like twelve hundred pinball machines at once. People crushed past us, spilling past the two open, massive carved doors to the courtroom. A faded reproduction of *The Signing of the Declaration of Independence* hung on the wall in front of us, and on the opposite wall near the entrance to the courtroom was a set of four portraits, guys in muttonchops, hair parted in the middle.

We watched loads of people—the Uribe family with every known relative, Gina's mom and her photographer guy from the newspaper, the man who had wanted to tow my car, the waitress from El Pancho's whose name I couldn't remember, Val Muñoz and her grandmother. Coach Stevens came in a skirt, which, I guess, would make her look more serious. A cop like a reincarnated Great Dane stood just outside the courtroom, his arms crossed and his eyes in a mile-long stare. Everyone who had to testify seemed like bleached versions of themselves. The witnesses had to wait in a separate area until they were called, so they stood down at the other end of the hallway.

Rachel leaned into me and pointed out the ex-cheers. "There."

Myla, Jaycee, Lisa, and Lorelei wore similar pale print dresses with drawstring waists, ruffled sleeves, and patterns of tiny flowers while standing straight in their white high-heeled Candie's slides. They were probably wearing little gold cross necklaces, too. *Please.*

"Now they want everyone to believe they're as pure as driven snow," said Gina.

I watched Lorelei, her head bowed, hair pulled back tight in a straight ponytail. Her dad, Ron, had turned the dial down on his personality, although he still waved to people, flashed a toothy smile, and shook some people's hands.

"Lorelei is so not fooling anyone," said Rachel.

"Yes, sir." I heard Nick's voice and my head whipped around. I watched him walk with an older version of himself, probably his dad, as they headed toward the witness area. The dad talked while Nick nodded. I was about to raise my hand up in the air to get his attention.

Gina leaned into me. "This is not the time to flirt with your pretend boyfriend."

Then we heard the squeaking patent-leather oxford shoes. Everyone looked over their shoulders. It was the sheriff. The too tight uniform. The buzz-sawed hair, the mirrored sunglasses, the broom mustache. His badge glinted, and two officers walked a half step behind, a mini police parade.

Rachel made a sound like a balloon losing its air really fast.

"That guy is like—" Gina started.

"Public enemy number one," I said.

We squeezed into the courtroom, but Diaz looked past us, waved, and called out, "Catalina!" A short, plump woman with dark cascading hair came toward us in a kelly-green dress and ankle-strap sandals. Carlos Uribe's wife. She carried a toddler in a pink dress and white tights on her hip. Delicate gold filigree earrings dangled from the little girl's ears. Two older children clutched her hem, a boy of about seven in a crisp white shirt and salt-and-pepper cords and a girl who could not have been much older, her eyes wide under dark bangs, her hand pressing a fold of her red velvet dress. Catalina and Diaz conferred. Then several other family members crowded up to him, speaking in Spanish, and swallowed him whole.

"Crusaders." Max ushered us to seats in the gallery.

He held a poster board with a white vellum cover under one arm. "Let's get a move on." He directed us to sit behind the Uribe family. I watched Catalina settle in her seat as the little girl in pink tested everyone's lap. The jury stood and waited for the judge. The place echoed like crazy. I was getting dizzy. We watched Diaz set up his files and briefcase on the defense table. Max leaned over to hand Diaz the poster board and a paper bag that looked like someone's week-old lunch.

A shackled Carlos Uribe came through the side door opposite the judge's box and jury gallery to the right, accompanied by a bailiff. He wore a charcoal suit, white shirt, black tie, and shiny black cowboy boots. His chair screeched as he sat down. He'd had his black hair cut short, and now it was parted on the side and slicked down. I saw the sheen of sweat on his forehead when he turned around in his seat before the bailiff uncuffed him. Catalina leaned in, willing herself closer to her husband, mouthing something to him. He looked at her with eyes like freshly dug graves. Diaz touched Uribe's arm to remind him to turn around. Uribe's left leg twitched slightly and made the fabric of his pant leg move. Catalina leaned back with the knuckles of her hand at her mouth; in her fist was a handkerchief with yellow and red embroidery.

The jury was a total joke. The crew included the man who owned most of the land surrounding Santa Raymunda, the orange groves, open fields, and hillsides not owned by independent ranchers. He was selling bits and pieces to developers, like Ron Miller, which made him even richer. Also, there was the mayor's brother, who stood at the far end next to a nun from the Catholic school. It didn't look a whole lot like a jury of Uribe's peers to me. Max talked to several people on the other side of the gallery, and at one point he slapped the mayor on the back and laughed.

"All rise," the bailiff announced. "The Honorable Edgar Ruttan presiding." Ruttan was a short man, and his robes dragged behind him. His bushy gray eyebrows dominated his face, but you could see his dark eyes zeroing in on people. His curly hair looked as if he'd just taken off a baseball cap, smoothed down on top and springing out at the sides.

The judge snapped his robe sleeves and ordered the bailiff to seat the jury.

"The case of *The People versus Carlos Uribe*." Ruttan looked at the district attorney, who sat at the table closest to the jury. He had long ash-blond hair, fuzzy sideburns, and invisible eyebrows, and wore a tan sports jacket and brown plaid pants. He was tall as a skyscraper. The judge looked at Diaz, asked each if they were both ready, and I started to think we would be here forever.

"Your Honor, ladies and gentlemen of the jury, the defendant, Carlos Uribe, has been charged with the murder of Merry Eloise Jacobs." Lance O'Brien started his opening statement, walking around his desk with his hands clasped behind his back. He stopped to make eye contact. "Merry was a star pupil, an outstanding leader at her school, and a true friend. Her parents told me she was committed to making a positive contribution to her community, to her team. So, it is especially disturbing that our community has lost this vibrant young woman, a positive future leader, and a great force for good in this world." O'Brien paused. "The evidence will show the defendant ended Merry's life, brutally murdering her by suffocating her to death between four p.m. and nine p.m. on Friday, May third."

Several gasps sounded in the gallery like soda bubbles.

"The following Monday morning," O'Brien resumed, "her body was found in the vicinity of the defendant's work area, directly outside the high school's maintenance shop, behind the girls' locker room, in a pile of leaves, in an unpaved area, alone. The evidence will show that the defendant had knowledge of the victim's daily school routine, and was observed to be in the company of Merry at school on the Friday afternoon prior to her death. The evidence will prove beyond a reasonable doubt that the defendant is guilty as charged." O'Brien continued, "Members of the jury, the court recognizes your important responsibility in the service within the justice system. This trial and the details are explored here for your benefit so that you may reach a decision, a just decision for Merry Jacobs, her family, and her community."

Catalina's head fell forward. Uribe sat rigid in his chair. I could see his hair had grooves in it like a record, it was so intensely combed.

Chatter flowed in English and Spanish. The woman to Catalina's left clutched a rosary. The little girl in pink cried out.

Ruttan settled back in his seat, folded his hands on the bench, and nodded at Diaz. "Does the defense wish to make its opening statement now?"

"Yes, your Honor." Diaz rose. "Members of the jury, first I want to recognize the importance of your service at this trial. We are grateful for your presence here today. You will be asked to conclude your judgment of the defendant on the basis of the evidence provided to you beyond a reasonable doubt. Your Honor and ladies and gentlemen of the jury, according to the laws of this state, my client is presumed innocent until proven guilty." Diaz looked down, then looked to the jury to make eye contact. "But there is no evidence that proves that my client is guilty. What the evidence will show is that the police unfairly biased their investigation against my client and failed to apprehend the real murderer, who remains at large and is a threat to the safety of our community, even possibly in this very courtroom." Diaz paused. "Now, while we hear the details of the death of Merry Eloise Jacobs, which we all agree is a terrible tragedy, the longer we persist in continuing this trial, the longer we withhold justice for her."

A rising tide of voices filled the air. Uribe's shoulders relaxed. Catalina raised her head. I looked at Max, who sat directly in front of me on the aisle. I'd never seen the guy sit up so straight.

"Quiet, everyone." Ruttan sat up and slapped his hands on top of the judge's box. "You may proceed, Mr. O'Brien."

"The People call Mr. Nick Stanley." O'Brien scratched the desk legs against the floor when he stood up.

I watched Uribe blink. I looked up as Nick solemnly took his oath, his eyes hollow, crossing and re-crossing his arms. He stated his name for the court reporter.

"Mr. Stanley, you told the police that you regularly saw the defendant with the victim. You said the defendant was interested in the victim—by that you meant physically interested. You reported that you saw the victim and the defendant after school on the day of the murder at approximately four p.m., which was the time the student ASB meeting was concluded. Is that correct?"

"Yes, but—"

"Thank you. No further questions."

You could hear people sit up and straighten their posture while they gradually absorbed what O'Brien was saying. I saw Catalina shaking her head as she held the hand of the woman next to her.

"Mr. Diaz? Questions?"

"Yes, Your Honor." Diaz rose and walked calmly to face Nick. "Mr. Stanley, is what you told the police true?"

"No, sir," said Nick.

People shifted in their seats.

"Were you near the school on the Friday afternoon that Merry Jacobs was murdered?"

"I was not," said Nick.

"Did you ever see Mr. Uribe talk to Merry?"

Nick sighed. "No, I did not."

"So, you gave the police a statement that was not true, is that correct?" said Diaz.

"Objection—assumes facts not in evidence and leading the witness," said O'Brien.

"Sustained." Ruttan looked at Diaz.

"Let me rephrase that." Diaz paused. "Why are you now denying what you previously stated to the police?"

The court seats creaked, as people in the back raised themselves slightly to hear what Nick would say.

"I—" Nick tilted his head back to look at the ceiling. Then he looked at Diaz. "I lied."

Voices trickled back and forth, and people looked at each other.

"I'm sorry, I couldn't hear you—could you repeat what you said?" asked Diaz.

"Objection, question asked and answered." O'Brien scooted his chair back as if to stand.

"Overruled. You may answer the question." Ruttan nodded.

"I lied," said Nick, and the words pierced the back wall like bullets.

"Is it true, Mr. Stanley, that sometimes people lie not because they mean to but because they feel they have to?"

"Objection—calls for expert opinion."

"Sustained," said Ruttan.

Diaz nodded and then continued his questioning. "Someone may even lie because they feel threatened, would you agree?"

"Objection—calls for expert opinion and leading the witness," O'Brien fumed.

"Withdrawn," said Diaz. He started again. "Mr. Stanley, why did you lie?"

"I lied because someone told me to," said Nick.

"Who told you to lie?"

"Um, it was—" Nick stopped, unable to get the words out.

"Mr. Stanley?" Diaz cocked his head at Nick like an expectant labrador. "Who told you to lie to the police about Mr. Uribe?"

"It was," Nick geared up, "Mr. Miller, Ron Miller. He asked me to, to identify whoever the police pointed out to me as their suspect. And it turned out to be him, Mr. Uribe, but I—"

The courtroom erupted as people rose from their seats to see Ron Miller, but he was still out in the witness area.

Ruttan smacked his gavel twice. "People, please. You must stay seated."

"Thank you, Mr. Stanley." Diaz turned, and Nick started to get up to leave the stand.

"Not so fast, Mr. Stanley," said O'Brien. "Your Honor, permission to treat the witness as hostile."

"Yes. Young man, you must remain seated until you are excused. Mr. O'Brien, would you like to re-cross the witness at this time?" Ruttan looked at Nick and then nodded at O'Brien.

"Yes, Your Honor. May I approach the witness?" O'Brien asked.

"You may." Ruttan leaned back.

"You were told to lie by Mr. Ron Miller, is that correct?" O'Brien asked with an edge to his voice.

"Yes, that's right," said Nick.

"I see, and—wait, let me make sure I follow this. You work for Mr. Miller, do you not?"

"Well, I did work for him."

My heart sped up to a solid 120 miles per hour. Oh, my God—

maybe Nick Stanley wasn't seeing Lorelei anymore. All of my wishes were coming true. He was a good guy after all.

"But at the time of the murder, at the time that you lied to the police, you worked for Mr. Miller, and Mr. Miller paid you money, is that true?"

"Yeah, but—"

"Objection—asked and answered," Diaz interrupted.

"Overruled; the witness may answer," said Ruttan.

"Your honor, Mr. Stanley has already testified that he lied to the police," said O'Brien. "I'm just exploring this further. It's obviously important to know when a witness is lying and when he's not."

"Objection—relevance." Diaz raised his voice.

"No, Mr. Diaz; you opened that door during your examination of the witness," said Ruttan.

"Thank you, Your Honor," said O'Brien. "Just to get this straight. When the man you worked for paid you money to lie, you did. So, would you have to be paid to tell the truth as well?" O'Brien paced back in front of the bench.

"No, I—I mean, I didn't have a choice." Nick twisted left and right in his seat; his hands took hold of the witness box shelf.

"I hope Diaz knows what he's doing," Gina whispered to me.

"Now, Mr. Stanley, I do need an answer to my question. Did you receive any money from Mr. Diaz to say what you just said? That you lied to the police?"

"No. I'm telling the truth—"

"Mr. O'Brien, I believe you've made your point." Ruttan held his hands in front of him fingertip to fingertip.

O'Brien made a short bow.

"What about the ex-cheers?" Gina whispered.

"No further questions, Your Honor."

"Mr. Diaz?"

"No further questions, Your Honor."

"You may step down, Mr. Stanley," said Ruttan, "but you are not excused in the event counsel wishes to recall you."

Nick dropped his chin to his chest, the veins visible on his temples and neck. He gripped the rails of the witness box when he stood up, really gripped, as if maybe he could pull the whole structure out of the flooring. When he did let go of the wood panels, they sprang back with a boom.

I was mad at Diaz. Now, Nick looked like a fool. "Why didn't Diaz prepare Nick for this?"

"It wasn't Diaz's fault," said Rachel.

"That O'Brien. Super-smug old-rock-band wannabe," said Gina. "He made Nick totally unreliable."

I tried to make eye contact with Nick, but with his curly hair flopped down, I couldn't see his face. His hands had frozen into fists. He was mad too.

"The People call Sheriff Lloyd Griffin, Your Honor," said O'Brien.

"Yes!" Rachel cried out.

O'Brien rolled his shoulders back like a rooster getting ready to blast his vocal cords in triumph.

Silence fell over us. Then the squeaking shoes broke the silence. The sheriff marched past O'Brien with so much power, O'Brien's hair flew back, and it was still fluttering down slowly even after Griffin was sworn in.

CHAPTER 37

The heat in the courtroom increased despite the box fans trying to circulate the air.

"Sheriff Griffin," said O'Brien. "What happened on the morning of May fifth?"

"We received a call through our dispatch that there was an emergency involving a student at the high school," said Griffin. "I drove to the site immediately with two backup officers. We confirmed that the victim had died. We called for the coroner, and I proceeded to question the young women who discovered the body."

"That's us," Rachel whispered.

"Was the defendant at the scene as well?" asked O'Brien.

"He was. He was the only one near the body. He was trying to take the victim's pulse; however, it was clear the victim was dead." Griffin took a minute to stare at Uribe and Diaz.

A gasp sounded from the back. People shifted in their seats to look at Uribe.

"Did you question the defendant?" asked O'Brien.

"I did not," said Griffin. "That was conducted by one of my deputies."

"Do you know the defendant?" asked O'Brien.

"I do."

"Could you explain how you know him?"

"Objection—lacks relevance, Your Honor," said Diaz.

"I'll allow it," said Ruttan.

"I had reason to arrest him in a case of stolen property several years ago. There was probable cause to consider him a suspect in that case. He was driving a van full of stolen car stereos." The longer Griffin got to talk about Uribe, the more his eyes bored straight into the man.

"And was he convicted of this crime?" O'Brien asked.

Griffin took his time to lean forward in the witness box. "No."

"Why wasn't he convicted?"

"There was not enough evidence to prove his involvement." Griffin looked at Uribe and then at Diaz.

"Objection, Your Honor. Lacks relevance. My client was found to be completely innocent," said Diaz, rising off his seat.

"It goes to character, Your Honor," said O'Brien.

"It does not, Your Honor. It only serves to bias the jury against my client," said Diaz.

"You've made your point, Mr. Diaz," said Ruttan. "Sit down, sir. Sustained."

Everyone took a deep breath. I looked at Gina, who shrugged and shook her head. Rachel bent forward with her elbows on her knees. How was Uribe going to have a fair trial?

"Sheriff, did you take Mr. Stanley's statement?" asked O'Brien.

"I did," said Griffin.

"Did you in any way suspect that Mr. Stanley was not telling you the truth at the time of his statement?" O'Brien stood in front of the jury.

"I did not," said Griffin.

"Thank you, Sheriff. No further questions."

Diaz waited to cross-examine the witness until ~~after~~ O'Brien sat back down and finished shuffling his papers.

"Sheriff, in this previous case of stolen goods, the stolen stereo equipment, you never actually charged the defendant with anything, is that correct?" Diaz looked at the jury.

"There was nothing to hold him on." Griffin narrowed his eyes at Diaz.

"Because he was in no way involved in any crime," said Diaz. "He had simply left his van overnight in a parking lot, and the thieves were able to break into his vehicle and store the stolen property. Wasn't that the conclusion of your police report?"

Griffin leaned back in his seat. The wood popped. I had to really concentrate on not blinking while I watched the sheriff.

"What you said is correct," said Griffin.

Diaz turned around. He took out a white handkerchief, blotted his forehead, and turned again to face Griffin.

"Sheriff, why did Nick Stanley make his statement to the police about my client two days after the body of Merry Jacobs was found?"

"Objection—calls for expert opinion."

"I'll allow it if the witness knows the answer."

"It's common for people to be in shock, and then later remember important facts."

"Objection—calls for expert opinion."

"Sustained. The witness's statement will be stricken from the record."

"Do you know Mr. Stanley?"

"I'm in contact with the mayor's office and with the city commissioners, and I know that Ron Miller has Mr. Stanley working for him. I have seen the boy at City Hall in that capacity."

"Do you talk to him?"

"As a courtesy, which I do with all of the good citizens in my jurisdiction." Griffin smiled, but it was really a show of his large white teeth, like shiny new bathroom tiles.

"You know Mr. Miller, and you know Mr. Stanley. You are familiar with both of these people?" asked Diaz.

"I'm friendly, Mr. Diaz, you know that." Griffin laughed and then everyone laughed as a kind of delayed reaction, the laugh track from a bad sitcom.

"Have you ever had any business dealings with Mr. Miller?"

"Objection, Your Honor," said O'Brien. "Where is this questioning going?"

"Overruled. However, Mr. Diaz, let's get to the point," said Ruttan.

"No." Griffin looked amused at Diaz.

"Did you tell Mr. Miller to have Mr. Stanley make a statement to the police so that my client would be a suspect in the murder of Merry Jacobs?"

People whispered back and forth to each other. The sheriff clenched his teeth and flicked his head in O'Brien's direction.

"Objection, Your Honor—assumes facts not in evidence," said O'Brien.

"Overruled." Ruttan nodded.

"I can answer that," said Griffin.

"No, no," said O'Brien. He stood up, his chair scraped the floor, and he flapped his arms as if to flag Griffin down.

"Mr. O'Brien." Ruttan shot a look at the DA. "The court will not tolerate your distraction!"

O'Brien bowed his head.

"I have no recollection of saying anything to Mr. Miller about Mr. Stanley whatsoever," Griffin bored into Diaz.

"No further questions, Your Honor," said Diaz.

A bunch of people started talking and standing up behind us. Ruttan clacked the gavel three times. "I will have order. Order, now, or you will be dismissed. Mr. O'Brien?"

People quieted.

O'Brien stood and kept his eyes closed for five seconds.

"Sheriff, how long have you served this community, the citizens of Santa Raymunda?"

"I've lived here all my life, started my career here on the force in 1952. I have been sheriff here for the past twenty years."

"Have you ever tried to influence a witness?"

"I have not. If I ever had, I would not be able to wear this badge." Griffin nodded at the judge.

"Thank you, Sheriff," said O'Brien. "Nothing further, Your Honor."

"Nothing further, Your Honor." Diaz looked straight at Griffin.

The sheriff stood up, towering over everyone. He put his mirrored aviator sunglasses back on and his shoes squeaked as he marched out of the courtroom.

"He thinks he's going to get away with framing Uribe. Well, he's not," Rachel whispered.

"We should keep tabs on him," said Gina.

"You know it," I said.

"The People call Mr. Ron Miller," said O'Brien.

Bench seats knocked and creaked. Miller took the stand. He was trying hard not to let his expression default into that mile-wide state senate campaign smile. The two flat plates of his blond hair that fused together on the right side of his head gleamed. He wore a sea-foam green leisure suit with a dark photo-print shirt. Miller unbuttoned his jacket and cleared his throat while the oath was read. I noticed the furrows of his forehead, the jutting chin. He ran a finger between his collar and his neck. He was squirming.

"Does Mr. Nick Stanley work for you?" O'Brien asked.

"Yes. He does odd jobs. That kind of thing," said Miller.

"Did you tell Mr. Stanley to make a statement to the police against the defendant?" O'Brien rolled onto the balls of his feet.

"Absolutely not." Miller shifted in his seat.

"Did you direct Mr. Stanley to lie?"

"I did nothing of the kind," said Miller.

"Thank you. No further questions." O'Brien took his time to sit.

"Mr. Miller," said Diaz.

Two trapped swallows flitted in and out of their nests under the eaves outside the windows behind the jury.

"Have you ever employed a high school student to do odd jobs for you? Before you took on Mr. Stanley?" Diaz asked.

"No." Miller cleared his throat.

"You recently hired Mr. Stanley to work for you, is that correct?"

"Yes."

"Who did you hire to do this kind of work, these odd jobs, before you hired Mr. Stanley?"

"No one." Miller shifted in his seat, which pulled the suit up and back so that it looked like it was too large for him. He looked like just a head propped up on a jacket collar. Ron in the Box.

"So, no one had done this work for you until a few months ago, and yet, having never had a position to fill, you suddenly hired Mr. Stanley. Is that correct?"

"Yes." Miller looked at O'Brien.

"Mr. Miller, why did you pay Mr. Stanley in the first place?" Diaz turned and looked directly at the jury.

Miller looked at Diaz, trying to think of something to say, to fill the gap. "For the jobs, I mean, the job—that's why, and it made sense—because Griffin thought it was a good idea, especially after the school murder. He said to pay the kid since I'd paid him for everything else —" Miller stopped and looked up.

"Objection! Hearsay!" O'Brien waved his hands at Ruttan.

"What did you say?" Diaz asked.

Static filled the air. I could feel my teeth buzzing. Rachel's eyes got glossy. Gina clenched her lip gloss container in both hands.

"Nothing. I don't know what I said."

"Could the court reporter please repeat the witness's previous statement?" Diaz asked.

The reporter started in a monotone voice: "Mr. Miller, why did you pay Mr. Stanley in the first place?" "For the jobs, I mean, the job—that's why, and it made sense—because Griffin thought it was a good idea, especially after the school murder. He said to pay the kid since I'd paid him for everything else—"

The gallery roiled into a roar of whispers, questions, and echoes.

"Your Honor." Diaz spoke over the noise. "This changes everything!"

"Your Honor." O'Brien approached the judge.

"Order!" Ruttan raised his voice.

People looked at Miller, who sat stock still while his eyes moved from O'Brien to the judge.

"Ladies and gentlemen of the jury, I think now would be a good time to break for lunch. We will reconvene at one o'clock this afternoon. Do not discuss this case with anyone, including each other." Ruttan smacked the gavel once.

"Did you hear *that*?" Rachel looked at me.

Uribe was escorted from the courtroom.

"Papa!" His little girl threw her arms up, and Catalina pressed the girl to her chest.

"That's it." I looked at Rachel. "That shows they framed Uribe."

"We don't know the jury will see it that way," said Gina.

We squeezed into the crowd, rushing for the exit. I tried to look for Nick's face in the hallway, but I couldn't see him.

CHAPTER 38

Outside, we felt the sun on our faces and made for the quad in front of the courthouse, where the grass grew in weedy patches and people disbanded into small groups.

"Hey, you guys." Val Muñoz waved at us from a bench under the shade of an old sycamore tree. Her grandmother was seated on the bench, chatting with another older woman who sat next to her. Val sprang up to meet us. I wondered if Val had ever been told by her aunt or her grandmother that her real dad was the sheriff. The thing is, she wasn't unique. I think the count of out-of-wedlock kids for Griffin was up to at least four.

"Val," said Rachel.

"What are you guys doing?" she asked.

"Just getting some air," I said.

"Yeah, wild in there." She nodded at the courthouse.

"Guess that's all we can say," said Gina.

"So, are you guys still poking around for Diaz?" she asked.

"Maybe," said Rachel, smiling.

"Well." Val swished her long ponytail when she bobbed her head. "Maybe you are, maybe you aren't. Anyway, not that this has anything to do with what's going on in *there,*" she lowered her voice, "but I've seen the sheriff driving around at night, like, late."

"What?" asked Rachel.

"I don't know what it means, but last Monday night, I couldn't sleep and came out to get a drink of water, just happened to look out the window, and the sheriff's in his car. Just parked across the street—you know, weird."

"Any clue why?" I asked.

"That's why I'm telling you, dodo brains—like, follow him, you know, get on it," said Val.

"Like, what time at night?" asked Gina.

"Midnight." Val squinted.

"Okay, good to know," I said. "We'll check it out."

"Look, I got grandma duty—see you later." She took Mrs. Muñoz by the arm and entered the courthouse.

"What does 'check it out' mean?" asked Rachel.

"Crusaders," Max called to us. He carried a box of tacos and drinks. "Sustenance," he said with a wink. "We're due back in there pretty soon. Eat."

"Where's Diaz?" asked Gina.

"He is with his client," said Max. He ate his taco in two bites.

"But—" Bits of taco shell dust puffed out of my mouth. "Max, *the sheriff—*"

"We can only do one case at a time. Right now, we need to get back into court. Hurry up." He ducked through the entrance and joined the stream of returnees.

O'Brien was standing at attention with his arms crossed, but his head was turned toward the back. Ron Miller was seated in the witness box. His perfectly straight hair had puffed out like stale cotton candy and the ruddiness in his cheeks had faded.

The bailiff counted the jury to make sure everyone was back before the judge returned.

"Ladies and gentlemen," said Ruttan as we sat down. "We are picking up where we left off and we have resolved the hearsay objection. The hearsay, as agreed in chambers, is recognized as admissible. So, I will allow it. The objection is overruled. Mr. Diaz?"

"Wow," Gina whispered.

Miller smoothed his suit jacket with an unsteady hand.

Diaz looked at Miller for a long time. "No further questions, Your Honor."

"Mr. O'Brien, you may re-cross," said Ruttan.

O'Brien turned his head to acknowledge the judge and set his hands on the edge of his desk to inspect the papers laid out under his gaze. Then he looked up. "No further questions for the witness, Your Honor."

"Mr. O'Brien, your next witness."

"No further witnesses, Your Honor. The People rest their case."

"Mr. Diaz, is the defense ready?" asked Ruttan.

"Yes, Your Honor. The defense calls Ms. Lisa Black," said Diaz.

Finally, he was calling the ex-cheers. Lisa entered the courtroom with her butter-blond Egyptian haircut. The silent, but probably just as deadly third ex-cheerleader, and Jaycee's best friend.

Lisa Black walked past us down the front aisle to the witness box. She seemed almost colorless in her pink gauze dress, and her eyes never left the ground. After Lisa, Diaz would call the rest, including Lorelei, and finally the whole truth would be out there. Justice for Merry. Justice for Uribe. We hoped!

The bailiff swore Lisa in before she sat down.

"Ms. Black, are you the teacher's aide for Mr. Boatman in first-period Biology? At Santa Raymunda High?"

"Objection, Your Honor—relevance?" said O'Brien.

"I'm allowing it," said Ruttan.

Lisa leaned forward. "Yes." But she didn't stop looking down.

"And did you take something from Mr. Boatman's dissection shelf that you shouldn't have?"

"I did, but—"

"What did you take?"

"It was a cat." Lisa took a few small breaths. "It was dead. It was for dissection." She put her face in her hands.

"Objection, Your Honor—assumes facts not in evidence; lacks relevance," said O'Brien.

"Overruled."

"Now, would you tell the court, Ms. Black, what you did with the cat?" Diaz stopped to gaze at the jury.

She sat up and cleared her throat. "Well . . ."

I had to keep my head from spinning so fast I'd be airborne before she said anything.

"Take your time," Diaz spoke calmly.

"We, we all, I mean, the four of us, Jaycee, Myla, me, and Lorelei, we—we had this idea—"

"Objection, Your Honor—hearsay. She cannot speak for others."

"Overruled, Mr. O'Brien; I'll let the witness explain." Ruttan leaned back in his seat and rubbed his face.

"Yes," said Diaz. "Go ahead."

Oh, my God, what was Lisa Black going to say? My skin got tight like Saran wrap. I couldn't look at anyone. All the stuff we had done? What if they got away with it?

"It was this idea we had for Merry."

"An idea? Could you be more specific?" said Diaz.

"Like, you know, a joke," said Lisa. For some reason she looked up.

"So, a joke you meant to play on Merry Jacobs?" said Diaz.

I couldn't breathe.

"We just wanted to scare her, you know. I mean, like, Merry started it first." Lisa's voice cracked and there was a well full of water way, way down inside her.

"This was for fun?" said Diaz.

"I mean, we were only pretending. God, we weren't going to make Merry *eat* the cat."

For about twenty seconds all you could hear were echoes: *Cat? Gato?*

"Order, please," Ruttan commanded.

"You have to understand." Lisa started panting. "Merry—she made so much noise."

"Objection, Your Honor—assumes facts not in evidence."

"Overruled."

Diaz raised his hand. "Ms. Black, please explain in more detail."

"We . . ." Lisa took a big breath and closed her eyes. "We were *pretending* to make her eat . . . the cat."

"Your Honor, may I approach the witness?" Diaz asked.

"Yes."

"Ms. Black, I'd like to show you a photograph and ask you to identify it. Mr. O'Brien, I have a copy for you too." Diaz handed photographs to the witness and prosecutor.

"It's a picture of a dead cat," Lisa said.

"Is this a picture of a particular dead cat?" Diaz asked.

"Yes, it's the cat I took from the classroom." Lisa shivered.

"Your Honor, I'd like to enter this photograph into evidence as Defense Exhibit D-1."

"Agreed," said the judge. "Please mark the photograph as Defense Exhibit D-1."

"Your Honor, I also have a display board of an enlargement of this same photo that I'd like to enter into evidence as Defense Exhibit D-2."

"Objection, Your Honor—cumulative."

"Overruled; I'll allow it," said Ruttan.

"Your Honor, may I publish Exhibit D-2 to the jury?" Diaz asked.

"Objection, Your Honor. This photograph is inflammatory and is intended solely to inflame the jury."

"Overruled." The judge glared at O'Brien.

Diaz unveiled the poster, flinging the cover back to show the court a five-foot magnified photo of the formaldehyde kitty.

The photo was clearly visible from the gallery, and we were definitely getting light-headed. Several women held handkerchiefs up to their faces. Gasps expelled from mouths like helium tanks all going off at the same time, including inside the jury box. *Hold on to your seat, Sister Mary Immaculata.*

Ruttan worked the gavel three times to cut through the noise.

"Ms. Black, please describe the picture in more detail," asked Diaz.

"It's a kitten; I don't know how old. It's floating in a big jar of formaldehyde or something."

People quieted. Diaz reached into a crumpled paper lunch bag and held up the cat in a jar.

"Objection, Your Honor! This performance is pure theater and extremely prejudicial to the prosecution!"

"Counsel, are you arguing that the best evidence rule should apply? Should I allow this preserved animal into evidence instead of the photographs?" Ruttan asked, his eyebrows raised.

"Why, no, no, Your Honor, I mean . . ." O'Brien tapped his shoe to think.

"Your Honor," Diaz said before O'Brien could finish his thought, "I submit this jar containing what is obviously the same kitten that appears in the photos into evidence as Defense Exhibit D-3, in accordance with the best evidence rule."

O'Brien shuffled the papers on his desk and sat down.

"Agreed. The clerk may mark the exhibit as Exhibit D-3," said Ruttan.

"Now," said Diaz, looking at the poster of the cat, "Ms. Black, if I understand your earlier testimony, is it true that you and your ex-cheerleader friends intended to somehow trick Merry Jacobs into thinking she was going to eat this kitten?"

"Objection, Your Honor—lacks relevance," O'Brien protested. "What is the point, exactly?"

"Overruled," said Ruttan.

"Ms. Black? Can you please explain to the jury how you attempted to trick Merry Jacobs into thinking she was going to eat the cat?"

"We had her pinned down, then we took the cat out of the jar. One of us covered her eyes, and then we just held the cat, like, just above her mouth, but then Merry was so—this screeching."

"Why didn't you stop?" asked Diaz.

"It was to just scare her. She had been reaming us. It was just a joke." Lisa put the palms of her hands up to her temples. "She was alive when we left her. I swear. You've got to believe me. She *was* breathing. She wasn't *dead*!"

I looked at Rachel, then at Gina. It was like we'd all jumped out of a plane, feeling for where our rip cords should be.

"You left her there," said Diaz.

"No. Yes. No, we left her—"

"Objection, Your Honor. Lacks relevance. How does this relate to the murder?" O'Brien waved at the judge.

"Overruled," said Ruttan.

"It was, so, like, awful, and then she had this foam stuff come up out of her mouth, and we thought she was trying to spit at us, you know? That's when I told Lorelei she should do something, and that's when Lorelei stuffed Merry's mouth, grabbed the cheerleader skirt and filled her mouth with it, you know, instead of the cat. And then Merry finally shut up—" Lisa stopped and took a breath. "But Merry was alive, I swear. I swear, I swear, I swear. Nick even said she was alive."

For about five seconds you couldn't hear a thing.

"Can you say that again, please?" said Diaz.

"We left. Nick said he would take Merry. We had to leave." Lisa heaved and cried.

"Wait, you said Nick. Are you talking about Nick Stanley?"

"Yes, but after the party, he told us Merry stopped breathing—"

"You left Merry Jacobs with Nick Stanley?"

I gripped the edge of my seat.

"Order!" the judge's voice rang out. Then he stared hard at Diaz.

"Thank you, Ms. Black; I have no further questions at this time," said Diaz.

"Mr. O'Brien?" said Ruttan, his voice raised.

"No questions, Your Honor," said O'Brien, seated at his desk, rubbing his forehead.

"The defense calls one more witness, Ms. Lorelei Miller, to the stand," said Diaz.

I couldn't help myself. I watched the bailiff escort Lorelei into the courtroom. She looked like she was shaking, and she looked at Nick, who stood up. And then everyone was standing up, trying to watch both of them.

"Ladies and gentlemen, you must remain seated." Ruttan smacked the gavel.

Lorelei got to the stand and was sworn in by the clerk. I don't know why, but I felt a wave of pity, or something like that, rush over me. Rachel bit her fingernails. Gina pressed her lip-glossed lips together.

"Ms. Miller," Diaz asked, "were you with Ms. Black the day Merry Jacobs died?"

"Yes," she replied.

"And was Merry Jacobs with both of you at some point that day?"

"Yeah," she said.

"And when Merry Jacobs was with you, did you and Ms. Black attempt to play a practical joke on Merry Jacobs?"

"Yes," Lorelei answered, but her voice barely registered.

"You must speak louder, Ms. Miller," said Ruttan.

"Yes, we were playing a practical joke," said Lorelei. Her eyelids looked puffy. Her cheeks were thin. She looked like she had almost drowned.

"Can you please describe what you did and what Merry Jacobs's reaction to that was?" Diaz asked.

"Like Lisa said. We—Myla and Jaycee and Lisa and me—we were just going to play a joke, a really mean joke, on Merry. We waited for her after school." Lorelei sniffed. "We got her pinned down outside the girls' locker room, and we put the cat up to her mouth. She," Lorelei dropped her head for a second, "she screamed so loud it was deafening, and then we couldn't get her to stop."

"Is it true that you ~~had~~ tried to stop Merry from screaming?" said Diaz.

"Yes."

"How did you do that?"

"I just wanted to make her stop. It just seemed like she was overreacting. I just wanted to scare her, and she was scared, and I didn't think she would scream. It was so awful. We'd stopped playing around, but she was still screaming, so I grabbed the bag with the uniforms, and I just pulled out the first thing, and shoved it in her mouth. I swear—" She started to tear up.

"What was it that you put in her mouth?" asked Diaz.

"It was this—it was a cheerleader skirt, just part of it. I grabbed it and got it in her mouth just to make her not so loud," said Lorelei.

"You were best friends with Merry Jacobs?"

"Yes, I would never have done any of it, I swear to God—"

"Ms. Miller, was Mr. Stanley there?" asked Diaz.

"Yes. He was there to pick me up." She wiped at a tear at the corner of her mouth. "We were supposed to go to a party. Merry had scratched me, and Nick saw us."

"He saw you with Merry?"

"Yes. He's my boyfriend. We have—I'm going to have his baby—"

The crowd exploded. Ruttan's sleeves waved as he pounded his gavel like a bad junior-high rock-band drummer.

"Silence!" Ruttan yelled.

The room died down.

Lorelei clung to the shelf of the witness box in front of her. "He told me not to worry. He'd calm Merry down. Everything was going to be fine for us."

"So, you left Merry with him, no one else?"

"Yes," Lorelei sniffed.

"Thank you, Ms. Miller. Is there anything else you can tell the jury about Merry Jacobs's condition when you left her?" asked Diaz.

"She was breathing; I could feel her breath." Lorelei looked up at the ceiling, raised her folded hands holding onto a ball of Kleenex. "Merry was really out of it, but she was breathing." Lorelei looked into the gallery. We heard people shifting in their seats. Lorelei dropped the Kleenex and stood up. "Merry never showed up, never came to the party. Nick said it was all my fault, mine and the other ex-cheerleaders', and I believed him." Everyone in the gallery turned their heads at the same time, like at a tennis match, to see Nick standing up, his eyes locked on Lorelei. "Nick said he'd take care of her, take her home. But he didn't. He lied!" Lorelei yelled out.

For a second Nick stood there, his face like stone. The edges of his mouth stretched down as if something was going to come out of his mouth.

"He did it, he killed Merry!" Lorelei pointed at Nick. The color drained out of her face and she toppled, a porcelain doll falling from its shelf, clattering to the floor.

We could feel the panic now from people. Watching Lorelei fall. Turning their heads again to watch Nick, who had climbed out into the aisle to make a run for it. People from the gallery, a small older man in overalls and a baseball cap and a larger man with a motorcycle jacket on, got in front of Nick just before the two cops at the back tackled him. Once they had him, they had to keep people away who had gathered in the center aisle to get at him. The cops finally got him trapped down between them in a seat in the back row. The courtroom noise climbed toward the ceiling.

"Order!" Ruttan waved his gavel. "I will not allow mob behavior in my courtroom." Ruttan spoke while he whacked the gavel until it was quiet enough to hear. He leaned toward the court from his bench with his bat-wing sleeves. "Ladies and gentlemen, you must return to your seats or you will be removed for the duration of the trial!" he shouted, and finally all was quiet.

"Addie." Rachel tugged my skirt. "You have to sit." I couldn't feel the floor I was standing on. Nick had killed Merry?

As I lowered myself into my seat, I watched the bailiff lift Lorelei up. She leaned on one arm of the chair in the witness box, her eyes bleary. The room was so soundless I could almost hear people blink.

O'Brien took hold of his desk and steadied himself.

Diaz crouched at the defense desk opposite Uribe, telling him something that had to be reassuring, and Uribe nodded yes.

"Mr. O'Brien, do you have any questions for this witness?" Ruttan asked.

"No, Your Honor," said O'Brien.

I turned around to see Nick Stanley between the two officers, his head hanging low. I felt like the stupidest person in the world. Jeez, even worse than that.

"Addie," Rachel whispered, and I turned back to see Diaz standing.

"Your Honor, I wish to call Mr. Uribe to the stand," Diaz's voice rang out.

After Uribe was sworn in, no one could keep still. Catalina hugged their little girl close.

"Mr. Uribe, will you tell the court what you did on the night of Merry Jacobs's murder, between four p.m. and nine p.m. on Friday, May third?"

"I left work early at three thirty. I had to take my boy to his T-ball game. Then I went home and got his bicycle, and then dropped it off to be fixed at the bike shop. I came back to the baseball field and watched the rest of the game. After that I took my son to his friend's house for pizza, and I went over to the bike shop to pick up the bike. Then I went home for dinner with my family."

"Did you go back to the high school after you left at three thirty p.m.?"

"I did not," said Uribe.

"When did you go back to the high school?"

"I went back on Monday, at seven a.m."

"Did you see the body of Merry Jacobs then?"

"No. One of the girls who found the body came into the shop before school and said there was an emergency. I called the school secretary from the shop and asked them to call the police."

"Did you know Merry Jacobs?"

"No."

"You checked the pulse of the body?"

"I did."

"Was there a pulse?"

"No."

"Then the police came?"

"Yes. They came right after I knew the girl didn't have a pulse."

"So just to review your testimony, Mr. Uribe: one, you were never at the high school during the time when Merry Jacobs was killed. As the jury heard earlier, Nick Stanley was the last person to be seen with Merry Jacobs when she was alive; two, you had just come to start work and had no idea that the body was at the scene at all on Monday morning. Only when you were made aware of the body did you see Merry, and take her pulse, something we would all probably do; and three, then the police arrived."

"Yes, that is what happened."

"Then you were arrested five days later and taken into custody."

"Yes."

"Nothing further, Your Honor," said Diaz.

"Mr. O'Brien?" Ruttan looked at Uribe and then at the DA.

People chattered.

"Your Honor." O'Brien took a deep breath and stood up. "The prosecution concedes the case against Mr. Uribe is over and agrees to drop all charges."

The voices piled one on top of the other like waves breaking.

"Agreed," said Ruttan. "Mr. Uribe, you are free to go. The jury is thanked and court is adjourned."

Then everything slowed down. My ears filled with this pounding, suffocating sound. It was like when you've gone under a wave and you come up way too soon, and the water takes you every which way, and half of you is twisted around this way and the other parts of you are being pulled out of their sockets, and you are just trying to get to the surface, and you start to think, but maybe you can't. That's what the sound inside the courtroom was doing. It bounced off the closest wall, and then bounced to the next wall, and the next, in a counter-clockwise motion.

Max waved to us, his eyes squinted, his cheeks all pink, and he gave us a thumbs-up. I looked at Rachel hugging Catalina and the little girl. I looked at Gina. She put her hand out for a high-five. I hit it with a smack. I saw Gina's mother standing and smiling at her, and Gina waved back. I couldn't help wondering what was happening with Nick.

Children squealed and played tag and hide-and-seek. People stopped to chat or pick a fight. A couple of pigeons ducked into the courtroom through the open windows and flapped low over arms that tried to protect heads. Rachel was playing peek-a-boo with the little girl. Gina was hugging her mom now. Out of the corner of my eye, I saw Lorelei—I mean, I didn't realize it was her at first because she was so, I don't know, you know, like, pale, like there might not be any life in her or something. I just had to get close; I had to say something. I squeezed in here, muscled in there, and then I was right behind her. All her hair was pulled tight against her perfect oval head into a ponytail, and I reached out for that rope of hair, closer and closer.

"Addie!" Max called.

Lorelei turned to look behind her, and she saw me. Her skin looked like that piece of raw chicken my dog brought home one night. But before I could say anything to Lorelei, Max guided me back to the row where everyone was still happy and excited. Then his face appeared right in front of me. The big cheeks, the gray mustache, and the gray hair that was meticulously shaved above his ears. He smelled of mouthwash and Old Spice. Diaz was there. He wiped his forehead with the back of his hand.

"Did you know it was Nick?" I asked.

"No, surprise to me," said Diaz.

"Those ex-cheers, they still hurt Merry," said Rachel.

"I can't believe it was Nick," I said. "I am such an idiot."

"You are not," said Gina. "He made everyone think it wasn't him, even me."

I closed my eyes super tight to get myself to believe that.

"It's a tough case," said Max. "His word. Their words."

"Great job." Diaz shook our hands.

"Thanks," I said. "I mean, we—thanks!" I didn't have any other words inside my head now.

"Carlos Uribe is a not going anywhere except home where he belongs," said Diaz. "That's a victory."

"Time to celebrate," said Max.

"Okay, Crusaders. Catch you later. I need to go to talk to the family," Diaz said.

The crowd dissipated.

"Mom?" I saw her standing just behind Max in her sky-blue corduroy jacket, and she was about to smile. I could tell because there was that way she would tilt her head up just before she smiled. I hugged her, the corduroy soft, and took in her Jean Naté bath splash smell. I opened my eyes and saw Rachel hugging her mom. I felt good and sad at the same time.

"I was so wrong," I said.

"I love you, my sweet girl." She hugged me again.

I heard Rachel's mom laugh. She held Rachel's hand.

The noise started to die down.

"Okay," I said. The room and everything in it finally came into focus. "I may have been wrong about Nick, but I am not wrong about the sheriff."

I mean, we had to show that Griffin had covered up for the murderer. He'd already tried to get an innocent man sent to prison. How many more people was he going to do that to? But before we did anything about the sheriff, I had to find Nick.

CHAPTER 39

I lost Rachel and Gina in the sea of bobbing heads in the crowded courtroom lobby.

"Excuse me, excuse me, thank you," I repeated.

I pushed past the cowboy hats, ranch shirts, bolo ties, flowered dresses, girls in pinafores, men in short-sleeved business shirts, all squeezing through the tiled hallway. I lost my balance for a second and got shoved into the crowd that spilled outside. I looked for Gina and Rachel. I heard voices. I turned and saw one of the cops who had caught Nick in the courthouse was standing at the edge of the walk, talking to Nick's dad. Had Nick run off again? No, just down from them at the side of the courthouse where no one was going, Nick sat hunched over on an iron bench. The other cop stood watch over him.

As I walked closer to Nick, I could see his curly sun-bleached hair was wilder, unrestrained. One tail of his dress shirt had come untucked and the knot of his tie had pulled to one side. I waved like crazy to try to get his attention. Automatic reflex, I guess. The cop stepped toward me which is I guess what got Nick's attention. I looked at the cop.

"I just need to talk to him for a second, officer," I said.

"Make it a really short second," the officer took a step back and spit.

Nick turned his head my way. When he saw me, he stood up straight and set his hands at his waist. He tried to make that familiar smile that showed his dimples. His eyes widened, shiny with that deep golden ore that made them so intense. I had to know. I had to ask.

"Why, Nick?" I looked at him. "I don't understand."

"I'd do anything to bring Merry back." He sounded sort of like himself, but more like he was trying to convince himself of what he was saying. "I was in love with her."

"But you were lying the whole time." I heard the catch in my throat.

"My life was already over, Chuck. Merry was never going to take me back. I was begging her—Merry kept saying it over and over. She didn't want me." The smile started to change. The golden light went out, and his eyes turned the color of dead kelp leaves.

"But you and Lorelei? I mean, this is high school, Nick, it's not forever."

"I had to have someone. I knew it made Merry mad."

"They were best friends, Nick." I wanted to shut my eyes and have this be one of those dreams you tell yourself is a dream, but you can't believe it even after you wake up. "You tried to get off, you tried to get someone else to take the blame. You used me." I could hear the whine in my voice. I thought he could say something that would make sense to me. A real answer.

"Hey, Chuck." Nick put out his hand. He tried that smile again, but it wasn't working. He'd totally used up his smile.

I couldn't take his hand. I couldn't touch him.

He looked away and crushed a bougainvillea blossom with his dress shoe, leaving a dark gooey gash on the walkway.

"Okay." The cop stepped towards me. "Move along," he barked. His radio made a garbled sound.

I nodded and walked fast past the cop talking to Nick's dad into the thick crowd gathered near the steps of the courthouse.

In the courtroom, I'd only felt shock. Shock that Nick had ended Merry's life, and shock that I'd been completely wrong about him. I'd bought it all, what he wanted people to see. I'd been so in love with him, I couldn't pay attention to what he really was. I was so wrapped up in him paying attention to me. So gullible. Why hadn't I been smart enough to see that Nick just manipulated me? Granted, I wasn't as smart or as perfect as Merry Jacobs, but—and that's when it occurred to me. What if Merry Jacobs was as gullible as me? I mean, when it came to Nick?

I felt light and heavy at the same time, and somehow connected to Merry. That maybe she was like me. Or I was like her. I closed my eyes for a second, as if I could talk to her. I wanted to say how sorry I was for all the mistakes I'd made not seeing that Nick was the murderer the whole time, that the sheriff had probably made it impossible for Nick to face the consequences for it, that her murder might remain unsolved, a shadow lingering in the dark corners of the high school, under the bleachers, in the girls' locker room, up near the maintenance building. A shadow that would never go away.

My eyes blinked open. Now, I knew. We had to destroy Sheriff Griffin. If anyone was going to pay for sure for Merry's death, it was the person at the very top, Sheriff Lloyd Griffin. He'd screwed everything up. We had to nail Griffin and show what a fraud he was. He had to be stopped. There was no telling what further harm he was going to do.

I stopped to watch Diaz and Uribe for a second on the courthouse steps, getting their pictures taken. The bronze justice symbol over the courthouse entry was one of those art deco numbers with a big Picasso-shaped justice lady. It glinted in the sun, but it didn't quite line up with the entryway. The *Gazette* photographer held up his camera for the shot. *Shi-ku, shi-ku, shi-ku*. Then Diaz and Uribe started to answer questions from three reporters in the crowd. A news van from the one small local TV station was setting up. I couldn't see Rachel or Gina.

"Addie!" Rachel yelled from behind me.

"Where did you go?" Gina asked.

We headed to El Pancho's. Rachel's Dr. Scholls snicked on the sidewalk. We stopped to cross the street while a crowd from the gallery went up to Los Buitres.

"I tried to talk to Nick," I said.

"Addie, that guy is a murderer."

"Right, I get it. He used me. I just thought, I thought he would have a good reason," I said.

"And?" Gina looked at me.

"He didn't have one," I said.

"Good," said Gina. "Finally, you're starting to sound like the genius you are."

"Guys, come on," said Rachel.

We booked it across the street to where the stairwell led down into the plaza.

"I'm sorry he wasn't who you thought he was," Rachel whispered to me.

"Thanks, Rae." I nodded. "Okay. About Griffin," I said just before we all headed down the stairs. "We follow him. Griffin. Tonight. You know, when he drives around, like Val said. That's your neighborhood." I looked at Rachel.

"Shouldn't we tell Diaz?" said Rachel.

"There is no way he would agree to us tailing Griffin," said Gina.

"Hey, *andale*, guys!" Diaz yelled to us from down below. Max waved, standing next to him.

"How did they get here so fast?" asked Rachel. She waved back.

"We do a stakeout. We take him down when he's driving and handing money around. It's perfect," I said.

"Oh, yeah, of course, that's good. A stakeout," said Gina full of skepticism.

"No, that *is* good," said Rachel.

"We'll take him by surprise. No one else will be around. Griffin will be in the palm of our hands. I bet you anything he's got something in that car. We find it; we show how corrupt he is." I couldn't believe I'd had such a good idea.

"Yeah, but my mom is off tonight," said Rachel. "The only way to sneak out of the house is out my window. I hate jumping off the roof."

"Just for tonight," I said. "We're coming!" I yelled to Max and Diaz waiting below.

Diaz actually smiled as we hopped off the last step. Psych—all this time, and I didn't know the guy had teeth.

"Thought you guys were going to try to fly down here," said Max as we walked past some tables and sat at the same one we had eaten at the time before.

"Now, Crusaders, we feast," said Diaz. "Thanks again for working so hard. Getting all that information, plus the cat, plus Stevens, all that work with the ex-cheers. Okay, here's to future victories." He grabbed his water glass for a toast.

There was a crash of dishes. Everyone in the restaurant looked up; a fork dropped on the ground; someone coughed. I could see in the distance the waitress's flowing skirt slowly unfurl. I heard the squeaking patent leather. Sheriff Griffin.

"Well, what all do we have here?" Griffin's voice resonated.

"No way, José." Rachel lost her balance, and I pulled her back toward me.

It was him. Lloyd Griffin. He was standing this close. It was like time freezing to the seventy-ninth power. I could hear the trickling in the fountain, the breath of people, the echo of the mariachi music not playing.

"Diaz." Griffin sawed off the name as if it were a limb.

"Griffin." Diaz spoke but didn't look at the sheriff.

"Walker." Griffin's breath rustled through the brush of his mustache.

"Lloyd." Max didn't move.

The restaurant returned to calm. People wandered back into conversations, wiped their mouths with their napkins. The mariachi band struck up a tune and strolled our way before regrouping to serenade an older couple three tables away. Man, it was like looking at another world behind glass. I couldn't stand it.

I squeezed my eyes tight and stood up. "You're a criminal, Sheriff Griffin, and you know it," I let loose like a busted sewage line.

"Hold on." Griffin stuck his hand out like he was trying to stop traffic.

"You totally framed Uribe." Rachel jumped up out of her chair.

"You broke the law," said Gina, standing next to Rachel and me.

"You stole evidence." Rachel gritted her teeth.

"Whoa, whoa, whoa." Griffin's smile was like a stuffed animal's from one of those carnival games that you can never win at. "What's with all the firepower? I'm doing what?" Griffin leaned in close, and I saw the mole in the middle of his forehead, the color of blue smoke. His patent-leather oxford scraped forward, almost touching my sandal.

"These are the Crusaders; they were crucial to Uribe's case." Diaz rose and moved closer to Griffin.

"The Crusaders, huh? Weren't they a disastrous failure in the end?"

"Caped Crusaders," I said.

"You know, Justice," said Rachel.

"Truth," said Gina.

"The American Way." I smiled, and I didn't know why.

"You heard the young lady on the stand: it was all an accident. I have to keep my little city safe, and my intent—"

"Your intent, my ass." Max faced Griffin. A thin glaze of sweat on his bald head reflected the waning sunlight in Griffin's sunglasses.

"Walker, you know I couldn't let Ron go off on some fantasy of his. You see what position he's in. Those young ladies apparently didn't mean to really hurt the Jacobs girl. The young man? It appears there's just not enough evidence. Too many unresolved issues. Don't even know that it *was* murder. Just remember, I'm letting you save Uribe, for now, and I'm saving you. After all, my job *is* to save people." The sheriff lifted his left hand, a toothpick wedged in his thick fingers. "Did I sacrifice some things? Yes. Okay, I'll take the rap for that. But I did it to make sure we didn't find another girl's dead body, if you know what I mean." He stuck the toothpick in his mouth and let it point up, then down, then up again.

"You do all this just to look good. You knew Uribe was innocent. You stole evidence, too, that cheerleader uniform, to get Miller totally under control. Why not, why not have something up your sleeve to zip Miller's mouth shut?" said Diaz. "He bought you first, and now you buy him back."

"What are you talking about?" Griffin's nostrils flared; he rolled the toothpick to the other side of his mouth.

"We're not stupid," said Gina.

"We're not giving up," said Rachel.

"We're not afraid of you," I said.

Griffin's cheeks squeezed up against his sunglasses when he

smiled. "You know, you better watch *these* girls, Diaz." Spit pooled in the corners of Griffin's mouth.

"You knew the Miller girl and the others had something to do with the murder of Merry Jacobs." Diaz squinted at Griffin. "Turns out the boy fooled you too. He was the murderer all along and because of you, he may go scot free."

"You heard them on the stand, Diaz. It was all a mistake, it was all a practical joke gone wrong," said Griffin.

"But you were going to sacrifice an innocent man," said Diaz.

"And you let Miller buy you to save his ass?" said Max. "Because when the banks start lending in droves, you make one hell of a profit from the developers."

"You realize, don't you, the whole routine with Miller didn't work. You realize the judge dismissed every last bit of Miller's testimony?" Griffin clenched the toothpick in his mouth. "Now, it doesn't matter what he said."

"Fine by me," said Max. "Cat's out of the bag now. You are guilty of framing an innocent man. And letting a guilty man go."

"The Stanley boy won't spend a day in jail and you know it. You want to question my police work? You haul me in on a charge."

"Oh, we will. The subpoena's coming for you in the mail," said Max.

"The subpoena!" Griffin bellowed. People in the restaurant hushed. Griffin waved to them, then turned to us, took off his sunglasses, and whispered, "I'll be sleeping with one eye open." He winked.

"That," said Max, "seems to be your natural state: only one eye on the murder scene, only one eye on the investigation."

"You are going to lose everything," said Diaz. "Your incompetence will catch up with you."

"Well, guess what? I'll be taking my incompetence all the way to the state capitol." Griffin grabbed at his wide belt with both hands, the holster with the gun at his right.

"What the hell does that mean?" asked Max.

"You're looking at your new state senator from the thirty-eighth district."

"No way, José." Rachel held her forehead like she was feeling her temperature.

"Someone's got to take over for Ron's campaign," said Griffin.

"You? You're going to run for state office? That's not possible," said Diaz.

"Headed over to City Hall to put my name in right now." Griffin choked out a laugh. "Maybe you ought to throw your hat in the ring, Diaz. As it stands, I have absolutely no competition, nada."

"There is no way in hell you can run for a state office." Diaz stared at Griffin.

The mariachi band started another tune.

"You were taking money from Miller on those land deals, Sheriff, and he cut a check for you just like he did for everyone else on the city council," said Diaz.

"You might try to shut Miller up," said Max, "but we're not shutting up. We don't owe you."

"You should know, Walker; you're on that city council." Griffin rubbed his thumb and forefinger. "Owe," he said, drawing the word out. "You really want to talk about owing, as in, you owe me?" His neck veins throbbed, his giant teeth chomped on his toothpick; it snapped and whizzed past. His face and neck were a mottle of pink and red. He put his sunglasses back on. He started to resemble a Gila monster. A Gila monster with a mustache and sunglasses.

"You used to be a clean cop," said Max.

"That's enough." Griffin spat the other half of the toothpick over his shoulder. "I became sheriff to help you clean house, and that's exactly what I did. Wiped this city clean, for you. You want to talk payoffs, you want to talk dirt? Maybe we'd better look closer at you, Walker, because I didn't get rid of you, *yet*." The "t" in the consonant struck like a match.

A pack of five men hustled out of the back room of the restaurant, making their way toward us. Their fancy shoes clopped on the tiles. Three of the men I'd never seen before, but the other two were the patriarchs of the two ruling families of Santa Raymunda when it came to land and construction. All the major development money combined.

"See you at the next meeting, Sheriff!" one of the men shouted.

Griffin made a salute with two fingers on his right hand to the center of his forehead. "Time for me to take my leave. Got to do some politicking."

"Nooooo!" I couldn't help myself.

"Addie." Diaz stepped in front of me.

"Send these girls back to Home Ec for me, Diaz," said Griffin.

"We're on to you," said Gina.

"Yeah, you just wait," said Rachel.

"Home Ec?" I shouted. "We'll show *you*!"

The pack of men crowded close to Griffin. They all hiked down the last set of stairs to the parking lot. We raced to the railing to watch them below. The sheriff got into his squad car; the other men piled into two sedans. The ignitions started, one, two, three. Bus boys cleared tables. I looked back at Diaz. I couldn't let him know we were going to get Griffin, no matter how much I wanted to.

"Hey," said Max. "Let's all calm down. We'll make a case against the sheriff. But it's a long game."

"Doesn't have to be," said Gina.

"You guys." Diaz looked at us. "No funny business."

"Us?" said Rachel. "You know it! No fun, and nooo business. That is for sure."

CHAPTER 40

At one forty-nine a.m., we were in the Pinto in the alley behind Griffin's backyard fence, under the shadows of willow and bougainvillea. We were on watch like 1-Adam-12 city. I had my Kodak Instamatic camera, Rachel was able to borrow some walkie-talkies from her brother, and Gina managed to get binoculars and a handheld tape recorder from her mom. She told her mom we were going bird-watching in the morning for extra credit in Biology. Griffin lived up the hill from Rachel's house. His place was one of the pastel-colored homes with red tile roofs and rock wall enclosures built in the 1920s.

We wore black pants, black tops, and black knit beanies. I could barely fit into my black cords, and they made this skitch-skitch sound when I walked fast. I kept telling myself it wasn't that loud. We had rubbed charcoal on our faces from Rachel's drawing set. We weren't totally indistinguishable, but we didn't look like ourselves.

"Gross me out." Gina leaned back into the car with lightning speed. She'd been watching for Griffin out the passenger-side window. She thrust the binoculars down toward her lap.

"Oh, my God, what?" I cried, and squeezed the steering wheel.

Rachel jumped up from the backseat.

"Gina, it's just a moth." Rachel pointed to the creature stuck on Gina's cheek.

"Get this thing off of me!" Gina squirmed, wiping at her face, the binoculars still looped around her neck.

"It's dead," said Rachel. "It *is* pretty big. Poor guy, now he's covered in charcoal."

I looked over to see Rachel peel what was left of the moth's wings and body, inspecting it.

"Gross, man. Just toss it." Gina wriggled.

"I really think we should have asked Diaz to come with us." Rachel leaned over and flicked the rest of the insect out Gina's window.

"Forget it. He would never have okayed us to do this in the first place," said Gina.

"But we could have given him one of *these*." Rachel held up her walkie-talkie.

"Rae, nothing's going to happen us," I said. "I mean, at this point, everything we've done has worked perfectly. We don't need any adult interference."

"Guys, let's focus." Gina picked up her binoculars.

"What if we wind up following Griffin on some old back road or something?" asked Rachel.

"We went over this. *We* have justice on our side," I said.

"You want Griffin pulling up at your house to arrest you for something you didn't do?" asked Gina.

"No," said Rachel. She shifted in the backseat. "Hey, why is Lorelei's diary back here, and the bag of uniforms?"

"We'll swing by the Millers' house tonight and put it all back, you know, after we're done with Griffin," I said.

"You have got to be kidding." Gina looked over her shoulder at me.

"Well, we might have to leave it at the *side* of the house," I said. "But we have to get rid of it before we go home."

"Man," said Rachel. "I can't believe I got out of the house with these." She held one of the walkie-talkies up to her mouth as if to speak. The antenna was out far enough that it poked my head and then glided along my temple.

"Ouch."

"That's going to take an eye out." Gina grabbed the antenna. "Do you mind?" She pointed the antenna away.

"We should test them," said Rachel.

Gina leaned farther out the passenger window, her knee on the side armrest, to track Griffin.

"SOS." Rachel clicked the button on her walkie-talkie. "Hey, turn yours on," she said, tapping my head.

"Yes!" Gina held up her left hand and waved to Rachel and me.

A light had turned on in Griffin's attic, a square of yellow. It gave you the impression the sheriff could take a look out and see the town below. Hopefully, he couldn't see us.

"That's him," I said.

Then the light went out.

"I'm just going to make sure he's leaving." Gina jumped out and disappeared around the corner to the side street where Griffin had parked his squad car. A big thump shook the Pinto, and I saw a huge opossum lumber off the front of my car. The passenger door was open. Gina had to make it back before Griffin drove too far ahead of us.

"God, that scared me," said Rachel.

A car started.

"Here we go," I said.

Gina ran back around the corner, holding the binocs. I took the emergency brake off and let the car roll forward in neutral. The passenger door winged out. I turned the key in the ignition and stepped on the gas. Gina caught hold of the door handle and ran along the car as it moved, then dove in while grabbing and then slamming the car door shut.

"Oh, my God, I can't believe I did that." Gina caught her breath.

"Wicked," I said.

"Don't turn the headlights on," said Rachel.

"It's so dark." I eased the car up to speed. There was only one streetlamp between here and the traffic light down by the mission.

Gina squeezed herself up on the dash against the windshield and focused her binocs.

We made it around the corner. Griffin's brake lights glowed in the distance.

"Don't lose him," Rachel gulped.

We crawled past the neighborhood's sleeping moon-washed houses, where vines and shadows splayed like veins. Griffin's red back lights winked on the horizon.

"Man, where do you think he's going?" said Rachel.

He coasted through the blinking yellow light at the mission and took a left. He was going east on Diego Highway over the interstate, the route all the bikers took in and out of town. There was a roadhouse out there where people fought with knives after too much drinking. My mom would totally have a cow if we ended up there. So far, we'd passed two closed gas stations, a couple of orange groves, and two farmhouses on property that sloped down on our right, in the direction of Santa Raymunda Creek.

"Hold it," said Gina.

Griffin slowed and made a left turn. So, he wasn't making for the roadhouse. He was on a new road. I'd never seen it before. It curved up the hill between white fencing on both sides. An occasional driveway on the right led out to new mansions being built on scrub-land. I didn't think anyone was living here yet.

"There's Griffin," said Gina. "He's all the way at the top."

"Wait a second," said Rachel. "I know where this goes."

"We lost him," said Gina.

"This is the new part of Casa Ridge," said Rachel. "It goes back to —" She was sitting so far up I could feel her breath.

"Casa Ridge?" I said. "The Millers' house?"

We made it to the top. The road changed to old crumbling asphalt, no shoulder, and went down steeply and up again. Luckily, we had the full moonlight to see. This was some old semi-used farm road. A big orange grove spilled through the valley on the whole eastern side.

"He's going to the Miller house?" said Gina.

"Oh, man," I said.

Griffin's brake lights bloomed at the bottom of the hill for a second and then he cruised up. I stepped on the gas just a little more to make sure that once he got over the next hill, we weren't too far behind. Even in my turtleneck and cords, I felt cold. A dead tree with gnarled branches on one side stood against the starlight on the right as we crested the slope.

"Yes! This is it!" Rachel bounced in her seat.

"Stop, stop, stop!" Gina grabbed my arm.

I stomped on the brakes. We were in Lorelei's neighborhood.

"Cut the engine now!" said Gina.

"It's the Miller house." Rachel pointed. "Are you guys sure we can do this?"

We were a few houses back. The streetlights didn't start until the second house down. But I'd gotten used to the moonlight. We could see Griffin's squad car in the Millers' driveway.

"Busted," said Gina. "We've got to record this—get the camera." She started to open her car door.

We planned to all sneak out through the passenger-side door, so Griffin wouldn't see us. I got to the sidewalk on all fours, following Gina. Rachel crawled from the backseat, and I grabbed her hand so she wouldn't fall on the concrete. Gina booked it on her hands and knees behind a utility box on the lawn next to the sidewalk. We did the same.

"He's out of the car," said Gina, handing me the binocs.

"Okay, he's got the trunk open—bingo," I said. "This is it—we have to get there now."

"Wait," said Rachel. She tossed me the other walkie-talkie.

"Gina," I whispered. "Tape recorder?"

"I got it," she said.

"Rae, where's my camera?" I asked. I looked for her, but she was back in the car, searching the backseat, her feet hanging out. I looked at the long lawns. The perfectly trimmed trees. My heart was beating like a boxing speed bag. I could feel the charcoal layer getting grainy on my face. I was sweating big time.

"Rachel, come on!" I said in a hushed voice.

"Just stay low," Gina whispered.

"Flashlight?" I turned to Rachel, who crouched beside me.

"Right here." Rachel turned it on and a little circle of light hovered just above the grass. Then she snapped it off.

Coming at the Miller house from this direction was different. I realized that the Millers were all home, and the sheriff was here, and I wasn't that fast on my feet across the three large lawns, much less crawling on my stomach, which we had to do to stay out of sight.

Gina looked through the binoculars. "He must be going to the front door," she whispered. "Follow me."

She'd stuck the little tape recorder in her back pocket, and I could see the metal flash as she crawled. She turned around to make sure we were behind her. My arms and legs felt shaky. Gina lunged forward, then ran and slid at a diagonal up to a planter with leafy shrubs on the other side of the Millers' front entrance. Rachel and I tried to do the same. Once I started running, I could hear the sound of my cords. I dropped and slid, then checked my front pocket for the camera and the back one for the walkie-talkie. I heard Rachel. We'd both made it, and I could hear my racing heartbeat in my eardrums.

Rachel and I curled up behind Gina, who was scrunched under a hibiscus bush near the front door. The iron fence divided the front yard from the side and back. The same fence we'd climbed over when we were here before. The light over the front door wasn't on. We heard a squeak. I held my breath. Griffin was here, right on the other side of the hibiscus bush. I strained to look at Gina. She was reaching for her recorder. I dug into my front pocket and fingered out the Instamatic.

Griffin knocked on the Millers' door. The sound echoed against the stucco walls of the front entry. I thought I could hear Griffin's heavy breathing, slow and methodical. Sweat dripped off my nose. Gina looked at me. I could see the smudged charcoal on her face, the beanie pulled over her eyebrows. She held the mini tape recorder close, and slowly pushed the RECORD button. The binocs were still around her neck. The door clicked open and Gina stuck the recorder out behind a big leaf. The indoor hallway light dissolved some of the darkness. As long as we could stay still, we could—

"Ron," we heard Griffin say. "We need to talk." We heard Griffin's shoes squeak inside. The door closed and the light was gone. I dropped the camera.

Pppfff, pppfff.

I looked at Rachel.

She shrugged.

I picked up the camera to put it in my pocket again. Gina turned around. She held the recorder in one hand and her binocs in the other.

Pppfff, pppfff. The sounded faded, then came back, and this panting—

"Aaa—" I started to speak, but Rachel clamped her hand over my mouth.

"It's the dog," said Rachel in a whisper as thin as a blade of grass.

Gina and I watched the dog sit and then lie on its front paws and start to lick Rachel's face.

Gina shook her head.

"Rae," I whispered.

"It's okay," said Rachel. "At least she's not barking."

The dog ran off.

I tried to reposition myself, so my feet wouldn't go to sleep. I heard the dog race up to us along the fence. I turned around. Rachel was gone.

I clicked on my walkie-talkie. "Rae?"

"Give me a second," she answered on hers.

I felt the sticky slime of a hibiscus petal on my neck.

"We should get over to his car, don't you think?" Gina whispered.

"Yeah," I said.

Just as I was about to stand up, the front door opened again. Light spilled out, and I almost froze, but Gina grabbed my ankle, and I dropped. I could see the shadowed leaves of the hibiscus wave at me. I clenched my teeth and looked at Gina. She had the recorder on. I could see the little red light at the top.

"I'm a man of my word, Ron," said Griffin. His voice made my spine turn to goo. It was louder somehow. It took forever for my hand to dig into my front pocket for the Instamatic. Once I'd retrieved it, I rolled onto my back to see if I could get Griffin and Miller together in the frame. I had to nudge into Gina. I punched the camera button twice.

"What are you talking about?" said Miller. I could see him and Griffin from my position upside down. Miller's robe was cinched at his waist, his hair was sticking out on one side, and his slippers scuffed on the concrete.

"One minute," said Griffin.

We heard his shoes squeak away, and the heels were loud on the concrete driveway. It seemed like forever, and now I worried about Rachel, wherever she was, and what about the dog, and Gina next to me? I wasn't sure how long I could maintain my pose on the hard ground like a pill bug, with my legs raised and my arms up holding the Instamatic, my head way over to the left. We heard the sheriff's footsteps again. Then they stopped.

"You can count it if you want to," said Griffin.

I watched Griffin hand Miller two small brown rectangular bricks. I held my breath and pressed the camera button.

"It's all there," said Griffin.

Miller was looking at the side of one of the packages.

"Look, I make the deals here, Lloyd. I get the investment, the builders. Casa Ridge? This? It's all me. You have nothing without me," said Ron.

"I met with the senate election committee. You're out. O-U-T. I'm taking the seat. Consider it a severance package."

"You can't do that. You, you can't," said Ron.

"You have too much on the domestic front. It's a liability."

I needed to get to Griffin's car now before he went back to it. I rolled slowly to my side, looked at Gina, and pointed my thumb in the direction of the car. She nodded and raised the recorder slightly. I nodded back. At least while Miller and Griffin were at the entry, I could sneak over. Plus, Gina was faster than me. She could race down to warn me when Griffin was coming back to his car. My lips started to dry out because I kept licking them. I squeezed my toes tight inside my shoes and chewed the inside of my mouth. I took off. I made it to the car and took a couple of gasps of air like I'd been underwater. I felt for the trunk latch, which hadn't shut all the way, and I pushed it open and leaned over. There it was—the legal gold mine—evidence that Griffin was a crooked cop.

Oh, man. An open silver lock box with brick-like brown-paper-wrapped stacks. I picked one up and tore off half a wrapper. Yep, it was cash. Bills in tight packs. I got out the camera and clicked shots, and then I saw the cheerleader skirt. It was folded in half, neat and tidy. I kept punching the camera button. I moved what looked like Griffin's jacket, and I saw a pad of graph paper with handwritten columns and names and amounts. I took more shots. I heard something. I looked up, but the trunk obscured half my view of the Millers' driveway and yard. I wanted to yell out to Gina to get her over here and see. Then I saw her head bob up. She was crawling on the lawn, and she was waving at me. Not a friendly wave. Her hand swiped in front of her. Like she wanted me to move back, away from the car.

I tried to back up. But it was too late. I felt Griffin's thick hand grab the neck of my shirt. It felt like he was going to choke me. I tried to run. The money I'd ripped open went everywhere; the graph pad with notes slapped on the driveway. I saw Gina racing toward me. I hit the ground as Griffin dragged me across the asphalt on the street just beyond the gutter. My hands pressed into the oil stains and little pebbles got stuck in my palms. I tried to feel around me for the camera. I needed the walkie-talkie. I saw Gina on the sidewalk so close I could touch her. I kept trying to run and pull, so the neck of my shirt would rip and I could get free, but I couldn't because when I got almost far enough, the fabric stretched but didn't rip. But then I couldn't breathe.

"Not so fast," said Griffin. He pulled me back once more, and I was on my knees. Then came a sound I'd never heard before, like an ice cube that cracks, just once, and it sounded pretty close to me, to my head. My brain started to pump adrenaline like lighter fluid. I saw both his feet behind me. He had my shirt collar in his left and something in his right that made the weird sound. I tried to turn my head, but I felt his fist touch my ear, so I only moved my eyes. In the pale shadow of the streetlight, I saw a piece of metal pointed above where his fingers held—I tried to make sense of it. I'd seen guns in pictures, on TV. Griffin was pointing the gun at Gina. She was holding the camera, trying to take his picture. The money had landed on the ground. Gina waved the cheerleader skirt.

"No!" I yelled at Gina. "Get away!" I rose and tried to run at her again. Trying to block her from Griffin's aim.

"What do you think you're doing?" Griffin pulled up on my collar so hard, I fell back hard on my tailbone.

"We've got all of it, Griffin," I said. "All your dirt." I tried to claw the skin on my neck because I couldn't get enough air.

"You think you've got me? Oh, that's very entertaining." Now, I felt the gun again near my head. I had to get his hand, his arm. Stop him from pointing in Gina's direction. "You're robbing me? Is that what's going on? I think you are." Griffin's voice was low, measured, calm. "You and your friend here. You picked the wrong person."

With each word he tugged at the neck of my shirt. The handle of the gun was so close to my temple, I thought my eyelashes might touch it if I closed my eyes. I was breathing in and out as quietly as I could, trying not to cry, not to move. Could he kill us? He could. We looked the part. We looked like robbers. I had screwed up, really screwed up. I had to think of something. Some way to save my friends' lives.

"Gina, get away!" I yelled.

"Oh." Griffin looked down at me. "You want to take the bullet? See, either way, I'm within my rights, because *you* are guilty of robbing me."

I felt the gun barrel graze my temple.

"I am perfectly within my rights. This is justice, just me getting justice."

I thought I was going to pee. I looked at Gina. I wanted to tell her to give it back, the skirt, the money, but I was too scared to say anything. Every time I opened my mouth, I couldn't get sound out. Gina looked more scared than me. I wanted her to see, in my eyes, that she needed to run, that she was my best friend and Rachel was my other best friend. I started to see my whole life like a washed-out film-strip show from first grade up to now. This was the stupidest thing I'd done, ever, getting my friends out here, way out of our league. My stupid, stupid plan.

I couldn't let them get hurt. I had to save them, but how? I was reckless, selfish, thoughtless. I'd got my friends into this horrible mess. I was never, ever going to see them again. Diaz was right. I couldn't just follow every wild idea I had. We needed someone like Diaz to run interference because if he didn't, we were totally cooked. Like right now. I should have said something. I should have asked Diaz.

"Gina!" Her name came out of my mouth.

I caught her hand somehow.

Griffin pointed the gun at my head now.

"You're the best person I know," I said, my voice strained by the sweater collar cutting at my neck. "I'm so sorry. And Rachel's the best person I know too. I failed you guys."

Griffin cocked the gun one more time.

"Go!" I managed this long, unending scream. Gina let go of my hand.

In a split second, the gun went off. I heard Rachel yelling. I was yelling. Gina was on the ground. Screaming. Then she propped her head up. *Oh, thank God!* I felt for Griffin's fingers, but he wasn't holding me anymore. I looked behind me. The dog had knocked Griffin face-down in the street and had his head pinned.

"Look." Gina pointed at Rachel.

"Here!" Rachel threw me the jump ropes we had in the car from Gina's little sister. I'd totally forgot about them. Rachel whipped the rope around Griffin's ankles. "Hurry, before he gets up!"

"Arghhh!" Griffin tried to grab for me, but the dog went for his face.

I tied a slip knot, caught one of his wrists and held it against the street, leaned over and winched his other wrist down, and clamped both wrists together. My sweat dripped on his pressed uniform.

The dog was running around now and every time Griffin started to make noise, it ran on top of him until he stopped. Rachel was up by the car.

"Rae, get me some more money," I said.

Rachel reached into the trunk and threw me two bricks of cash.

"Here you go, Sheriff." I managed to stuff the bricks in his jaws. "Here's your money. And your justice. Special delivery."

All Griffin could do was grunt and thrash his head, trying to jerk it out of his mouth.

"Come on, you guys," said Gina. "Everyone's going to wake up."

"Where's the camera?" I asked.

"Here." Gina ran up to me, and I grabbed the Instamatic.

"Where's the skirt?" I asked.

"Come on, puppy," said Gina. "She's got it." Behind her the dog carried the skirt in its mouth.

"Hey!" I grabbed for the skirt, but the dog took off ahead of us.

"Just run, and she'll follow us," said Rachel.

We took off for the car. Our sneakers, my cords, the dog's collar, everything echoed. I looked over my shoulder. A few people were coming out of their houses, standing at the edges of their driveway, the moonlight making their pajamas glow. I saw the Millers. Lorelei in her nightgown. But I couldn't stop to look closer.

We jumped in the car. I cranked the ignition. We burned rubber.

"Good dog," said Rachel.

The dog panted in the back of the car. All the windows steamed up. I kept the headlights off.

"Think Griffin knows it was us?" asked Rachel.

"Of course," said Gina. "At least he won't get that senate seat."

"I know," I said. "But he does have a gun."

"That doesn't mean he gets to do whatever he wants," said Rachel.

"He's going to keep on going until someone stops him," I said. My hands gripped the steering wheel super tight; my arms were shaking.

"Or *we* do," said Gina. Her face was streaked with the charcoal.

"I think we have to," I said. "We just have to avoid, you know, certain death."

"Oh, man," said Rachel. "I put Lorelei's diary in his trunk and the bag of ex-cheerleader uniforms."

"Good one, Rae," I said.

"Excellent," said Gina. "Can we go any faster?"

I floored the Pinto down the steep grade of the farm road. In this valley there were just dark patterns of rows across the dark fields. All I really wanted to see was that blinking yellow light in the middle of town. My boring little town. We sped, hopping culverts, the shocks thumping us with the jolts. I weaved on the road just so I didn't have to slow down. I would get us to town. Get us safe and sound. We'd get all of this over to Diaz. Start the long game on Sheriff Griffin.

Rachel tapped me on the shoulder. "What's the plan?"

"I don't know," I said. "Yet."

ACKNOWLEDGMENTS

There are so many talented and supportive people who helped create *A Mouthful of Murder*. I am truly grateful for so much time and attention from you all. To Konstellation Press and Cornelia Feye for steering this project and whose great wisdom and vision have made my characters and story more powerful than I had imagined. To Lisa Wolff for her amazing editorial expertise. To Jim Gripp for his detailed legal authority. To my brother, William Carter, whose graphic work "drives" the front cover art. To Scott Pridham for his insight and suggestions in early revisions. To Gretchen Days Brunk and James Warren Boyd for their time and tireless reading and commentary. To the coolest teen readers ever, Ariana and Brooke Verdugo, who helped me make sure this is truly a teenagers' story. To the Independent Writers' Studio, and Mary Gillilan and Norman Green who provided editing and encouragement as well as publishing a version of Chapter 5 in *Clover: A Literary Rag* in the early days of drafting the story as a complete novel. Finally, thank you to my friends and family everywhere for your interest, excitement, and love, without which this dream would never come true

CPSIA information can be obtained
at www.ICGtesting.com
Printed in the USA
FSHW021524270719
60457FS